Praise for Silvia Violet's Magic in the Blood

4 Cups "SENSATIONAL! This vampire romance will rock your world. Lots of action and adventure is just a start for this fantastic fantasy. Carrying forward is also exciting spells and loads of magic. Interesting characters and extremely spicy sex scenes tie this mystical story together for one spellbinding, spine tingling read." ~ *Wateena, Coffee Time Romance*

4.5 Magical Wands "The central relationship develops as the two struggle against their 'forbidden' relationship. Liz's gradually developing trust in the vampire was very well done, as were his reactions to her mistrust. ...The deep magician concept was interesting, and I was intrigued by the deep-seated fears over 'changing' magicians to vampires. I am hoping these two ideas will be more fully explored in future stories. Overall, an enjoyable mix of vampires, magic and sleuth-work. Good job, Ms. Violet!" ~ *Tee Bee, Enchanted Ramblings*

"An excitable tale full of twists and turns, with interesting secondary characters to help carry the story along, Silvia Violet's MAGIC IN THE BLOOD is not to be missed!" ~ *Courtney Michelle, Romance Reviews Today*

Magic in the Blood

By Silvia Violet

A SAMHAIN PUBLISHING, LTD. publication.

Samhain Publishing, Ltd.
2932 Ross Clark Circle, #384
Dothan, AL 36301

Magic In The Blood
Copyright © 2006 by Silvia Violet
Cover by Scott Carpenter
Print ISBN: 1-59998-214-5
Digital ISBN: 1-59998-027-4
www.samhainpublishing.com

First Samhain Publishing, Ltd. electronic publication: May 2006
First Samhain Publishing, Ltd. print publication: August 2006

Chapter 1

Was Avran Niccolayic a vampire? Liz shivered at the thought. She peered into his study from her crouched position below the window sill.

Focusing on the part of her mind that allowed her to read other people's emotions and surface thoughts, Liz sent a mental probe toward Avran. She tried every trick she knew to get around his impressive shielding but couldn't find a single chink.

His mind was like nothing she'd encountered before, and his shields blocked every attempt at entry. He wasn't a normal human. That was certain, but he wasn't necessarily a vampire. He could be a psychic or a shapeshifter, or any of a number of creatures humans relegated to the world of fantasy.

Suddenly, Avran turned her way. She ducked. Had he seen her?

After a few long, slow breaths, she had to assume he hadn't. She heard no movement and felt no stir of anger or apprehension.

Once again, her practical nature told her to flee. But she couldn't. The sanctity of her home town was at stake. When the Save the Square Committee had drawn up a list of potential donors for their cause, Avran's name had been mentioned. He'd donated a considerable sum to the local historical preservation society over the last few years. And it was well known that he was worth millions. Several committee members had qualms about approaching the mysterious man, but Liz volunteered to contact him.

She was the only person in town who knew the true identity of Max Liftkin, the builder who wanted to tear down the historic Mercer building and replace it with a modern structure. In truth, he was a Deep Magician, like herself. She didn't know the true motives behind his desire to purchase the Mercer building, but she knew every move he made was an attempt to gain power. And he wasn't afraid to kill anyone who got in his path.

If she could convince Avran to make a donation to their cause, then the committee would be able to keep their legal battle alive, thus giving her more time to discover Liftkin's true reason for coming to Granville. And if Avran was indeed a vampire, he would make a powerful ally. Of course, the laws that Deep Magicians lived by forbade her to share her knowledge with him, but she had to do something to save the town from Liftkin.

Stepping back into the shadows, Liz calmed herself with another slow breath. She'd only seen Avran one other time, at a concert in a local pub. He'd only recently returned to town after a long absence, and Liz had been intrigued by the wild rumors circulating town. The people of Granville had a number of theories about the enigmatic man. The two most prominent were that he was either a vampire or a CIA agent. Of course some people thought he was both.

She'd hoped to get a better read on Avran's character with her mental probe, but she couldn't wait outside all night. She'd just have to go in, armed with nothing more than the knowledge that he wasn't your average man and that he was as sinfully beautiful as he'd been the first time she'd seen him.

Liz walked around the side of his imposing Victorian mansion, easily the largest home in town, and the most mysterious. The Niccolayic family had owned it for over a hundred years. Yet, it had stood unoccupied for many of those years, sometimes for decades at a time. The men who'd lived there never married and secluded themselves for the whole of their tenure in Granville.

These facts were often quoted by proponents of the vampire theory, and Liz had to agree that they made a good argument, but vampires were few in number. And if she believed what she'd been taught during her magical training, only a handful lived in America. The creatures appeared to prefer the old world to the new. Still, she couldn't rule out the idea of a vampire spending at least part of his years in Granville.

A jolt of fear raced up her spine.

She could defend herself against almost anything. But if Avran truly was a blood drinker, she wasn't confident she could outsmart him.

*****

Avran's study said much about his love of all things sensual. Rich burgundy leather covered the sofa, and matching armchairs surrounded the huge stone fireplace. His desk was fashioned from wood so dark it was almost black. Thick rugs covered the floor, and floor-to-ceiling bookshelves lined the walls on two sides. Visitors often remarked that the room resembled the lair of a nineteenth-century gentleman. Avran had enjoyed that century and was pleased to have preserved a bit of it for himself.

He sat at his desk, flipping through a packet of papers from his broker. A cool breeze wafted in from the window. He breathed deep and noted the delicious smell of a woman close by. His instincts told him she meant no harm.

The wind increased, and her scent assaulted him, breaking through his control. His mouth watered and tingled. Mmmm. A woman all alone. In his territory. Easy prey.

No, he said to himself, shaking his head to clear it. He would not treat a guest in such a fashion. At his age, he could go days without feeding. This woman's scent had stirred a powerful hunger, but he would have to restrain his baser needs.

In the ten years he had lived in Granville during this 'lifetime', no woman had ever come to see him. With rumors circulating about his being a vampire, a werewolf, or a demon, none had dared. This night might prove far more interesting than he had anticipated.

The doorbell rang. His butler, Gregory, the only human in Granville who knew what he really was, would answer it and show the young woman in. Avran took advantage of the time to sit and quiet his body, returning his heart rate and breathing back to their normal, nearly imperceptible level.

His hunger receded. He would attend to it later, but first, he would play the part of a civilized host. In the century and a half that he'd owned this particular home, he'd made certain to always treat the population of Granville with perfect courtesy. He'd settled here because he truly loved the town and its surrounding terrain. He had no intention of taking any action that might bring suspicion down on himself.

The door to his study opened. "Ms. Elizabeth Carlson," Gregory announced.

Avran forced himself to appear nonchalant. He finished scanning through the stock report he'd been reading and set it aside before he looked up. When he did, his hunger returned, stronger than ever. Ms. Carlson, whom he knew as the proprietor of Carlson's Fine and Rare Books, stood before him in a clinging tank top of silver velvet. The fabric caught the light as she moved, drawing attention to her curves. Tight jeans accentuated the firm muscles of her legs. After nearly a century of seeing women in pants, the sight still aroused him. He supposed a part of him would never leave the fourteenth century when such a sight was tantamount to seeing a woman naked.

If only he'd fed earlier, such compulsion might not grip him. As it was, his need rendered him incapable of anything but taking in the wonders of her body. His eyes followed the line of her long blond braid as it fell over her shoulder, skimmed her perfectly rounded breasts, and curled against her waist. The tender pulse at her neck drew him. He could hear her heart thundering, pushing blood through her veins.

"Good evening, Ms. Carlson," he said, keeping his voice neutral.

"Good evening, Mr. Niccolayic. I won't take up much of your time. I have a business matter to discuss with you."

Nervous energy radiated from her. Her hand ran up and down her braid.

"Please, call me Avran." He deepened his voice and let it brush over her. Her fidgeting increased, and he couldn't stop watching all the small movements of her body.

She spoke rapidly, explaining something about the preservation of the Town Square and how much his support would mean. Her words rushed out as though she feared he would stop her at any moment, but he wasn't listening. All he could think about was stroking her smooth skin and sinking his fangs into her neck. What was wrong with him? Only a fledgling would be so affected. He was over six hundred years old, he ought to have better control.

Her blood would taste so rich. He would only drink a little, he told himself. Just to take the edge off his hunger. Then he could listen to her. He would erase her memory. It wouldn't hurt her, not really. How easy it was to convince himself of that.

*****

Mr. Niccolayic suddenly stood. Terror gripped her body. Humans could not move like that. He pressed against her mental shields, telling her not to be afraid. He wrapped her braid around one hand and pulled her head to the side.

"What...what're you doing?" she asked, fear mounting.

He ran a finger down the side of her neck and made a noise between a purr and a growl. She struggled against him. "Let go!"

He continued to caress her neck with the knuckles of one hand as his eyes darkened to the color of smoke. "But you look so delicious."

She struggled harder, taking hold of the hand fisted in her hair, squeezing it with a grip that would bring a human man to his knees.

All he did was smile. Then she saw them. His fangs. "Oh gods. You're really—"

"Hush." His soothing touch rubbed against her body and moved inside her, as if he could caress her mind, her emotions. "You will feel no pain. You will not remember." His voice echoed inside her mind.

Sensual heat enveloped her. Desire rushed like a flood. She wanted him to kiss her, wanted his teeth on her flesh.

"No!" She fought her way out of the fog.

Then heat and desire again, stronger than before. Her legs weakened, but his arms held her. She told herself to fight, but a sensuous languor enveloped her.

Only the scrape of his teeth against her skin ended her stupor. She called to the Lord and Lady, asking for strength and help. Focusing her mind as much as she was able, she gathered energy, pulling it to her hand, visualizing a line of blue fire.

He jerked away before she sent the energy into him, but the shock still knocked him to the floor. She stood over him, freed from his mind control. But her body still thrummed with desire.

She should run before he recovered. But she couldn't make herself go. How had he broken through her shields? She'd worked hard to develop her own powers—how could she have been so careless? He could have killed her, if he'd only been a bit faster.

*****

Seconds passed. Avran made no attempt to rise. He'd already made a big mistake, one a vampire with his experience and power should never have made. He wasn't about to make another and let this woman get away before he found out how she'd been able to best him.

Never had he met a human as strong as she. A few of his potential victims had been able to block his initial probe of their minds, but he'd always gotten through in the end. No one had seriously challenged him in centuries.

More seconds ticked away. Then, ever so slowly, Avran rose, careful to keep distance between them. "Your power is most impressive. Do tell me how you came to such knowledge." He let the sensual quality of his voice caress her, smiling when he noted her sharp intake of breath.

"Why are you here?" she asked, ignoring his question.

The urge to taunt her, to frighten her, overrode all his good intentions. "I love the land, the town, the women who come to me longing to be bitten."

Again he saw her react. A mortal wouldn't have noticed it, but she'd lifted her foot to step back from him before planting if firmly and standing her ground.

"Why are *you* here?" he asked.

"I told you. I came to ask your support in the fight to save the Langley Square. Obviously, I made a big mistake."

"I would be glad to assist you."

"No, thanks. I don't require help that involves my blood being drained." She turned to go.

"Some vampires love the kill. That's not what it's about for me. It's about the give and take of pleasure."

"I'm sure it is. Your victim gives and you take."

"I assure you, I never take more than I need, and I give pure pleasure in return."

His words slid over her like satin caressing her skin. She turned to look at him, trying to resist, but pulled by a desire she couldn't explain. "I don't need your help or anything else you wish to give me."

"Perhaps you need me far more than you realize."

His soft words ran through her, heating her, the promise in his voice unmistakable. Years had passed since she'd gone on a date, much less been to bed with a man. But no matter how much pleasure he could give her, it wasn't worth the risk. Even the best sex in the world wasn't worth dying for.

"I must go." She turned toward the door.

"I trust you wouldn't want others to know of your powers."

She froze. "Don't try to blackmail me."

"Blackmail was not what I had in mind. I was thinking of a mutual agreement. We're both creatures with secrets that require protection."

"I have no intention of revealing your identity, and I have better sense than to enter into an agreement with a blood drinker." She slammed the door on her way out.

*****

When Liz pulled into her driveway, Ares, her Siberian Husky, ran to greet her, temporarily helping her forget the pounding of her heart. She'd expected to sense Mr. Niccolayic's pursuit, but apparently, she'd truly escaped.

When she pushed her door open, Ares nearly knocked her down. "Calm down, boy. I'm sorry it's so late."

He continued to stand on his hind legs and lick her face while Saffron, her twenty-five pound Maine Coon cat, wrapped herself around Liz's legs and purred, making it clear she believed herself far more deserving of attention than any dog. "You two have to let me move, or I can't feed either of you." Liz smiled despite the fear still coursing through her body.

At the word "feed" Ares bounded toward the front door. Saffron leapt onto the porch railing, not wanting anyone to think she was actually so crass as to run to her food bowl.

Liz's hands shook as she put food and water in their respective bowls. She supposed she should be scared after so narrowly escaping Avran's fangs. But it wasn't Avran, or the knowledge that she could have died, that terrified her.

Despite what she'd been taught about vampires, despite the fact Avran clearly intended to drink from her, she wasn't afraid of him. She was afraid of her reaction.

He was far too potent. For a few seconds, even after she'd registered his thrall, she'd wanted to surrender to him. As much as she hated to admit it, the lust wasn't all a product of his mind games.

Liz sank into the supple leather cushions of her sofa. Her head fell back, and she exhaled slowly. When most of the tension had oozed from her muscles, she opened her eyes. Looking around the room, she thought how much she loved the quaint little house. Though the whole house would probably fit in Avran's foyer, it was perfect for her. Normally she felt cozy and very much at home there, but at that moment, she shivered with cold and loneliness.

She'd inherited the house when her father died. She missed him desperately. He hadn't known about her powers, so she wouldn't have been able to share her problems with him, but at least he would have given her a hug and told her he loved her. Since her parents had divorced, contact with her mother had been minimal, and she didn't have many friends. It was hard to get close to anyone when she had to hide who she truly was. She supposed, being a vampire, Avran had much the same problem.

She shook her head. She should never have sought him out She'd had been foolish beyond measure to think anyone would help her defeat Max Liftkin. Deep Magician law stated that her kind took care of their own problems. Telling anyone what she knew about Liftkin would only risk exposing her secrets.

The laws were there for a reason. Most people would consider her a witch if they learned something of her powers. And in truth, Deep Magicians had many things in common with those who considered themselves witches such as a faith based on the cycles of nature, the ability to manipulate energy to perform magic, and a variety of psychic gifts. However Deep Magicians powers were far stronger. With little more than a thought Liz could call a ball of energy into existence that would annihilate a crowd of normal humans. If their powers were ever made known to non-paranormals, Deep Magicians would all be hunted. Such powerful creatures as they would never be allowed to roam free.

Liz had been alone with her secrets for years and that is how she would remain. Alone.

*****

Max Liftkin stood outside Liz's bedroom window, watching her shadowed form climb onto the bed to comfort the animals who'd sensed his presence. He'd not counted on finding another Deep Magician in Granville, but he'd be damned if he let her ruin his plans.

Killing her outright would draw too much attention. So he'd been studying her, learning what he could from those who knew her. She was tenderhearted. Overly so. If he hurt enough of the people she loved, she would back down and let him have his way. She'd do anything to protect the mere mortals she thought of as friends.

Chapter 2

The next morning, after hitting the snooze button for the fifth time, Liz dragged herself from under the covers. The minute she was on her feet, Saffron jumped to the floor and raced for the bathroom counter, nearly tripping Liz in the process. Wiping the sleep from her eyes, she turned on the faucet so the cat could drink from it.

Liz wanted nothing more than to crawl back under the covers and sleep for several more hours. All night she'd been plagued by images of Avran. His silky voice lulled her, while his skilled hands roamed her body and his fangs sank into her neck. All of it—even his bite—had been delicious.

He still haunted her as she stood in the shower. The water running over her reminded her of his hands. In her dreams, they'd been hot and fluid, not at all what she expected from one of his kind. Of course, her dreams were nothing but fantasy. The reality would probably involve less pleasure and far more pain.

Ares waited for her in the kitchen. She stopped to pet him before putting food in his bowl and starting the coffee brewing.

He whined and she bent down and patted his nose. "I'm sorry we can't walk now. I'm running late. We'll go when I get home, boy." He accepted her apology by nuzzling her leg.

When Liz pulled into her spot in the tiny parking lot behind her shop, she saw an ambulance and a police car parked behind the Cumberland Gallery. Her heart rate sped up as she surveyed the scene. A few cops and several people she recognized as morning regulars at The Coffee Bean stood at the gallery's back entrance. One of the women appeared to be crying, and all of them looked pale and shaken.

A feeling of dread settled in Liz's stomach. Two paramedics came out of the gallery, carrying a stretcher. One of them held an oxygen mask over the patient's nose, but despite her obscured view, Liz could tell it was Mrs. Cumberland.

Liz took a deep breath and approached the small crowd by the door, "What happened?" she asked a man whose face she recognized, but whose name she couldn't remember.

"Someone hit her over the head. That's all I know."

Then she spotted Stephanie, one of the few people Liz could consider a close friend. Rushing over to her, Liz asked about Mrs. Cumberland's daughter, Dorothy.

"She wasn't hurt," Stephanie said. "She wanted to follow her mother to the hospital, but the police still have some questions for her. She's inside."

"Did she find her mother?"

"No. Trevor, Rob, and I did." Stephanie gestured to indicate the owner of The Coffee Bean and the man Liz had been speaking to earlier.

"Will Mrs. Cumberland be okay?"

"I don't know. We found her on the floor in the back room. The police and the paramedics got here quickly, but we think she'd been unconscious for hours."

Before Liz had a chance to ask Steph another question, one of the cops approached her. He introduced himself as Officer Thompson, then asked her name.

"I'm Liz Carlson."

He pulled a small notebook and pen from his pocket. "You own the bookstore next door?"

She nodded. "How can I help?"

"We want to talk to everyone who saw Mrs. Cumberland on a daily basis. How well do you know her and her daughter?"

"Quite well. The bookstore has been in my family for a long time. I've known Mrs. Cumberland since I was a baby. Her daughter and I went to school together."

He wrote something down then looked back up at her, holding her gaze as though expecting her to look away. "Do you know anyone who would want to hurt them, or ruin their business?"

"No. Everyone loves Mrs. Cumberland." Then it hit her. Liftkin had done this. She was sure of it, but she couldn't say anything, at least not yet. The police were no match for a Deep Magician.

Officer Thompson raised his brows. "Did you think of something, Ms. Carlson?"

She shook her head rapidly. "No, I'm sorry. I'm just a bit overwhelmed."

"Of course. I'm sorry to upset you, but I need to ask a few more questions."

"I'll be okay." She forced herself to focus on his words.

"Have you seen anyone unusual hanging around the gallery, maybe someone you haven't seen before?"

Liz made it appear that she was considering the question. "No, sir."

"Have Mrs. Cumberland or her daughter received any strange or threatening phone calls or gotten any unusual letters?"

"No," Liz said. "At least they didn't mention anything like that to me."

He closed his notebook and put it back in his pocket. "Well, thank you for your time, Ms. Carlson." He handed Liz a card. "Call me at this number if you think of anything that might be useful, no matter how insignificant it might seem."

"I will," Liz assured him, sticking the card in her pocket. She had no intention of calling unless something made her doubt Liftkin's involvement.

As she approached the back door of her shop, icy fear consumed her. What if Liftkin had been in her shop too? When she got the door open, she walked through the store, taking a survey. All the shelves looked normal. The computer on the counter was untouched, and the comfy reading chairs still sat in the window nook.

Only one thing was out of place. A thick red book Liz didn't recognize lay on the floor by the front door. A black ribbon encircled the leather cover. Liz knelt on the floor and bent her head down to look for a title, being careful not to touch it. There was no writing on either the front cover or the spine. She held her hands above it, close but still not touching. She felt nothing, no malevolent energy, no indication that it could do her harm.

Gathering her defenses, she ran her hand along the spine. Her heart pounded, but nothing happened. She untied the ribbon and opened the cover. Light flashed, and a holographic image appeared a few feet above the book.

Liz watched a scene play out before her. A man dressed in black and wearing a mask opened the back door of the Cumberland Gallery. He didn't pick the lock or break it—the door simply opened as if it was already unlocked. Once inside, he encountered Mrs. Cumberland. The older woman screamed when she saw him. A bolt of energy shot from one of his hands, knocking her back.

He arranged her body facedown on the floor and sent another bolt of energy into the back of her head, making it look as if she'd been hit by a blunt instrument. Then, he held up his hands and sent chaotic energy throughout the gallery. Sculptures exploded, paintings fell off the wall, papers flew, and smoke poured from the computer at Mrs. Cumberland's desk. He did it all with magic, leaving no fingerprints and no way for the police to explain how the damage occurred. Before the image disappeared, the man turned toward Liz. "Continue fighting me, and more will be harmed."

Without seeing his face, Liz knew the man was Max Liftkin. Holographic recordings were a common form of communication between Deep Magicians. Liftkin would have known that only another Magician would be able to see the image he had recorded. A normal human would have found nothing out of the ordinary when he or she opened the book.

Liz had hoped to have the advantage of surprise, but she should have known better. Clearly Liftkin knew who and what she was. Despite her attempts to mask her powers, he had probably sensed her presence as easily as she had his.

How could she answer this threat? She desperately needed some help. Avran's compelling face appeared in her mind. She shook her head. She couldn't trust him. She needed another Magician. But she knew there was little chance of that. Deep Magicians rarely worked together, and the only one she'd ever been close to—her mentor, Elspeth—was dead.

As a last resort, she could request an inquiry from the Synod. But their system of justice was more painfully slow than the one for normals. As often as not, the innocent party was the one truly punished.

Resigning herself to a lost day of work, she put out a sign, indicating the shop would be opening late and apologizing for the inconvenience. She hated to lose customers, but devising a way to defeat Liftkin was far more important than selling books. She regretted having to perform her ritual of inquiry in such a small space, but she didn't have time to go home. Her office would have to do.

Liz cleared a circular space on the floor of her office and placed four candles at the cross points of the circle. She lit a stick of incense and carried it as she walked the perimeter of her circle three times, sealing herself in and keeping any negative energy from reaching her while she was vulnerable. When she finished, she sat down, crossed her legs, and began to slow her breathing.

She drew each breath in deep and held it. After each exhale, she waited, letting herself rest in the space between breaths, feeling the darkness, the emptiness. She stretched herself into it, finding the place where she could communicate with divine forces and draw in magical energy.

She asked the Lord and Lady to honor her with their presence, and a warm surge of energy surrounded her. Sometimes they appeared before her in human form, other times they remained nebulous, moving about her as pure energy. It was these times, when they took no form, that she perceived them with all her senses. Their energy caressed her body. The pop and crackle of it brushed at her ears. She could even smell them. Exotic spice and floral herbs floated by her nose. She inhaled deeply.

"What is your question, my daughter?" They spoke in unison.

"I am in need of help. Another Magician is in Granville, and he seeks to do harm with his power. I am not strong enough to battle him on my own. Whom can I trust to help me?"

For several long minutes, she sat in silence. She had learned years ago not to expect an immediate response. Sometimes no response came at all, only more questions for her to consider.

Finally, the Lady spoke. "You already know the answer, my dear, but you fear it. Trust your deep instincts. Be led not by fear, but by what resides within your soul."

Then the Lord's voice came into her mind. "I feel your frustration. Let it go. Rest here for a while. Let the darkness speak to you."

A few times before, when they had a vision to show her, Liz had been asked to remain there in the darkness of the void. Not once had she liked the results. The Lord and Lady inevitably showed her something about herself she would rather not see, but she couldn't deny the Lord's request.

It was easier to let herself go if she allowed her physical body to rest as well, so she unfolded her legs and lay back against the cold floor, arms resting along her sides, palms facing the ceiling. Blackness swirled around her. Fear closed in, but then the Lady sent warm energy through her and she calmed. Eventually she drifted deeper to a state near sleep.

She felt a touch, silken pressure running down the inside of her arm. It was Avran. She wanted to protest, but the sight of him paralyzed her. He smiled, continuing to stroke her. She looked into his silver eyes and fell under his spell. Somewhere, far above, on the surface of her thoughts, she knew she could fight him, but she didn't want to.

Reaching up, she cupped his face and stroked his cheek with her thumb. His skin was smooth and cold. She wanted it pressed against her, but even more, she wanted him to taste her. She, who had kept herself aloof, who had always prided herself on controlling her life, wanted to surrender to him, to fall into his eyes and feel his teeth piercing her.

She traced the line of his jaw and ran her fingers along his neck, down across his chest, feeling the hardness of the muscles there. He caught her wrist before she could move lower and placed her hand back on the floor.

He bent over her and used his tongue to trace the path his fingers had followed. Starting at her palm, he ran his tongue up and over her wrist, stopping ever so briefly on the pulse point there. Then he drew a wet line up her arm to the pulse that beat in the curve of her elbow. Back and forth he stroked her.

How could something so simple be so arousing? Each time he licked her pulse points, her heartbeat accelerated. The throbbing of her heart echoed between her legs. Lines of searing heat ran from her arm to her center. She felt ripe and heavy, ready to be taken. Never had a man made her feel like this. She should be afraid, but she wasn't. Everything was exactly as it should be, as if she'd been waiting for this her whole life, waiting to surrender.

When his tongue reached her wrist again, he stopped. He laced his fingers with hers and placed his other hand on her forearm, all the while stroking her wrist with his tongue. His fangs brushed her. Once. Twice. Then a sharp pain jolted her as his teeth sank into her flesh. It was immediately overshadowed by the most intense pleasure imaginable.

As his mouth sucked at her wrist, waves of heated bliss swam over her. She felt the pull of his lips all the way to her core. If she hadn't seen him bent over her arm, she would have sworn he was licking her swollen clit.

She writhed and twisted, praying he wouldn't stop. Reality rushed in for a moment. She wondered how much blood he could take without killing her. Would he stop in time? Then she was lost again to her passion. Her free arm fisted in his hair, locking him to her. She cried out, begging him not to stop. Then, she went over the edge and darkness consumed her.

Moments later, she opened her eyes. Where was she? What had happened? She looked around and slowly recognized her office.

Oh, gods, Avran. Where was he? She looked around again, but she was alone.

Then she remembered her trance and her meeting with the Lord and Lady. She must have fallen asleep and dreamed. She lifted her arm and stared at it as if it belonged to someone else. No bite marks. The moisture between her legs was real, but such a dream would make any woman wet.

Had she fallen asleep? It had been years since she'd been unable to stay awake during a meditation. What had happened?

She raked her hand through her hair. Her head felt fuzzy. It took several minutes to clear it, but finally, she remembered. She'd performed the ritual of inquiry. Had her question been answered?

The Lady's voice echoed in her head. *You already knew the answer.*

They had asked her to stay, to rest in the void, and—no! It couldn't be. She wanted it to have been a dream, not a vision. She wanted to deny it, but their message was clear.

She should have expected something like this. Divine visions were invariably frustrating. How could they want her to go to Avran, to surrender to him?

A little voice inside her reminded her she always regretted ignoring the Lord and Lady, no matter how much she resented their advice. She told the voice to shut up. Going to Avran was out of the question. She would have to find another solution.

Chapter 3

When Liz had left him the night before, Avran had been far more shaken than he wanted to admit. She had managed to stir an undeniable hunger in him *and* mask her power until she was ready to strike. A man who'd seen as much death and destruction as he had was damned hard to shock, but she'd done it.

Her strength was both unsettling and arousing. The idea of how fiercely she would react to him in bed excited him more than anything had in years.

Who was she really? Obviously she was more than a bookstore owner. He cursed himself for not listening more closely to what she'd said about needing his help in the effort to preserve Langley Square. Something about the man who wanted to rebuild the square had disturbed her. Instinctively, Avran knew Ms. Carlson would never have risked coming to him if her problem was not serious, but what could frighten a woman with power like hers?

When he woke in the late afternoon, he summoned Gregory to his study. Before going to sleep with the dawn, he'd asked his man to go into town and learn what he could about this intriguing woman and her dilemma.

"Good evening, sir," Gregory said.

"Good evening." Avran gestured toward the wine, indicating that Gregory should pour himself a glass. "Did you have any success in your quest?"

"I did. I learned quite a lot about the young woman's background, but the most interesting thing I discovered was that Mrs. Cumberland, the owner of the Cumberland Gallery, was attacked last night. The gallery was also viciously vandalized but nothing appears to have actually been stolen. Apparently some of the business owners are blaming Max Liftkin, the prospective buyer of the square. They think he's hoping to scare people off."

"If this was what Ms. Carlson was worried about, why wouldn't she go to the police? Why come to me?"

"I don't know, sir."

"Then we shall find out. Tell me what you learned of her."

"Ms. Carlson has lived in Granville all her life. Her father died almost a year ago, leaving her the sole owner of Carlson Fine and Rare Books. Her closest living relatives are her mother, who is currently on a tour of Europe, and her father's parents who live in Charleston. She's twenty-nine. She lives alone, hasn't dated anyone in years, and has few close friends."

Avran's brow rose. "And her powers? Has she roused no suspicions?"

Gregory took a sip of wine and shook his head. "She's openly Pagan, but I found no indication anyone suspects she has any greater power than a solid knowledge of herbal medicine."

Avran's curiosity grew once he learned how well Ms. Carlson had hidden herself. In a town the size of Granville, the slightest abnormality made for great gossip. Not only determination but great skill and planning would be needed to mask her true nature so thoroughly.

A thought crossed his mind. Could she possibly be— No. That was absurd. She couldn't be a Deep Magician. The fabled practitioners figured prominently in the oldest legends of his kind. Though if that *was* her secret, he would do best to stay far away from her.

But he had no intention of doing that. Once the light had dimmed enough for him to venture forth, he would visit Ms. Carlson and do whatever it took to win her over.

*****

Liz kept the shop open later than usual. By the time the last customer left, the sun rode low in the sky.

Her head throbbed, and she wanted nothing more than a long hot bath, but before she left, she wrote an email to the Synod asking them to investigate Liftkin's presence in Granville. She didn't put much stock in their efforts, but she had to make use of her limited resources.

Her hopes for a long soak in the tub were ruined when she stepped onto her porch. The cool energy of her own magic should have greeted her, but the air was calm and still. Her wards had been breached.

She laid her hand on the doorknob, sliding the lock back with her magic as she charged inside. Ares never failed to come running when she got home, but he was nowhere to be seen.

"Ares!" A cold, sick feeling came over her as she ran from room to room, finding no sign of either Ares or Saffron. "Ares! Where are you?Oh, Lord and Lady, please let them be okay!" Tears ran down her face. Why hadn't she thought to increase the strength of her wards?

When she'd searched the entire house, she ran onto her deck, praying her animals were in the back yard. She heard a meow. Her heart skipped a beat, but the sound hadn't come from Saffron. Her neighbor's gray tabby sat at the base of a tree, eyeing a squirrel.

Frantic, she paced the deck.

Liz had no doubt Liftkin was behind this. Who else could have gotten into her home? Maybe he'd left another message. She went inside and began to look for anything he might have left behind. She found nothing, but the message button on her answering machine blinking. Surely he wouldn't use such a conventional method of communication, but she had to check.

BEEEEEP! Liz...Are you home? It's Stephanie. I found Ares and Saffron wandering around when I went for a walk. They looked a little dazed, but they're all right. I've got them here. Come over as soon as you get in.

She ran out the door before the machine clicked off, realizing she was leaving the house completely unprotected, but unable to stop. She had to see for herself that Ares and Saffron were okay.

Her lungs burned by the time she reached Stephanie's yard. Her friend sat on her porch with Ares lying at her feet. Saffron stood inside the screen door, looking indignant. Relief washed over her as she bent to catch her breath.

"Liz, I'm so glad to see you," Stephanie said. "I was really worried when I found them."

Liz pulled herself together and raced up the steps. "Thank you so much!" She hugged Stephanie, and Ares jumped between them, trying to lick Liz's face. "Where did you find them?"

"I was taking a walk, and I saw them down on Hyacinth Street. Their eyes were a bit glassy, and they both kept tripping over their feet. If I didn't know better, I'd have thought they were drunk. But they're better now, so I wouldn't worry."

Saffron chose that moment to meow loudly and attempt to climb the screen. Liz let the cat out and stroked her back. "Did you have a fright today, darling?"

Once Saffron had settled in Liz's lap, Steph continued her story. "I took them back to your house, thinking somehow a door must have been left open, but everything was locked up tight. Were they inside when you left?"

Liz didn't know what to say. She knew exactly where she'd left Ares and Saffron that morning, but she would rather have Steph believe the incident had a logical explanation. "I thought they were, but I did leave the door open for a bit while I was loading some books. I don't see how I could have missed their escape."

Stephanie eyes narrowed. "It's not like you to be that distracted."

Liz forced herself to smile. "I know. This whole mess with Liftkin Construction has me exhausted."

Stephanie smiled, the scrutinizing look gone from her eyes. "I'm sure. How're things going?"

"Not very well." Not wanting to dwell on that subject, Liz scooped up Saffron. "Thanks so much for taking care of them. I'd love to talk more, but I've got a meeting later tonight."

Stephanie leaned against her porch railing. Concern was again evident in the way she scrunched up her nose and bit her lip. "What kind of meeting?"

Liz fought to think quickly. "Umm, a meeting for the business owner's association."

Stephanie frowned. "Liz, you're acting very strange. Are you sure you're all right?"

Butterflies flitted in Liz's stomach but she forced herself to keep her tone even. "I'm fine. I just really busy."

Liz called to Ares and headed home. As she walked, she convinced herself she hadn't really lied to Stephanie. She did have business to attend to. The clear message from the Lord and Lady hadn't been enough, but this incident made it obvious. She had no choice but to see Avran again.

After enduring Saffron's squirming for two blocks, she let the cat down, trusting her to walk the last few yards to the house. She was looking down, monitoring the cat's movements and patting Ares' back when she ran smack into a wall. At least it felt as hard as a wall. When she looked, Avran stood in front of her.

"For a woman with your powers, you are frightfully unaware of your surroundings."

How dare he? Anger rushed through her. Ares growled, either sensing her apprehension or simply finding Avran's nature objectionable. "It's all right. Go wait by the door." The dog shot a menacing look at Avran, but he obeyed.

"What're you doing here?" Anger, wariness, nervousness, and worst of all, arousal rushed through Liz's body. She prayed none of them came through in her words.

"We did not finish our conversation last night."

"I think we did." She wasn't about to tell him she'd planned to come to him.

He reached out a hand as if he were going to touch her but let it fall. "You're in trouble. Clearly you believe I can help you. So I'm here to lend my assistance."

She wished she could believe that was all he wanted, but the sensuality swirling around him and the low, velvety tone of his voice said he wanted far more.

Liz clenched her hands, barely able to stop herself from touching him. Her traitorous body had no concern for her safety. "If you're truly willing to help, then I need to explain some things."

"Shall we go inside? I don't think we should have this conversation in your front yard." He inclined his head toward the neighbors sitting on their porch across the street.

Liz nodded and turned toward the house. "I'm surprised you didn't let yourself in."

"I would not be so presumptuous, though I was concerned to find your home unguarded. Your door's standing wide open."

"I...something important came up. I had to leave suddenly." She failed to keep her voice steady. The thought of what happened still had her shaken.

Avran followed her onto the porch, but he stopped at the door and turned to face her. "After you." He bowed and gestured toward the door.

Then she remembered. Some of the myths about his kind were surely true. "You can't go in, can you? You have to wait for me to invite you."

Avran stared into her eyes for a few seconds, and she stopped breathing. "Yes, I must be invited."

"Once I ask you in, can you return whenever you want, no matter whether I wish it or not?"

"If you were a normal human then yes, I could. But I think you could keep me out if you truly wanted to." He said the last words as though he planned to make sure she would want him to come back every night.

Resigning herself to her fate, Liz extended her invitation, showed him into the kitchen, and offered him one of the stools at the marble-covered island.

"Do you...would you like a glass of wine?"

He smiled, his eyes assessing her with a look that was far too knowing. "I would love one."

Forcing herself to focus on the wine, she poured two glasses and handed him one. He brought the glass to his lips and stroked the side of it with his tongue, wiping away a drop that had spilled. Liz instantly remembered him doing the same thing to her wrist.

She swallowed hard, and he chose that moment to look up. His gaze captured hers. Waves of heat rushed through her body. She gripped the counter to steady herself.

Oh, gods, this wasn't going to work. She had to get him out of her house as quickly as possible. The best way to do that was to focus on the reason he was there. "I suppose you want me to explain why I came to see you last night."

He nodded, still studying her intently, his gray eyes dark and sensuous. She concentrated on closing her shields tightly. She wasn't sure what mind-reading powers he had, but she wasn't taking any chances.

"Before I start, I want you to understand that I came to you, because you are the only person in town who might understand what is happening, and well, the universe seems to be conspiring to put you in my path. Still, I don't trust you, and I have no intention of becoming your next meal."

Anger flashed across his face. "I understood your sentiments yesterday." His voice held a distinct chill.

Liz waited for him to say something else. When he didn't, she continued. "A development company, Liftkin Construction, wishes to purchase the city-owned park in the middle of Langley Square and the Mercer building. They intend to destroy the park, tear down the Mercer building and fill the area with modern high-rise condos."

"I am aware of Liftkin's bid for the land. I was saddened to read that the city was actually considering it."

"Most people assume this is all about money. The city is desperate for more revenue, and Liftkin thinks to make a sizeable profit off his condos. But I don't think Liftkin is the least bit interested in money. I think he wants the land for another purpose." She paused, unsure how to continue.

"What makes you think this?"

Here it was, the moment of truth. Could she risk telling her secret to a vampire?

His eyes narrowed as he held her gaze. "What are you, Liz?"

Could she really tell him what she'd only told a few others in her life? She took a deep breath. "I'm a Deep Magician and so is Max Liftkin."

He made no visible reaction, but tension emanated from him. "Long ago, I met a few of your kind. Their power had devastating strength. It is fortunate most of you follow the rules set down by your leaders. I take it Liftkin does not?"

"No, he's already injured and maybe killed one woman, and..." Tears came to her eyes. She stopped speaking. She could not let this man see her cry.

"What else has he done?"

She felt Avran's tension, as if at any moment he might spring and attack.

"When I came home from work, Ares and Saffron, my dog and cat, were gone. I knew he was behind it. No one else could have gotten through my wards. I thought he had killed them. But my friend, Stephanie, left me a message, saying she'd found them outside. I was at her house when you arrived."

At the sound of her name, Saffron looked up from the spot where she lay curled on the rug. The huge cat walked over to Avran, wrapped herself against his ankles and began to purr. He reached down to stroke her. The purring grew louder.

Liz stared. Saffron normally had nothing to do with strangers. Sometimes she even shunned Liz's affection.

"What can I do to help you stop him?" Avran's voice carried the force of steel.

Liz shook her head. "I wish I knew. Unfortunately, all Deep Magicians' powers differ slightly. I don't know what Liftkin is capable of, and worse, I don't know his real reason for being here."

Liz took a deep breath, again wondering how much she should say. "The area under the Mercer building is a place of strong elemental power. That's why my grandparents opened the bookstore near it. But there has to be more to Liftkin's plan. Elemental power centers aren't that rare. There's no need to go to such trouble to be near one."

Avran's gaze still hadn't left hers. The scrutiny was making her sweat. He smiled as if he knew the effect he had. "Do you know if Liftkin frequents a particular restaurant or bar at night?"

Liz shook her head. "No. I don't know anything about his personal life."

Avran nodded. "I'll send my man to find out what he can. Then, I'll arrange to run into Liftkin tomorrow night and see what I can pluck from his mind. I'm assuming mind-reading is not one of your powers, or else you've tried to read his mind and been unsuccessful."

Liz hesitated. She didn't want Avran to know what powers she held and what she didn't. Such knowledge gave him too much control over her.

Anger flashed in his eyes. "If you truly want my help, you must be honest with me. Ignorance is dangerous for both of us."

Liz knew he was right, but she still hated it. "I can't read minds. I can sense emotion and motivation but not concrete thoughts. I don't think you'll be able to read Liftkin, unless you are far more powerful than I imagine. His shields will be strong, and he will instantly detect a breach. Don't underestimate his power."

"Don't underestimate mine, either." Avran's voice was nearly a purr. His words flowed over and around Liz, making her shiver. "Come to my house around midnight tomorrow. I will tell you what I've learned and we will make further plans."

Liz hesitated to respond. She doubted the wisdom of meeting him at night in his own home. If he tried to seduce her again, would she be able to resist? But she knew if she wanted his help, she would have to learn to reign in her desire for him. "I'll be there. But, please be careful. I understand you have great confidence in your powers, but he's very dangerous."

Avran's smile was positively sinful. "You're dangerous, but I'm here, and I'm not afraid."

Liz feared she was already in over her head. She had to get rid of him quickly. "I appreciate your willingness to help, but I think you should go now."

"I dreamed about you this morning." His words rubbed over her skin like satin. Picking up her wrist, he turned it over and kissed the tender skin where her veins showed clearly. "You tasted wonderful."

Oh, no. He couldn't possibly have seen the same vision she had. She had no hope if he knew how easily he could pleasure her. "I asked you to leave."

"Don't deny your desire for me. You've made it clear you don't want to act on it now, but don't pretend it doesn't exist."

He was too beautiful, too alluring. It would be so easy to admit her feelings *and* act on them. "Avran. Please. Just go."

He stood, and Liz followed him to the door. As he was about to leave, he turned to her. He stood so close she could feel energy radiating from his body. The power he contained overwhelmed her. She'd been able to repel him when he wasn't expecting it, but she doubted she could defeat him if he was prepared.

His gaze dropped to her lips. She meant to step back, to tell him again that she wanted him gone. Instead, she watched the beautiful planes of his face. He lifted his hand and brushed her cheek ever so lightly. Then, he was gone.

Chapter 4

Max Liftkin was riding high. Only a few barriers stood between him and success. Liz Carlson was a woman who followed rules. She didn't have the courage to destroy him. All he had to do was continue threatening those she loved, and he would break her.

He glanced down at the ugly red scratch on his hand. Who in their right mind would keep a cat that grew so enormous? He should have killed the damn beast when he had the chance. But he only wanted to scare Liz, because even the most cowardly woman could be pushed too far. He preferred not to risk testing his magic against hers. Especially not when his plan was working so well.

Bribing several members of the town council to vote in his favor had been laughably easy. God, he loved his ability to read people. He'd been prepared to pay twice as much to assure that the city would sell the property he needed.

Soon his greatest dream would come true. And then he could get rid of his so-called ally. She thought she was using him, but once he got what he needed from her, the tables would turn. Yes, his life was looking up, and tonight, he was going to celebrate.

✶✶✶✶✶

Avran moved silently through the alley behind The Black Cat. He'd been waiting by the back entrance, opening his mind to the roar of mental voices inside. He'd waded through the mass of unshielded minds until he felt what he was looking foran unconscious reaction to power. He felt it every time he approached a potential victim. For some there was fear, for some attraction or envy, but always there was a reaction. When several people made that mental jump, he knew Liftkin had entered.

Avran walked to the front entrance of the bar, ready to size up the man who had dared to challenge Liz. He smelled Liftkin as soon as he opened the door. Like Liz, the Magician had an earthy scent, but his was more pungent, more male, not nearly so clean or pure.

Avran found a seat at a table near Liftkin's and resisted using his persuasive powers to call a waitress to his table. He couldn't risk disturbing the energy of the room and losing the element of surprise.

When a waitress finally approached him, he ordered a stout. She offered him a dinner menu, but he had to decline. Eating was the mortal pleasure he missed most. Vampires need only blood to survive, but their bodies could metabolize other liquids. Solids, however, were not tolerated. In the months following his Change, Avran had tried again and again to eat his favorite foods, thinking surely something would agree with his new constitution. But every time he'd eaten even the smallest portion of food, he'd been gut-wrenchingly ill. Finally, he'd accepted that he'd never taste solid food again. Still, it had galled him not to be able to try all the unfamiliar delicacies he'd encountered as he'd traveled the world over the last six centuries.

At least he could still drink, and drinking a beer as dark and thick as this as this micro-brewed stout was a lot like eating a loaf of the dark peasant bread he had enjoyed growing up in Brittany.

He slid into the corner of his booth, wishing he could appear less conspicuous. Unfortunately, the tales of vampires melting into the darkness or cloaking themselves with invisibility were complete fiction. Going unnoticed had never been easy for Avran, even when he was human. He'd been the tallest, strongest man in his village, the one always sent to war as their champion. Once he'd gone through the Change and gained that special vampire beauty, vanishing in a crowd had become impossible.

Avran could turn all the heads in a room if he wanted, especially if he dressed the part. Tonight, he'd dressed like a modern human man—jeans and a plain black T-shirt, but many of the women in the bar, and a few of the men, watched him like they were the ones who needed to feed. At least he wasn't the only one attracting attention. Liftkin drew his own share of glances.

Max Liftkin was a tall Nordic blond. He wore his hair long, and it curled across his face, giving him a boyish look that belied his power. Avran studied the table where Liftkin sat. Four women hung on his every word, and Avran required no mind-reading talent to know Liftkin hoped to take one, two, or even three of them home.

One advantage of becoming a vampire was one gained a lot of patience. Avran could sit still for hours, his breathing slowed to almost nothing. So he sat and watched while the women at Liftkin's table downed drink after drink. Once Liftkin's companions began giggling loudly and draping themselves around the blond man, Avran reached out with his mind and caught the musky scent of lust swirling around their table. Avran decided Liftkin was as distracted as he would get before leaving the bar.

Letting his mental touch fall as lightly as he could, Avran made contact with the edge of Liftkin's shields. Feeling no reaction, he probed into Liftkin's surface thoughts, but all he saw was slight inebriation and intense lust.

To his vampire senses, Liftkin's mind was like an onion, full of layers of thought with the subconscious at the center. He peeled back the first layer of Liftkin's mind with the delicate touch of a surgeon and moved deeper. At the next level, he found nothing but a jumble of thoughts about the women at the table—what Liftkin fantasized about doing to them and the man's observations of others in the bar. Nothing about Liz.

Avran needed to get deeper, but Liftkin's shields pressed tightly against his probe. He had a few seconds, at most, before they closed against him. Rather than use the time to move deeper, he tried another tactic.

The dark haired girl sitting on Liftkin's lap had a vapid mind that was easily guided. The barest suggestion from Avran convinced her to reach under the table and stroke Liftkin's cock.

Success. Liftkin's shields loosened. Avran probed deep, but all he caught was the word 'treasure' before Liftkin's shields snapped shut, and his eyes locked with Avran's.

Avran's first instinct was to feign confusion, pretend he had no idea how he had offended Liftkin. But if Liftkin was half as strong as Liz suggested, he would know without question that Avran was not an average human.

Liftkin stood, dumping the dark-haired woman off his lap. He crossed towards Avran's table, and the vampire threw up a mental disguise. If he could hold onto the glamour, Liftkin would think Avran was a powerful witch who had enough mental abilities to be dangerous, but he wouldn't see any of Avran's true nature.

"What were you staring at?" Liftkin asked when he stood less than a foot from Avran's table. At least, that was what he asked out loud. Avran heard something different in his head.

You've just written your death warrant. No one gets behind my shields and lives.

For the benefit of those around them, Avran responded aloud. "I was wondering what your companions saw in someone so crass." *You're welcome to try, but killing me won't be easy.*

Liftkin continued to stare. Avran felt his sharp probe, but the vampire's illusion held. Hopefully, Liftkin would think he was an upstart witch who didn't know what he was playing with.

"Leave," Liftkin said aloud.

"Since you obviously don't know how to behave in civilized company, I'll oblige you."

Liftkin returned to his table and threw several bills on the table. Avran walked out slowly, all his senses focused on Liftkin. He could sense the man tracking his movements. He doubted the Magician wanted to cause a public scene, not when he was already hated by most of the community. If he could get Avran in private though, Liftkin's pride wouldn't let him back down from a fight.

Avran considered leaving the area quickly to avoid the confrontation. With his vampiric abilities, he could arrive home before Liftkin left the bar, but he knew Liftkin would come for him sooner or later. If Liftkin didn't already know who he was, he could easily find out by asking around. While Avran had little contact with the citizens of Granville, many of them recognized him. He'd rather deal with a challenge now, than have Gregory at risk while he slept.

So Avran walked slowly to the parking garage where he'd left his black Mercedes. As he reached for the door handle, he sensed Liftkin approaching. There was no one else near them, but the garage was still a public place. Would Liftkin risk using magic?

Avran stood still as Liftkin came closer, turning only when he was less than two car lengths away. Avran expected a lecture on respecting one's magical superior, but Liftkin said nothing. Rather, he punched Avran's jaw with stunning force.

Avran's head flew back, but he caught himself against his car. Blood poured from his mouth as he steadied himself.

His vampire reflexes allowed him to grab Liftkin before the man could land another blow. Avran fisted his hands in Liftkin's shirt and threw him against the truck in the next parking space. He could have made it a fatal blow, at least to a human, but he held back.

Liftkin staggered to his feet. Avran sensed the gathering of energy too late. A bolt of light shot out. Liftkin had aimed for his chest, but Avran turned, shielding his body against his car. The energy sliced through his leg like a knife.

Avran grabbed Liftkin and pulled him into a choke hold. The urge to kill the man swamped him. As he squeezed to cut off Liftkin's air, he could smell the man's blood. For years, he'd refrained from killing anyone with his bite, even those who deserved it. When the life left a body, the dissipating energy surged into him, giving him a high unlike any other. Such pleasure was too delicious, too addictive.

Perhaps he would have broken his reserve and ended Liftkin's life, but he didn't have the chance. The door to the stairs opened, and a car beeped. He would not risk being caught with Liftkin's body in his arms. He let the man go.

"You will die for what you've done." Liftkin snarled as he rubbed his throat. Then the Magician turned and walked toward the elevator.

Avran slammed his fist against the roof of his car. Liz would be furious. At least he'd kept enough control to keep Liftkin from reading any of his thoughts. The man would have no reason to connect him to Liz. Anger and hunger threatened to snap his control. He stood still for a few moments, trying to calm himself.

When he thought he had his rage under control, he examined his injuries. Blood had soaked his jeans where Liftkin had cut his leg with energy. It also poured freely from his nose. He would need to feed again, but not here.

He looked at the clock in the dash of his car as he opened the door. Fifteen minutes after midnight. Liz would be waiting at his house, wondering why he wasn't there. At least he prayed she was. If Liftkin had gone after her, he would kill the man, even if Avran died in the process.

*****

Liz paced back and forth in Avran's study. Gregory had shown her in, saying Avran had not returned but was expected any minute. The vampire's absence disturbed her. She rubbed her arms, trying to warm herself, but no amount of friction could remove the chill of her fear.

She had no reason to assume Avran was stronger than Liftkin, no matter how well-protected he thought he was. Liftkin was ruthless. If he caught Avran prying into his thoughts, Liftkin wouldn't hesitate to kill him. She knew far too little about vampires, but she was certain it was possible to kill one. Immortality was not a guarantee.

The thought of Avran dying at Liftkin's hand made her shivers increase. Any harm that came to him would be her fault. This was her fight. She shouldn't have let him get involved, no matter how desperate she was for help. Deep Magicians were supposed to save others, not lead them into danger.

Just when Liz had determined to go after Avran, she saw lights coming up the driveway. Reaching through the darkness with her mind, she detected Avran's presence and breathed a sigh of relief. There was just enough moonlight to see him as he exited the car. He appeared to be limping.

She rushed toward the front door, arriving in the foyer just as he entered.

"What happened?"

"I pushed too hard. Liftkin caught me."

"Are you okay?"

He took her arm and led her back toward his study. "I will heal. My injuries are the least of our concerns."

Liz's heart raced and to her shame, she felt tears prick behind her eyes. "I...I was worried about you. I'd decided to come after you but then I heard your car and saw you limping."

"If Liftkin had seen us together, he would have killed you. He held back with me, but he was struggling to keep his temper in check."

"I know, but I would have come anyway." Her voice was soft, almost a whisper.

Avran sucked in his breath. "Thank you." His voice held the promise of wild pleasure.

When they stepped into the light of the foyer, Liz gasped. Blood had crusted on Avran's lips, a savage cut marred his beautiful cheek, and she could see a bruise forming above it. She couldn't stop herself from reaching out to touch his face. But feeling him tense under her touch, she dropped her hand.

Gregory came to see if they needed anything. Liz asked him to bring her a dish of water and a soft cloth. Then she began rummaging in her purse. After resorting to dumping out its contents, she found the small jar she needed. "This salve should work." She grabbed his arm and tugged gently. "You need to sit down. Let's go to your study."

★★★★★

Liz's assumption that he needed taking care of both amused and amazed Avran. This woman was truly a force of nature, one so strong she could affect a man as jaded as he.

"This really isn't necessary," he said, following Liz to his study. "My kind heal rapidly."

"It goes against all I believe in to leave anyone in pain. Now sit." She pointed toward the sofa and turned to light some candles.

Avran wanted to protest again, but his leg was throbbing, so he sat down. He turned himself so his injured thigh wasn't visible in the dim light. "We need to talk about what happened."

"You can talk to me while I work, but healing you is my priority."

Avran felt uneasy allowing her to take care of him, yet he was touched more deeply than he thought possible. Never had anyone put his care above everything else.

Gregory entered with the supplies Liz had requested. She sat the bowl down on a table and surrounded it with four of the candles she had lit. Avran assumed she was going to bless the water before she used it on him.

He enjoyed watching her work. She looked very serious bent over the bowl with her brow furrowed in concentration. Her golden hair sparkled in the candlelight. She extracted another container from her purse and poured a few drops from it into the water. After a few moments of silence, she straightened and picked up the cloth. He watched her while she immersed it in the water and wrung it out.

"I really don't mind if you talk while I heal you." Her words made Avran realize he'd intended to do just that but had gotten distracted by her beauty.

"I found Liftkin at The Black Cat. He sat with a group of women, and I thought him sufficiently distracted for me to probe his mind. I got through his surface thoughts and had entered his deeper layers when he detected me. All I saw before he pushed me out was the word "treasure". I'm sorry. I misjudged the situation, and now I've put you in greater danger."

Liz frowned. "I'm just glad you escaped. Was he able to learn anything about you?"

"I don't think so. I had to struggle to keep him out of my mind while we fought, but I believe I succeeded."

She pulled an ottoman over so she could sit beside him, placing the bowl of water on the floor and holding the cloth. "I'm going to wash your cuts. Then I can give you some healing energy and cover them with plantain salve to reduce the pain. Where else are you hurt?" She brushed a finger gently over the bruises on his face.

"Liz, this really isn't necessary." He'd lost a lot of blood. He knew that if she touched him again the temptation to feed from her would be nearly impossible to resist.

"Avran, I won't argue with you about this. You need healing energy, and I'm going to give it to you."

Not since his human life, and rarely even then, had a woman used such a commanding tone with him. He wanted to protest again, but he knew she wouldn't relent. He'd simply steel himself as well as he could.

"I have a cut on my right leg." He turned so she could see it.

She looked down at the red stain, which covered most of his thigh, and the color drained from her face. "Did Liftkin use a knife on you?"

"No, he cut me with energy."

Liz gasped. "In public?"

Avran nodded.

She laid her hand gently on his knee and Avran saw fear in her eyes. "Why would he take such a risk?"

"I think his control was slipping."

She nodded. "What happened after he did this?"

Avran decided not to tell her that he'd nearly drained Liftkin and left him to die. "Someone saw us, and he had to walk away."

He could hear her heart beating wildly. Liftkin's erratic behavior truly terrified her. "Where were you?"

"In the High Street parking garage. I left the bar after he detected my probe. He followed and attacked me by my car."

She shook her head as if attempting to banish her fear. "We'll talk about this more after I've healed you."

Avran gripped her wrist, trying one last time to stop her. "I assure you these cuts will heal on their own, in a matter of hours."

"Avran, I'm not discussing this anymore." She began washing the blood off his face. The cloth smelled like lavender, and he breathed deeply, enjoying the sweet scent. The water was cool and soothing, but her touch made him hot with need. His skin felt feverish where her hands brushed him. He could see the pulse beating at her neck and the rich clean scent of her surrounded him. He needed more distraction. "Tell me about your day. Did you learn anything else that might help us?"

"I gathered the names of each of the owners of the Mercer building, the dates on which it changed hands, and the names of all the businesses that have rented spaces in it. I'm hoping to find a clue about Liftkin's interest about the building but I've not had any luck so far."

Liz laid her hand over Avran's face. Tingling warmth spread across his cheek as she sent healing energy into him. His whole body felt invigorated, renewed. His cock felt impossibly hard. Her wrist hung over his mouth. Instantaneously, he could bite into the thin covering of flesh and feel her hot blood pouring into his mouth.

He had to keep her talking or he would lose his battle with himself. Finally, she lifted her hands and bent to dip the cloth in the water. "Do you remember the names of the first owners? I might have known them. The Mercer building was under construction when I bought this house."

"So it *has* been you living here all these years. I'd wondered."

She rinsed out the cloth several times and then looked up. The color drained from her face.

"What's wrong?" Avran asked, frightened by her reaction.

"The cuts and bruises on your face. They're completely gone." She brushed her hand across his cheek, studying it intently.

Her touch brought a wave of need crashing over him. He squeezed his hands into fists to keep from grabbing her arm and satisfying his hunger. "As I told you, we heal very quickly on our own. Apparently, with the addition of your power, we heal instantaneously."

*****

Liz took a deep breath, attempting to calm herself. The prospect of instant healing excited her mind, but touching his skin had sent fire racing through her body. She had never allowed herself to be distracted from healing someone and was ashamed that she couldn't separate her sexual hunger from her desire to relieve his pain.

She looked down at his thigh. Before she could heal it, she would have to remove his blood-soaked jeans. "Where would I find a pair of scissors?" Heat crept into her cheeks when she heard the raspy tone of her voice.

"In the top drawer of my desk." His voice sounded strained too. Was he in worse pain than she'd thought, or was he also affected by their closeness?

She got the scissors and cut the fabric of his jeans away from the gash, thus saving herself from seeing him without his pants. Still, she could hardly keep from squirming as she looked down at the thick muscles of his thigh and couldn't help but notice the huge erection that pressed against his jeans only inches from her hands. At least she wasn't the only one feeling the sexual tension leaping in the air.

The cut on Avran's thigh was long and deep. "If you were human, this would need stitches. Will it heal correctly without them?"

"Yes...my body will...regenerate the skin." Each word sounded as if he'd squeezed it from his body. Liz felt hot energy pulsating from him. She slid her hand further from his crotch.

As quickly as she could, she washed his cut with the lavender water. When she laid her hands on his leg to send energy into it, an image flashed through her mind. In it, she was using her tongue instead of her hand. Only the greatest effort kept her from doing just that.

When the flow of energy ceased, she lifted her hands and looked up at Avran's face. His skin was paler than she'd ever seen it. His eyes were squeezed shut, and he didn't seem to be breathing.

"Avran?"

He didn't move. "Call Gregory and leave."

Her heart hammered. "What's wrong?"

"Blood loss."

Heat crept into Liz's face. How could she have been so foolish? Of course he'd need to replenish the blood he'd lost. No wonder her presence seemed like torture.

Two days earlier, the thought of Avran biting her had been horrifying, but now, it sent a tingle of desire through her. Unbidden, her eyes went to his lips. She remembered them on her wrist and imagined them brushing against her neck. She saw the muscles in his arms tense.

"Liz, please."

She'd gotten him into this situation. The least she could do was offer her blood to complete his healing. She shivered but not from fear of him. Her only fear was that his feeding would feel as good as it had in her vision.

"Avran, if you need blood, you can take mine."

"No!" He choked out the single word.

"I said I would heal you. If giving blood is necessary then I will do it."

He shook his head. "You don't understand."

"Then explain."

She watched his chest rise with a deep shuddering breath. "You would have to drop your shields completely. And taking blood is linked to...sex."

Liz swallowed hard. "I know, but I'm still willing."

"Your desire would be stronger than anything you've ever felt."

Dear Lord and Lady, it would be just like her vision, but she had to follow through anyway. "I can handle it."

"No."

"Is there any way you can drink from me without making me lose control?"

"Only by hurting you, and that I will not do.

She took a deep breath. "I can handle a little pain."

His eyes closed again and the muscles of his face tensed. "When we bite without mind control it is excruciating for our victims."

Liz shivered at his words. Part of her wanted to run, and part of her desperately wanted to tell him to bite her, loss of control be damned.

Avran opened his eyes. Liz gasped. They'd gone solid black, and they sparkled like precious stone. The cords in his neck stood out prominently. "Leave now!"

She ran for the door.

Chapter 5

Liz woke the next morning in a strange bed. She felt the weight of Ares across her feet. When she opened her eyes, she saw Saffron staring at her from the window sill. She squeezed her eyes shut and then opened them again slowly, thinking the room would right itself. She would be at home, the strange surroundings merely the vestiges of a dream.

But nothing changed. She was truly in one of the numerous guest suites in Avran's home. He had insisted she sleep there, not wanting her to be home in bed when he began his dawn sleep and could not come to her aid. They'd gone to her house to get Ares and Saffron, because she refused to leave them alone all night. Then they'd talked more about her research and his encounter with Liftkin, both being careful not to mention the incident in Avran's study. It had almost been dawn when she'd gone to bed.

Strong bright sunlight streamed in through the thin curtains. It must be near noon. Panic hit her. The store. Then she remembered it was Saturday, and Cindy, the college student who assisted her, had the opening shift.

Within half an hour, she was showered, dressed, and ready to go. Gregory offered to make her breakfast, but she declined, thinking she would pick something up at Eccles Bakery since she needed to talk to the Eccleses anyway. She did, however, ask if there was a computer she could use. She wanted to see if anyone from the council had emailed her.

Surprisingly, a message from Rosalia sat in her inbox. Liz opened the message and scanned it quickly. Rosalia informed her the Synod did not have time to look into a matter where there was no proof of ill intent. If Liz found concrete evidence of wrong doing, she could contact them later.

Of all the nerve. What were they there for, anyway? Obviously not to give the protection they supposedly promised.

She looked at the clock on the screen. She still had time to make it to the yoga class she usually attended on Saturdays. Stephanie should be there, and Liz would be able to find out how Mrs. Cumberland was doing. Steph might also know what, if anything, the police had discovered about the gallery.

Then, she could stop by Eccles Bakery. The bakery was always a good source of gossip, and Mr. and Mrs. Eccles were both in their seventies, so they might remember something about one of the Mercer Building's previous owners.

Liz knew Avran would be livid if he woke and found her gone, but she refused to sit around all day waiting for him. The city council would decide whether to sell the property to Liftkin in a matter of days. She couldn't afford to waste what time she had. She doubted Liftkin would make an outright attack in broad daylight. If he did, she would have to rely on her own magic to save her.

She got to the yoga studio a few minutes early and found a spot for her mat near Steph's. "How's Mrs. Cumberland doing?" she whispered, not wanting to disturb the people who were stretching or meditating before class began.

Steph rolled to her side to face Liz. "Not very well. She hasn't regained consciousness. Dorothy's only left the hospital for a few hours and then only because I forced her to. She's really run herself down."

"Is there anything I can do?"

Steph shifted to a seated position and scooted closer to Liz. "Do you have any of your restorative tincture? The one you were showing me how to make last week."

Liz nodded. "I think I've got a bottle in the cabinet at the store."

"Great. I'm going to the hospital to bring Dorothy some lunch after class. Could we stop by the store when we're done here?"

Liz leaned forward over her legs, relishing the deep stretch. "Sure. Do the doctors think she will wake up eventually?"

Stephanie exhaled loudly. "They don't know. She had some internal bleeding, but they stopped it. Apparently, all they can do now is wait."

"Do the police have any leads on who did this?"

"None. They can't find evidence of anyone, other than Mrs. Cumberland and Dorothy being in the store that night. It's almost like the vandals were invisible."

Liz's stomach flip-flopped. "Do the police know for certain there was more than one man involved?"

"It's unlikely that one person could cause that much destruction."

Liz forced herself to nod in agreement.

The instructor came in then, and they had to stop talking. Liz was relieved to hear that the police weren't taking the accusations against Liftkin seriously. He would only become more dangerous if his chances of getting the land and necessary permits decreased.

After class, Liz and Stephanie walked to Liz's store to get the tincture. Once her friend had left, Liz explained to Cindy that she was very upset by the incident at the gallery, and she felt like the energy around the store was too weak. They needed to intensify the protection around them. Cindy was unaware of the existence of Deep Magicians, but she knew Liz followed a

Pagan path, and she'd started attending the Goddess Circle Liz led.

Liz pulled the shades on the windows and stuck the *'Sorry to have missed you. Be back in fifteen minutes.'* sign on the door. "Cindy, if you would stand here." Liz pointed to a spot approximately in the center of the store. "I'm going to walk a circle around us. Then I will come and seal you and the store with protective energy."

Liz called on the protection of the Lord and Lady, asking them to be present with her as she blessed Cindy. She lay her hands on the younger woman's shoulders and let her energy flow in and around Cindy, sealing her from any harm Liftkin might have planned. If the spell worked, anything he threw at Cindy would bounce right off.

When they'd finished with the ritual, Liz and Cindy cleaned up and re-opened the store. Liz asked if Cindy would mind working the rest of the day, and fortunately, the young woman agreed.

By the time Liz left the store, she was starving, so she headed to the bakery. Mrs. Eccles frowned when Liz approached the counter. "You look tired, dear. You've been working yourself too hard."

"I'm fine," she said, smiling at the older woman's concern. If only Mrs. Eccles knew what Liz had been up to. "I'm just worried about the square."

"Did you ever get around to seeing Mr. Niccolayic?"

Why hadn't she expected this question? She had to scramble for something that sounded sensible and wasn't too far from the truth. "I did. He does support our cause, and I think he's willing to speak at the public hearing. I need to talk to him again though."

"That's wonderful news. Did he behave like a gentleman?"

Liz shivered involuntarily. "He's a bit flirtatious, but he did nothing out of line." She almost laughed at the thought of how Mrs. Eccles would react to Avran's actual behavior.

Mrs. Eccles reached behind the counter and pulled out a cupcake. "Here you go, dear. You look like you need this."

Liz smiled. She was twenty-nine years old, but Mrs. Eccles still thought a cupcake could solve all Liz'a problems. She wished that were true and had to admit it would give her a few moments of distracting pleasure. "Thank you. Could I get a soy latte and a spinach and cheese scone as well?"

Liz pulled out her purse, but Mrs. Eccles held up her hand. "It's on the house today. You deserve a treat."

"Are you sure?"

"Absolutely"

"Thank you. By the way, I was wondering if you or your husband know any stories or legends about the Mercer Building. I thought if we could find more concrete evidence of the building's historical significance, we might have a better chance of saving it."

"I grew up a bit north of here, and we didn't travel into town much, but Robert might know more. Go ahead and take a seat. I'll send him out to you when your coffee's ready."

Liz took a seat at her favorite table. Slowly, she peeled the wrapper of her cupcake, a chocolate one with white icing—the same kind Mrs. Eccles had been giving her since she was a little girl. She could remember being carried in on her father's shoulders and having Mrs. Eccles hand her a treat. That was only one of the many wonderful memories of her life here in Granville. Whatever Liftkin had planned, she wasn't going to let him hurt any more of the people she loved.

She heard the squeak of the half door at the end of the counter and looked up. It was Mr. Eccles, carrying her latté and scone.

He smiled as he sat the tray down. "Margaret says you want to talk to me."

"I do, if you have a few minutes."

He pulled out a chair and sat. "I always have time for you, dear."

Liz smiled. "Thanks. I'm trying to find out more about the Mercer Building. Do you know anything about its previous owners, or have you heard any interesting stories about the square that I might not know?"

"Well now, let me think. Who was that feller who owned it when I was a boy? Bedford. Mr. Miles Bedford. He owned most of the buildings in the square back in the thirties and forties. He was a real character. He used to tell us some crazy stories about things that had gone on in the town, but I don't know if any of those old stories would help you."

"I'm looking for anything that might make the building more valuable or show its importance as a local landmark. Anything tied to the town's history in a special way."

"Well, I don't rightly think this one would make the building valuable. In fact, it might encourage people to tear it down. But Old Mr. Bedford used to say that there was an Indian treasure buried under that building. I believe it was supposed to be a huge big bundle of silver coins."

Liz nearly jumped out of her chair. Liftkin had been thinking about a treasure before he attacked Avran. "Do you know anything else about this supposed treasure?"

"Not much. Mr. Bedford said he never knew exactly where it was or he'd a gone diggin' himself. It was supposed to have been buried long before the town was built but the Indians thought it was cursed, so they never dug it up. By the time anyone might have tried, the buildings were already there. Besides, no one knew exactly where to dig."

Liz was itching to get up and head for the library, but she had to be polite. "Can you think of anything else that might help?"

"No, I guess I'm not much help after all. I'll let you know if I remember anything else."

Liz wished she could tell him how much help he'd actually been, but she didn't want to put him in danger. "That's okay. I appreciate you talking to me."

"Any time. You should come in and sit with us more often."

"Maybe when this hearing is past I'll be able to."

Liz quickly finished her scone and walked to the library, praying she'd be able to find more information about this buried treasure. She talked to three different reference librarians. They told her about a local legend involving a lost silver mine, but none of them had ever heard it connected to the Mercer building. They recommended she visit the Native American cultural center, but it wouldn't be open again until Monday.

She left with an armload of books on local legends involving silver coins and a stack of pages of photocopies from old journals and other documents she couldn't check out. The librarians promised to keep looking and let her know if they found anything useful. She hoped Avran would be willing to do some reading that night.

*****

"What the hell were you thinking leaving like that?"

Liz took a deep breath. She'd known Avran would be angry but she'd hoped to get in the door before he attacked her. As it was, she stood in the doorway dripping wet, having been caught in the rain walking back to her car from the library. "I was continuing my investigation."

I can only protect you when I'm awake. The point of you staying here last night was so Liftkin wouldn't be able to corner you alone."

"Attacking me in broad daylight in the middle of downtown would blow his cover. He's not going to do that."

Avran shook his head, and Liz felt his power roar to life. "All he needs is to get you alone for a few minutes."

She stepped past Avran into the foyer and gathered her wet hair and pulled it over her shoulder so she could wring more of the water from it. "I'm hardly defenseless. I do have abilities of my own."

Avran smiled and nodded. "Indeed you do, but you admitted you don't know the extent of Liftkin's powers. You have a far better chance of survival if we work together. Otherwise, you never would have approached me."

Liz kicked off her wet sandals. "I couldn't afford to waste a day. The hearing to decide about the park and the Mercer building will happen next week. If I don't find a way to stop Liftkin by then, the whole town could be in serious danger. My safety is far less important than that."

"If Liftkin eliminates you, he will get what he wants regardless."

"Then I just have to be smarter than he is. Going out today was a calculated risk, one that turned out to be profitable. If you would stop arguing with me about something you can't change, I could tell you what I learned."

Avran's eyes flashed and Liz felt another burst of power radiate from him. "While I have every intention of finding out what you learned, where you went, and who you talked to, our conversation will have to wait."

He walked out the door. Liz was stunned. "How dare you attack me for going out alone then walk out the door without even an explanation?"

He was suddenly standing in front of her, so close a deep breath would bring her in contact with his body. "Unless you are offering to be my dinner, I'm going out to eat."

Liz's heart raced. Avran's eyes glowed like black jewels, the way they had the night before. She could feel herself falling into them. Her body didn't want to resist. How easy it would be to tilt her head, offer her throat. She knew her vision hadn't lied. He would make his bite feel like pure bliss.

No! She shook her head and pulled back. She couldn't let him gain such control over her, no matter how good it would feel. "I'll be in your study when you return. We have lots of reading to do tonight."

She walked away, forcing herself not to look back.

*****

Avran sat in a chair on the balcony off his study, reading by the last rays of the summer sun. The sun was so low in the sky he didn't have to cover himself or wear shades to keep it from burning him, and he loved to watch the sunset. He also loved to watch Liz. Since her human eyes needed more light, she sat inside. She leaned against the armrest of the sofa with her legs stretched out. The long, swirling black skirt she wore spilled down onto the floor, and her long braid snaked across her body. She looked exactly like what she was, a woman filled with magic.

He could smell her earthy scent as it floated to him on the breeze. If he opened all his senses, he could hear the blood rushing in her veins. She smelled so alive, so vital, and he wanted her badly. His anger at the risk she'd taken had caused his hunger to rise in a way it hadn't in years.

Just the scent of her brought his blood lust curling up through his body, and any strong emotion made it worse. Even now, after he'd fed, he wanted to taste her. The thought of her hot blood filling his mouth had his cock throbbing. He would have her, sooner or later. His body wouldn't have it any other way. He would make sure she screamed in pleasure before he was through with her.

He forced himself to look down at the book he was studying, but before he'd read a paragraph, Liz called him. Bracing himself for the hunger her nearness would bring, he walked inside and seated himself on the sofa as she swung her legs to the floor.

"This is a section from a journal kept by Ida Lu Mazey, the wife of the man who first owned the Mercer building. Here's what she says—*John talked to an Indian the other day who told him he should not have bought that building in town. He said it was cursed, that a man from his tribe had buried silver coins there long ago. No one wanted to dig them up because the man had filled them with magic, and his magic always brought evil. When he died, nobody looked for his treasure. They just left it be and he said us white folks should do the same.*

John told him the man he didn't believe in magic, but the old Indian said he ought to. He said John ought to open his eyes and ears to what was really around him. John seems to have forgotten all about it, but I haven't. Something about that Indian's words made me shiver, but then part of me is glad John did buy that building, because that way nobody's going to come and try to get the treasure.

"Somehow Liftkin found out about these coins, I just know it, but he must know more than Ida Lu's words tell us. He must know what kind of magic the coins hold, and he must believe he can benefit from it. Otherwise the risk wouldn't be worth it."

"Perhaps not, but I've seen men kill for much less," Avran said, remembering his mortal days as a soldier and his meetings with vampires who'd let their beastly side rule them.

She turned her head to look up at him, and his gaze locked with hers. Her breathing stopped, and her heartbeat accelerated rapidly. Hunger vibrated through him. Did she understand the danger? Did she know how much he wanted her, how uncontrolled his desire could be? He expected her to look away or get up. But she didn't move.

He leaned down, closing the distance between them. Her tongue darted out to lick her lips, and he took it as an invitation. He kissed her gently at first. When he felt no resistance, he increased the pressure on her lips and pressed against their seam with his tongue. She tasted delightful.

He could feel the wildness building inside him. He forced himself to hold back. She had to open freely to him. Force was not the way to encourage her. But he burned, and he needed to taste her to quench the fire.

His tongue explored her mouth. He felt the heat of her body increase. She melted against him, her body so pliable he was able to bend her back over the arm of the sofa. Her breasts pressed into his chest. He had to grip the thin straps of her tank to keep from moving his hands up to cup them.

*****

Liz's body throbbed with need, The ache between her legs consumed her. She struggled to grasp a rational thought. What was she doing? Why had she let Avran kiss her? This was madness, exactly what she'd tried to avoid. Yet she didn't want it to stop.

If this was a taste of the pleasure he could give her, she wanted it all. The feelings he inspired were even more intense than those in her vision. She felt his fangs scrape against her neck. Did vampires always bite during sex? How would it feel? She longed to know. She no longer cared if her relationship with

Avran got complicated or dangerous. She wanted the passion and the danger. She wanted to feel his teeth in her.

Liz stroked his back while he returned to his assault to her mouth. Never had she experienced a kiss so varied and so intense. He lapped at her mouth, making her feel the sensations all the way to her core. His teeth gripped her lower lip. Once again, she felt the sharpness of his fangs. Only the barest hint of restraint kept her from pressing her lip against them and letting her blood spill against his tongue.

She was falling, descending into a world of nothing but pleasure.

Then she froze. Avran's mind pressed against her shields.

"Let me in." His velvet voice swirled around her, caressing her as surely as his hands.

She didn't move. Her shields remained firmly in place.

"I smell your desire. Drop your shields, and let me in."

She wanted him with a desperation she thought never to feel, but she couldn't do it. She pulled air into her lungs, working to calm herself, trying to let go, but her shields wouldn't release. "I can't."

"I won't hurt you."

She wanted the pleasure he offered. She wished she had the courage to accept it, but she didn't. The thought of him seeing inside her, having access to her deepest secrets, panicked her. "I can't let you in. I just can't."

He nuzzled her neck. "I only want to project my feelings into you. That's how I make my bite pleasurable, by letting you feel the pleasure it gives me. Our minds will be linked, but you will still be in control of your thoughts and your body."

She shook her head and pulled away. "No. I don't want you to see my secrets. It's too intimate." She pushed at his shoulders.

He sat up, but he kept a grip on her arms, pulling her with him. "Why are you so afraid?"

"We're taught not to share the secrets of our power with anyone."

"When I'm in the throes of passion, I haven't the ability to discern anything but your emotions."

"Avran, I'd be a fool to believe that."

"So you *don't* trust me."

"No, that's not what I meant."

Avran stood and picked up a stack of photocopies and another book. "I'm going to the greenhouse to read these. Let me know if you find more references to the treasure."

He walked out without a backward glance. The residual energy of his anger filled the air.

Chapter 6

Liz took several long, full breaths, trying to order the chaos in her mind. Avran was right. She wasn't telling him everything. Her fear stemmed directly from her experience with another.

John had been charming and gorgeous, though his looks were nothing to rival Avran's. She had trusted him enough to consider marrying him, but when she opened herself up and showed him who she really was, their relationship ended in disaster. Never would she make that mistake again.

But she owed Avran a better explanation of her behavior. He had risked much for her, and she had left him believing she doubted his integrity, when that was no longer true. He unnerved her, but as much as she might be loathe to admit it, she knew he was honorable.

She stacked her books on Avran's desk and went in search of him.

He was sitting on a bench in the greenhouse, his head bent over a book. He didn't look up when she entered, so she stood near the door for a few moments, just watching him. He'd tied his hair back to keep it from getting in his way, and it revealed more plainly the strong line of his face. His red T-shirt clung to his muscular arms, and the paleness of his skin gave him an unearthly beauty.

How she wished she could let herself open to him. Her practical side knew a relationship with him was impossible, if for no other reason than that he was immortal. Her powers allowed her to extend her life a few decades beyond that of an average human but no more.

Avran was a man to be savored, but she dared not let someone into her life the way she had John. She'd already told Avran far too much about herself. At least he couldn't dismiss her power as the product of an overactive imagination or the influence of "kooks who think they are witches", as John had described the women in the coven she'd joined in college.

Finally, Avran looked up at her. "Are you going to stand there for the rest of the night, or do you have something to say?"

The anger on his face and the bitterness of his tone gave her pause, but she forced herself to stay and talk to him. "Actually, I have a lot to say, if you're willing to listen. I want to explain my reaction."

Avran said nothing.

A few seconds later, the words of her story seemed to tumble out of her mouth. "A few months before my college graduation, the guy I was dating asked me to marry him."

Avran turned back to her, interest showing in his eyes.

"I didn't know what to say. I very much wanted to marry him and have a normal family, but I couldn't be a typical wife and mother, not with the powers I had. I'd never told John about my magic, but I knew I couldn't hide it if we were married."

Liz paused to take a long deep breath. Avran laid his book on the bench and stood. He inclined his head toward her as if asking her to continue, so she did. "I told John I needed some time to think. For a week, I railed at the fact that I was a Deep Magician. I even prayed that my powers would go away. The Lord and Lady laughed at me and told me the powers were entrusted to me for life, and they expected me to use them wisely.

"Finally, I decided that if I really loved John, I had to trust him. I had to share everything about who I really was. I called him and asked him to come over to my apartment that night."

Liz turned away from Avran, unable to meet his gaze. She didn't want him seeing the pain that surely showed in her eyes. "When I told him the truth, he laughed at me. I should have stopped right then, but I kept trying to make him listen. A man who loved me the way a husband should would not have called me a lunatic. He might not have accepted my story easily, but he would have at least heard me out.

"I wasn't going to let him walk away thinking I was crazy. I believed I loved him, and I had to make him see that I was telling the truth. I asked his consent to send him a vision. He thought it was ridiculous, but he agreed to let me 'play my little game'. So I let him see inside me. He experienced the day my powers awakened as if were watching a movie in his mind."

Liz turned back around and saw anger burning in Avran's eyes. She felt his power vibrating in the air. He reached for her, but she stepped back. She wouldn't be able to finish her story if she let him touch her.

"John looked at me like I was a monster. He couldn't get away fast enough. That alone brought me more pain than I thought I could bear, but the next time I saw him, he seemed unbalanced, as if what I'd revealed had sent him over the edge. He still denied the truth, but he knew. Deep inside, he knew.

"He started spreading rumors about me, saying I was a dangerous witch and that I'd tried to put a spell on him. Luckily, few people were inclined to believe him. Those who were knew me too well to think that I'd harm anyone." To her mortification, tears flooded her eyes. She couldn't stop them. They ran down her cheeks in hot streams. She sat down on a bench and turned away from Avran, unable to bear him watching her cry.

*****

Liz projected her pain so loudly Avran could feel it as if it were his own. Anger vibrated through his body. If he'd known where to look for the man who'd hurt her, he would've tracked him down and drained him until he was nothing but a dry husk.

Instead, he watched Liz as her shoulders shook from her sobs, feeling strangely helpless. He wanted to ease her pain, but he didn't know how. Comforting women was not something he was used to.

He looked down at the night phlox growing in the pot beside him. The lacy white blooms and the rich smell of almond and vanilla emanating from it reminded him of Liz. Suddenly inspired, he picked the blossom and walked over to her.

He allowed his hand to trace the line of her spine. "Look at me."

Several seconds passed, but eventually, she did as he asked. Seeing her red, puffy eyes and tearstained face brought his rage back to the surface. How could a man be so cruel?

He held up the flower for her to see. "You are as intricate, beautiful, and rare as this flower. That any man would dare to crush such pure beauty disgusts me. If he didn't cherish you as a man should something so beautiful, he did not deserve to be near you."

She started crying again. Avran pulled her into his arms, unable to resist holding her any longer. He held her head against his chest and rocked her.

She took a long breath and made a few hiccuping coughs. "When you say things like that, I don't know whether to try harder to find the courage to open up or to run as fast as I can from such temptation."

He squeezed her tightly, unable to say anything. He wasn't sure of the answer himself.

*****

When Liz woke up the next morning, it was nearly noon. She asked Gregory to bring her a sandwich and a cup of coffee in the study. She worked on reading through the rest of the books and papers she'd collected while she ate. She'd nearly given up on finding anything else, but as she neared the bottom of the stack of photocopies, she came across another reference to the treasure in a letter written to Mrs. Mazey.

She assumed the letter had been written by a Native American woman, since it was signed Flowing River. From the context it looked as though Mrs. Mazey had written Flowing River first, asking about the treasure. Liz read the letter greedily, hoping to hit on something new. In the second paragraph she hit pay dirt.

Red Bird's coins enhance the magical powers of anyone who holds them, but they are dangerous. The more they are used, the harder it becomes to control them. This enhancing of power can cause the coins' owner to lose control of the new powers. They have unbalanced many men and they must be kept hidden.

In the last paragraph, Flowing River once again implored Mrs. Mazey to keep the coins buried, saying many in her tribe had died as a result of their magic and Red Bird had eventually killed himself in a wild rage.

Liz wondered how much Liftkin knew about the coins' dangers. She doubted he would heed any warnings, even if he knew they had destroyed their creator. The desire to strengthen his powers would blind him to everything else. He was already one of the most powerful Deep Magicians, but he wanted to be the best.

Liz wanted to go to the library and see if anyone in reference knew where she might contact one of the Mazeys' descendants, but the library would be closed until Monday morning. She needed to act immediately. Now that she knew what to look for, she needed to know where to find the treasure. Then she could remove the coins and hopefully neutralize the magic.

Liftkin had been in her house and in the gallery. If she could find something he'd touched, she might be able to pick up some of the thoughts Liftkin left behind. Assuming the treasure was always at the forefront of his mind, those thoughts could reveal its location.

Liz had promised Avran she would stay at his house until he woke, but time was running out. She couldn't afford to wait. She wrote a note explaining what she intended to do and headed back upstairs to place it on her bed. Ares and Saffron were both in her room, sunning themselves by the big bay window.

She gave Saffron's silky fur a few strokes and was rewarded with a swat. Ares was more appreciative of her attention. He needed exercise, so she decided to take him with her. She encouraged him to be quiet as they snuck downstairs. To keep Gregory from detecting their departure, they exited through the greenhouse door.

When they reached her house, Liz sensed mental imprints on her wards. Someone had tried to get in. She sensed Liftkin but also another. The energy of the other presence seemed familiar, but she couldn't place it. Who would be working with Liftkin that she would recognize? She hoped the answer would come to her later. She thought it best not to risk facing two assailants. So she decided to go to the gallery first and return home later with Avran.

She stopped by her store before going to the gallery. Ares took his usual spot in one of the reading chairs by the window while she quickly processed a few web orders that had come in overnight. When she was done, she looked through the desk in her office until she found some bay leaves. Burning them and inhaling the smoke would enhance her ability to discern Liftkin's thoughts, so she collected a handful, a bowl, a lighter, and a charcoal tablet.

She considered leaving Ares at the shop but decided she would rather have him with her. He wouldn't be much protection against Liftkin's magic, but Deep Magicians were as susceptible to dog's teeth as normal humans.

Liz snapped Ares' leash on and they walked through the employee parking area to the back door of the gallery. If anyone saw her, she would simply say she was as a friend of the Cumberlands who'd come to cleanse the gallery of negative energy, something she truly intended to do later. The police would think her silly and harmless if they caught her and would likely only be mildly annoyed that she'd let herself in. By now, they had surely collected all the evidence they could.

Someone, either Dorothy or the police, had placed a padlock on the back door, but Liz used her magic to manipulate the energy in the metal and coax it to release. She took a deep breath and held firmly to Ares leash as they stepped inside.

She'd seen the destruction through the windows before the police had draped blankets in front of them, and she'd seen it in the holographic image Liftkin had left her, but the state of the building still shocked her. She had to watch her step—some of the shards of glass were sharp enough to cut through her canvas shoes. Menacing power swirled in the air, and Ares kept sniffing around and growling low in his throat. He held his tail low and still, a sure sign of unease.

Ares' fear fueled her own. Her hands shook as she lit the charcoal and laid the bay leaves on top of it. Ignoring her pounding heart, she began to walk through the office and the showroom, breathing deeply of the pungent scent and reaching out with her mind for any visuals of Liftkin. Carefully, with her free hand, she touched the pedestals where sculptures had set, the broken pieces lying on the floor, the walls, anything that might hold residual energy from Liftkin's magic.

When she touched a piece of glass from what she thought had been a fairy sculpture, a barrage of images flew across her mind. She couldn't hold any of them though. Everything came in bits and pieces.

Frustrated, she set the piece of glass back on the floor. She'd started to pick up a marble bowl when Ares growled loudly and began to bark. Glass crunched in the office. Taking hold of Ares leash, she moved in the direction of the noise, gathering energy and preparing to defend herself.

When she stepped around the corner, she froze. Liftkin stood in front of her.

"When I didn't find you at home or at your precious store, I thought you would be here." His quiet, calm voice was tinged with a hint of madness.

"You should leave." Liz hoped she sounded far more confident than she felt.

It was against her moral code to make the first move in a fight, but she decided this was an extenuating circumstance. Praying Ares would know what to do when she released him, she sent a bolt of energy slamming into Liftkin's chest.

Ares cleared the distance to Liftkin in one leap. Before the man could right himself, Ares tore into his leg. No matter how Liftkin shook himself, Ares held on, gnawing and tearing the man's flesh.

Liftkin tried to throw an energy bolt at Liz, but she deflected it with her hand. It cut and burned her palm, but it was too weak to do her serious injury.

Liz formed a force field around herself that would protect her from all but the strongest energy surge. Then she let her mind press against Liftkin's shields. She couldn't break through them, but she could feel his energy draining as Ares savaged his leg. He hadn't enough strength now to attack her. She didn't dare try to take him out on her own, but at least she could get rid of him for now. "If you promise to leave, I will call him off."

Liftkin's face was pale and covered in sweat. He nodded. "I promise." As soon as Ares let him go, he staggered toward the door and stumbled into the parking lot.

Liz wanted to go after him, but without Avran, she couldn't risk it. If she'd underestimated the extent of his injury, he could regain his strength before she'd sufficiently incapacitated him.

When she felt confident Liftkin had truly left. She sank to the floor, her shaky legs no longer able to support her. Her fear and anger hit her in a rush, and she buried her face in Ares fur. Sobs shook her body as she let out all the fear and anguish that had been building in her for the last few days. Fear of being unable to stop Liftkin, fear of her feelings for Avran, anguish over the fact that John had hurt her so deeply.

Chapter 7

Liz was crying when Avran found her.

"Liz! Liz, are you all right?" He ran across the room, oblivious to the broken glass, and sank down next to her.

When she looked up, the pain and fear in her eyes nearly knocked him over. He stroked her hair and reached out to pet Ares, trying to reassure the dog that he was there to help.

"What happened? Are you hurt?"

"No, I'm fine. Liftkin was here."

"Shit, it *was* him."

"Where?"

"I saw a man getting into a car in the back lot. He was limping, and his leg was all bloody. I thought it was Liftkin, but I had to find you."

"That was him. Ares bit him. Nearly chewed his leg in two." She smiled, but then pain crossed her face again. "I've pledged to be kind to all beings and to send a dog on someone, to want them to be hurt, it goes against all I've been taught."

"Liz, he would've killed you. He doesn't deserve any kindness from you."

She shook her head. "No, he doesn't but if I treated everyone like they deserve, I would be in violation of all my principles."

Avran couldn't help but smile. "I suppose I should consider myself lucky you feel that way. Now, tell me everything that happened."

Liz stood. "We'd better go over to my store first in case someone comes to investigate all the commotion here."

Avran could tell she was far from steady on her feet so he gave her his arm. "We'll do as you say, but then you're going to tell me exactly what went on here."

Liz opened the gallery's back door, and Avran shielded his eyes from the brightness.

She slammed the door shut and turned to face him. "Are you okay?"

He nodded, forcing himself to open his eyes and look at her despite the pain the sun inflicted on him. "I'll be fine. Let's go."

"Why did you come out in the light?"

"The light was the least of my worries." Liz stared at him, obviously not satisfied with his answer. "It was overcast the whole way here and I took precautions. I'm fine."

"But you could have been badly burned."

He nodded. "Yes, if the sun had come out while I was driving, I could have been, but I wasn't."

"What were you doing awake so early?"

"Did you think of me or wish for my help?"

Her teeth worried her lower lip. "When I saw Liftkin in the doorway, I wished you were here."

"If someone I've pledged to help is in danger, their distress call can wake me."

Liz frowned. "Avran, I never asked for your protection. I—"

"When I told you I would help you stop Liftkin, I was promising you protection. Now let's get out of here before he comes back."

Liz shook her head. "You can't leave with the sun out."

Avran fought the urge to scoop her up and carry her the distance to her store. "At the worst, I will get what you would consider a mild sunburn."

"Let me go first and unlock the door."

He clenched his fists. "You aren't going out alone."

"Avran—"

"No."

"Fine. Burn yourself then."

Avran couldn't help but smile at the exasperation in her voice. He was glad she'd been able to get rid of Liftkin on her own, but he had no intention of testing the outcome of a repeat performance.

Avran followed her as she ran to the door of Carlson's Books with Ares leading the way. Knowing his eyes were the only part of him likely to suffer from such brief sun exposure, he focused on the ground while Liz unlocked the door.

Once he was inside, Liz slammed the door behind him. "Are you all right?" she asked.

He tried not to read too much into the worry in her voice. But satisfaction coursed through him when he realized how concerned she'd truly been. "I thought you decided it would be fine if I burned."

"You know I only said that because you were being so stubborn."

"You're one to talk about stubborn."

She gave him a look meant to send chills down his spine. Instead, it flamed his desire for her. She was safe now, but adrenaline still coursed through his body, rapidly turning his fear into sexual hunger.

"I'm fine." And he truly thought he was. His hands and face might pinken slightly, but he would not suffer.

Ares curled up in one of the reading chairs, looking ready for a nap after defending Liz so well. Liz paced in front of the counter, her face pale and her hands in constant motion.

Avran sat down, seeing no reason to add to her agitation by looming over her. "Start from the moment you woke up and tell me what you've been up to and why the hell you disobeyed me and left the house."

Anger flashed in her eyes when she turned to him, but at least the pain he'd seen earlier was gone. "I am not a servant who needs to obey you. I asked you to assist me, not to be my keeper."

He fought the urge to argue, knowing it would get him nowhere. But despite waking six hours too early, his body was charged and spoiling for a fight. After a deep breath, he said, "Just tell me what happened."

She began by explaining what she'd read in Flowing River's letter. Then she explained her desire to find an object Liftkin had recently touched and search for thoughts about the treasure.

"And Liftkin found you while you were searching the debris."

"Yes. I don't know if he knew why I was in the gallery. He just said he'd looked for me at home and in my store and concluded I must be there." As she spoke, Liz lifted her hand to push her hair back from her face.

Avran noticed an angry red gash on her palm and froze. Anger coiled in his belly, bringing his power to life. He fought to keep his voice steady. "What happened to your hand?"

She looked down as if she'd never seen her own hand before. Her eyes grew wide. "It's nothing. I'll be fine."

"It's not nothing." Avran walked toward her. "Let me see it."

She put her hand behind her back, but he grabbed her arm, lifting her hand so he could see it. A long cut ran diagonally down from the inner corner of her palm. The edges were hot and puffy, and smaller abrasions streaked out from it. "Liftkin hit you with energy."

She sighed. "Yes."

Avran remembered the painful throbbing of the cut he'd received. "Your hand needs attention."

"I'll worry about it later."

"When I was injured you said healing was priority. No one should be left in pain."

"Oh." Her cheeks turned bright pink. "I guess I only feel like that when it's someone else that needs healing."

"You deserve to be cared for too," he said, capturing her gaze with his. Avran wanted to kill the bastard who'd made her close herself off from others. "Let me heal you, Liz."

She nodded her consent. He knew she expected him to ask her for some salve or first aid supplies, but he would use his own form of magic. He put his hands on her waist and lifted her so she sat on the edge of the counter. Then, he brought her palm to his mouth and ran his tongue along the cut.

He reveled in the taste of her blood, but the overtones of evil left from Liftkin's magic soured it. He swept his tongue back and forth until the heat of her hand became a natural warmth caused by his ministrations, not by the poison of dark magic. The antiseptics in his saliva would prevent infection, and her hand would heal completely within hours.

*****

Liz hadn't realized what Avran intended until his tongue touched her palm, but her shock of pleasure stopped her from protesting. She simply stared at his bent head, mesmerized and overwhelmed by the ecstasy his tongue could produce. He wasn't going to drink from her—at least she didn't think he was—and she wasn't enthralled by him, but his attentions felt much like they had in her vision.

The pain in her hand eased, but he didn't stop licking her. Each stroke of his tongue relaxed her. She felt like she was sinking under the surface of a pool, a magic one where she could breathe under the water. She floated, warm and content. Then her shields dropped, and her mind reached for his.

Avran's head flew up as she touched his shields. His eyes opened wide. Liz met his gaze and nodded, unable to articulate what she wanted. He opened to her, and burning hot need overtook her as he poured his lust and hunger into her. At that moment, if he'd wanted to drink her dry, she would have let him.

He brought her hand to his mouth once more and ran his tongue all the way up her arm, stopping at her pulse points like he had in her vision. He continued along her upper arm, over the curve of her shoulder and across her collarbone to her neck.

When his arms came around her, she tensed. Fear rushed through her, but she kept herself open to the stream of his desire. She had no idea how erotic it could be to know exactly how hot her partner was for her. She could feel the dangerous animal instinct in him. It called to the primitive nature inside her.

His fangs brushed her neck, and a bolt of heat ran through her. She pushed her hands into his hair and pulled his head closer. Cutting pain hit her for a second, then she was lost to sensation. Nothing, not even her vision, had prepared her for how good his bite would feel.

She could feel the pull of his mouth on her neck, but there was no pain. She felt him inside her head, swirling pleasure and lust around all her fears, her hopes, her dreams. It felt wonderful.

Liz knew why he'd insisted she'd be unable to resist him after he bit her. She'd never felt such raging need. If he kept drinking, she would climax from that sensation alone. He wouldn't even have to touch her.

Her body tightened, climbing toward release. A deep groan escaped her lips. She sank her fingers into the flesh of Avran's shoulders. Pleasure mounted with every movement of Avran's lips and tongue. She felt herself hanging on the edge, ready to go over.

Just when she thought her world would explode, Avran stopped drinking and pulled away from her neck. Anguish washed over her. She tried to protest, but she couldn't form words. All that came out was a whimper.

He stayed in her mind as he licked the wound closed. When he was done, he put his hands on either side of her face and turned her to look at him. She tried to focus but struggled. Her body was on fire. All she could think about was how much she needed him to finish what he'd started.

"Please." Her pleading tone shocked and embarrassed her.

He smiled like a satisfied cat and brought his lips to hers as he pushed his hand under her stretchy T-shirt. She rarely wore a bra, and that day was no exception, so there was nothing between him and the skin of her breasts. She arched against his hands, her nipples longing for his touch.

She needed to feel his skin under her hands. Her fingers fumbled with the buttons of his soft linen shirt. When she finally got her hands on him, the heat of him shocked her. He moaned as she stroked the hard, smooth muscles of his chest and back. She reached for his fly, wanting to see his magnificent body. She'd fantasized about since the first time she'd seen him.

His tongue thrust deeply into her mouth. She gripped his shoulders, pulling herself against him. His fingers toyed with her nipples, tugging and pulling at them until she wanted to scream. She was torn between wanting to draw out this first joining with him and wanting his cock inside her immediately. Her need won out, and she tore at the button of his jeans.

When she began to lower his zipper, he growled and grabbed her wrists. "Not yet. I want this to last." He pulled her arms up and tugged her shirt over her head. Then he lowered his mouth to her breasts while his hands worked on raising her long skirt.

She gripped the counter to steady herself when she felt his fangs against her skin. She thought he would bite her again, but he only nipped softly, never breaking the skin. She moaned in longing. Then his mouth closed on her nipple, and the world seemed to narrow to that single point. She speared her fingers into his hair and pressed his head to her, arching under him, begging him not to stop.

Her wildness nearly broke Avran's control, but he was determined to bring her to the point of pure frenzy before he buried both his fangs and his cock inside her. He'd forced himself to stop after taking only a little blood. He knew he would need more while he fucked her. He wanted to taste her essence as he pumped himself into her.

He knelt in front of her when he'd gotten her skirt bunched to her waist. Taking her satin panties in one hand, he ripped them off. She gasped but didn't protest. He pushed her thighs further apart, wrapping his hands around them. His tongue brushed her clit and she jerked, crying out. He licked her again, pressing against her more firmly. She moaned and her nails dug into his shoulders.

Avran sucked and licked and nibbled until Liz was whimpered and bucked her hips against his mouth. He released one of her thighs and pushed his fingers into her wet sheath, curling them up as if trying to touch his own tongue. She convulsed against him, screaming in her elation.

When he thought she'd regained enough control to hold herself up, he stood. Her hands tangled with his in their mutual haste to undo his pants. She reached around him, pushing her hands under the waistband of his jeans and shoving them down with surprising force. He lifted her off the counter and onto his shaft, lowering her until she'd taken all of him.

Her groaned as her tight pussy gripped his shaft. She wiggled her hips, but he held her still, wanting to slow her pace. Ever so slowly, he lifted her off him. He held her in the air with only the tip of him inside her.

She growled, her eyes shining with her passion. "More."

He waited a few more seconds then let her slide down. He wanted to keep it slow, but her enthusiasm and his increasing hunger did him in. His next thrust came hard and fast. He didn't slow down again. He worried he might hurt her, but she continued to beg for more with her mind and her body.

Liz couldn't pull any thoughts together. She seemed impossibly stretched by Avran's enormous cock. His mind continued to caress hers, and through their connection, she felt his hunger rising again as he thrust deeply into her. She gripped his shoulders tightly and met him stroke for stroke, loving the feel of his flexed muscles under her hands as he lifted her up and down on his shaft.

He captured her nipple in his mouth once again. His nipping and suckling were almost more than she could bear. She felt herself spiraling out of control again, nearing the brink of orgasm once again. She tried to hang onto Avran, but her hands slipped off his sweat-soaked shoulders. She fell back into the cradle of his arms. As he brought her down against him, she screamed. Her body writhed in pleasure.

Avran sank his fangs into her breast, near her heart. The taste of her heart's blood pouring into him shredded his last bit of control. He pulled her against him once more, and exploded inside her, his climax seeming to go on forever.

When he'd recovered enough to think, he cleansed and sealed her wound. She was loose, limber, and nearly unconscious. He lifted her off him and took a few steps, so he could sit her down in the chair that wasn't occupied by a still-sleeping Ares. Nearly as exhausted as she was, he sank to his knees and laid his head in her lap.

Chapter 8

Liftkin lay on the bed in his hotel room, pressing a healing poultice against the ragged, burning cuts on his leg. He'd stitched several of them together himself, having no desire to explain the incident to emergency room attendants. His work was adequate, but he would be left with scars.

The herbs were already making the pain subside, but his thoughts were filled with ways to get his revenge on Liz and her canine protector. When he'd finished his mission in Granville, he would go after her. This time he wouldn't hesitate to finish her and her vicious animals off.

When he'd satisfied himself that Liz would never thwart anyone again with her sickening morals, he would tend to Avran Niccolayic. Liftkin had returned to The Black Cat after their run in. By asking a few questions, he'd found out his opponent's name and where he lived.

Liftkin had also learned how some people in town thought Avran was a vampire or a demon. Liftkin dismissed this as nonsense. He'd felt the man's mind. Avran was nothing but a witch with low level powers. He needed to be taught a lesson, and Liftkin would thoroughly enjoy being the teacher.

*****

Liz sighed, her body boneless, as if Avran's heat had melted her. She wanted nothing more than to sink into sleep, but she couldn't. Liftkin could have tended to his leg by now and returned for her. The last thing she wanted was for him to find her with her clothes askew and Avran draped across her.

She felt the weight of Avran's head against her thighs. One of his arms was wrapped around her waist, and without realizing it, she had reached out to stroke his hair. Touching him seemed like the most natural thing in the world.

Just as she had feared, the more time she spent with him, the more easily she felt his pull. Making love with him had been better than her most lurid fantasy, but it was not an experience she could afford to repeat. If she didn't back away now, she would become addicted to the lush pleasure he could provide. Then she would get hurt.

She could never hope for a serious relationship with a vampire. He would have to move on before people realized he wasn't aging. Then she would feel more alone than she had before he entered her life.

Avran began to stir. Liz took a deep breath as he raised his head and looked at her. Passion had turned his usually silver-gray eyes to the color of dark smoke. He reached up and ran his knuckles along her cheek. "You are so beautiful," he said. "Both inside and out."

Embarrassment brought heat to her cheeks, and worse, tears flooded her eyes. Avran had seen her secrets, and he had not rejected her. But he was dangerous and forbidden. She would be wise to walk away from him immediately. Even if it meant she had to fight Liftkin on her own.

"Avran, I didn't mean for this to happen."

He shook his head, looking thoroughly exasperated. "It is pointless to deny your attraction to me, or how much you enjoyed feeling me inside your mind and your body. I don't want to hear any guilt or regrets. I want us to find our clothes, go back to my house, and spend the rest of the night in bed together."

Panicked, unsure if she could resist such a delicious offer, Liz shook her head and pushed him away from her lap. "No, we can't do this again."

"If you're worried I'll take too much blood, don't. I don't have to drink from you to enjoy your body."

She tried not to look at him as she re-braided her hair. "I'm not worried about the blood. This was a mistake. I gave into temptation, but I can't let it happen again."

Avran gripped both her arms and forced her to face him. "How dare you take something so beautiful and turn it into something shameful? I know you've been badly hurt, but you don't have to let that control you."

She pushed his arms away and stood, shaking her skirt down and looking around for her T-shirt. "I'm done with this discussion."

Avran made no effort to dress. He sat on the floor and stared at her, his eyes still smoldering but from anger now, not desire. "Sooner or later, you're going to have to confront your desires."

"Avran, please. At least give me some time to think about what happened."

"The last thing you need to do is think about how you feel. You need to fuck me again. And again, and again, until you no longer feel guilty afterwards, until you long for nothing else."

"Until I'm completely wrapped around your finger, willing to do whatever you say? And when you decide you've been here long enough and it's time to move on, then where will I be?" Heat from anger and embarrassment burned Liz's cheeks. She picked up her T-shirt from the floor by the counter and jammed her arms into the sleeves.

Avran stared at her for several seconds, his face looking paler than was normal. "Fine, you've made your point. Vampires aren't very good at relationships. But if you decide you're interested in some fabulous no-strings-attached sex, be sure to inform me. You certainly didn't complain while we were doing it."

Liz wanted to be angry at his cold words, but she heard the hint of pain in his tone.

She watched him dress, not knowing what to say. They needed to make a plan for defending themselves against Liftkin, but how could she talk about that now? Was she supposed to pretend she'd never let her shields down and given into her hunger?

When he'd finished buttoning his shirt, Avran walked toward the back door. "Liftkin could come back anytime. Let's get the hell out of here."

"But what about the sun?"

He gestured toward the window. "It's raining now. The sky's too overcast for me to come to harm, especially this late in the afternoon."

Liz frowned, still uncertain that he would be safe. Why the hell did she care so much? "You're sure?"

"Yes, let's just get going."

"I need to search my house since I didn't have any luck at the gallery."

"Not now."

"What?"

"You're too weak from the loss of blood. I took more than I should have. You'll be weak for several hours. If Liftkin were to come for you, you wouldn't have the strength to defend yourself. I'm taking you back to my house."

"You have no right to tell me where I can and can't go. This can't be put off." She paused as she searched for her sandals. She had no memory of removing them. "I came to the gallery first, because I sensed Liftkin's energy along the outside of my house wards. I waited until you were awake to search the house, because I wanted you to come with me, but I'm not waiting any longer. Either you come with me, or I go alone."

"No."

"What the hell do you mean, 'no'?"

"Neither of us are in any condition for a confrontation. You are physically drained and emotionally in turmoil. From the look on your face and the tightness around your eyes, I would guess you have one hell of a headache. We need our senses on high alert when we search your house. Right now, you're too weak, and I'm too angry."

The blood loss, combined with anger at Avran and at herself, had brought on a searing tension headache. Avran was right. She wasn't fit to confront Liftkin. Avran's commanding tone made her want to balk anyway, but she ultimately gave in. "Fine. You win. I'll put off searching my house, but only until I've rested a bit."

He turned without saying another word and walked to the back door. Liz called Ares. The dog looked none too pleased to be woken from his nap, but he hurried after them. When they entered the parking lot, Liz headed for her Jeep, but Avran grabbed her arm and pulled her in the opposite direction. "You'll ride with me. We can come back for your car later."

"Avran, that's just a waste of time."

"I will not let him catch you alone again, no matter how angry it makes you."

Her anger simmered under the surface, threatening to explode. She'd never used her powers in anger before. Avran was obviously itching to be her first victim. She took a deep breath, got herself under control, and followed him to his car. "As soon as you've deemed me recovered, I expect to be brought back to my car. I have no intention of being trapped at your house without transportation."

"You're welcome to use any of my cars if you need them."

"As if Gregory is going to let me leave without you. I'm sure you'll have him watching me when you sleep after catching me escaping again."

Avran said nothing. Instead he opened the door of his Mercedes and gestured for her to get in the car. The leather interior felt delightfully soft against her legs as she seated herself. Avran was right. She was so exhausted the comfortable car made her want to lay back and fall asleep.

He got in and started the car. As they pulled out of the parking lot, she gazed out the window to avoid looking at Avran. At first she didn't see the world as it raced by, but then something caught her eye. A petite woman with dark hair was walking toward them. She looked exactly like Rosalia, but why would a Synod member be in Granville?

"Avran. Pull over." When he didn't slow down, she shouted. "Now! It's important. Here." She gestured to the right. "There's a spot in that lot."

"Liz, what the hell did you see? Liftkin?" he asked, pulling into the spot.

"No. Someone I know. Someone who shouldn't be here." She wrestled with the unfamiliar seatbelt and door handle. Watching from the side mirror, she saw the woman disappear into a dress shop.

Avran followed her as she rushed down the street.

"We're looking for a woman. She's Italian, dark Mediterranean complexion, very short, maybe five feet or less."

"Who is she?"

"I'll explain later."

Liz pushed open the door of the dress shop and looked around. It was the kind of shop she would never normally enter, knowing she couldn't even afford the scarves or belts that set off the five hundred dollar dresses.

She looked around, but she saw no one besides the exotic, painfully thin young woman at the counter. The woman looked at her with disdain, but Liz continued to approach her. Avran was close on her heels, and when the woman saw him, she broke into a smile and ignored Liz completely. "How may I help you, sir?"

Avran effected a French accent. "I am looking for a young woman. Perhaps you have seen her. She is tres petite with dark hair."

"I'm terribly sorry. I haven't seen anyone who would fit that description." The woman let her gaze travel up and down over Avran's body. "But I would be glad to assist you in some other way."

Liz was thoroughly disgusted. She'd forgotten Rosalia had the power to make herself disappear. She couldn't truly become invisible, not even the strongest Deep Magician could do that, but as long as she wasn't in a crowd, she could use mind tricks to make certain those around her did not perceive her as part of their reality.

Rosalia could have used this power on the woman in the shop, but she couldn't hide herself from Liz. So if she had come in, where was she now? Liz hadn't seen anyone leave the store. And if the woman she saw wasn't Rosalia, then she couldn't have disappeared. Could Liz have been mistaken about which shop she'd entered?

Avran draped his arm around Liz and caressed her upper arm with his fingertips. "I don't think our friend is here, darling. We must have been mistaken." Then he bent down and kissed Liz on the lips. The woman at the counter's eyes opened wide with shock. Liz was only slightly less surprised.

"Thank you for your help," Avran said, looking up at the woman. Liz couldn't help but give her a wickedly pleased smile.

"Thank you," Liz whispered to Avran as they left. "That woman was insufferable."

"I would never enjoy such a woman. Her blood would be cold, not full of passion likes yours." His tone was low and sensuous. His voice wrapped around Liz, making her shiver.

Once they were back at the car, Avran stopped playing the lover. Liz was thankful they weren't arguing anymore, but she refused to think about how easily he'd made her hot for him again.

Avran put the car in gear and backed out of the lot. "Who do you think you saw, and why is she so important?" he asked as he unlocked the car.

Liz sighed. It was forbidden on punishment of death to tell another of the Magician Synod. Telling a vampire would probably earn her a very painful death indeed, but Avran wasn't going to relent until she told him something. "I thought she was a friend of mine from college. I don't know what she would've been doing here anyway. I was probably mistaken."

Only the hum of the car's motor filled the silence as they waited through a long light cycle. Liz felt Avran looking at her, but she resisted meeting his gaze, certain he would see the nervousness on her face.

"When you're ready to tell me the truth, please do so." The bitterness of his tone made her stomach flip. Rather than reply and start another argument, she remained silent for the rest of the drive. With every twist and turn the car made, her headache grew worse, and her stomach churned. By the time they reached Avran's house, she desperately needed to lie down.

Gregory opened the door as they stepped onto the porch. "Are you all right, Ms. Carlson?"

Liz knew she must look like hell. She certainly felt like it. "I've got a terrible headache. I'll be fine, but I need to rest."

"Shall I bring you something for your head?"

Gregory's concern was touching, and she tried to smile. "I don't suppose you have any fennel tea?"

"No, but I would be glad to get you some."

"Don't go to any trouble. I'll be all right if I can lie still and quiet for a bit."

Gregory frowned. "Are you certain?"

"Yes, thank you."

"Don't hesitate to call for me if you change your mind." Gregory headed off in the direction of the kitchen.

Liz started toward the stairs, trying to ignore Avran's presence behind her. He grabbed her arm just as she reached the first step.

"You need to eat something first or at least drink some juice. It's imperative that you restore what was lost when I drank from you."

His voice was tight, overly controlled. She could see tension in the line of his jaw, and his hand gripped her arm a bit too firmly. Both anger and concern poured out of him, but Liz couldn't bear to be around him right then. "Avran, let me go. I'm nauseous and my head is pounding. I can't possibly eat anything right now. I need to lie down and meditate to help the pain go away."

"It's the blood loss that's making you sick. At least try to drink some juice."

"Fine, ask Gregory to bring me something sugary and a glass of juice in half an hour. I promise to drink some water when I get to my room, but I need to work on my headache before I have anything else."

He dropped her arm, but the look he gave her made her ache inside. On his face, she saw hurt, concern, and cold anger. She wouldn't blame him if he told her to leave and never spoke to her again. She'd shunned his attention, refused to acknowledge the incredible pleasure he'd brought her, and lied to him.

The knot in her stomach tightened. She ran the last few yards to her room, barely making it to the bathroom before she was sick. When her stomach was empty, she curled up on the cold bathroom floor and cried. She felt nearly as bad as she had the night John ran from her.

Dizzy and unable to stand, she crawled to the bed and just managed to pull herself up. She stretched out on her back and tried to calm her body and her mind. If she could relax her facial muscles, she would feel better.

Her meditative healing technique usually worked wonders, but her mind would not still. A jumble of thoughts about Avran, Liftkin, and Rosalia ran through her mind, refusing to go away, no matter how often she tried to banish them. Finally, exhaustion overcame her. She turned onto her stomach and fell asleep.

Chapter 9

Gentle hands rubbed Liz's back. Someone breathed against her ear, whispering soft words she could not understand. A cool breeze blew over her, yet she was warm. Something firm pressed against her side. She felt safe and loved. She didn't want to wake, but then the voice called her name, and the hand on her back shook her gently.

As she came back to reality, she realized the hand and the voice belonged to Avran. He was telling her that it was time for her to wake up and eat. Ever so slowly, she opened her eyes and turned over so she could see him. His silky black hair hung in his face, but she could see his silver eyes sparkling. He was so beautiful he didn't seem real. She could almost believe she was still dreaming.

"How do you feel?"

She forced herself to focus on her body. Her headache had reduced to a dull pounding. She no longer felt sick to her stomach, only a little shaky. She wasn't sure if she would be able to stand without wobbling, and she knew she needed more sleep. "Better, but still weak."

"That won't change until you've eaten. Are you hungry now?"

Her stomach growled before she could respond. Heat rushed to her cheeks. "I guess so."

He smiled. "I brought you some orange juice and a sandwich. There's also a cup of fennel tea if you still need that for your head and a piece of cake to help restore your sugar level."

"I told Gregory he didn't to have to go out."

"He didn't. I did."

Liz frowned. "Why are you doing this after the way I treated you?"

He sat the tray on her lap as she sat up and then arranged pillows behind her back. "I care about you, Liz. And I'm foolish enough to believe that under that stubborn exterior, you care about me too."

Liz nodded. She wanted to say something, but she couldn't make the words come.

"Eat." He gestured toward the tray, and she was glad for the distraction from thoughts too painful to acknowledge.

She bit into her sandwich without even looking at it and was pleasantly surprised. It was stuffed with rich tangy brie and rare roast beef. The bread had been covered in sweet-hot honey mustard. "Mmmm. How did you know roast beef and brie was my favorite?"

Avran turned away and looked out the window without answering. Anger flared at his dismissal but then she realized he must have picked up some of her likes and dislikes when their minds touched. The last thing she wanted was another argument about her issues with intimacy. "Never mind, you don't have to explain."

He turned around and gave her a slight smile.

"Thank you for the sandwich. It's delicious."

He nodded. "You're welcome. I have some business to attend to. Gregory will collect your tray later." He stood and walked toward the door.

Liz had assumed he would stay and talk with her while she ate. She didn't want to be alone, but what could she say to make him stay?

She remembered the whispered words she'd heard as she lay half awake. "What did you say to me right before you woke me?"

"Nothing." He shifted position slightly, but she knew she'd made him uncomfortable.

"It wasn't in English, but I know you whispered something to me."

"It was nothing significant." He reached for the doorknob.

Desperation rushed through her. "Please stay."

*****

Avran's heart raced, not a common feeling for a vampire. He longed to pull Liz into his arms and give her the comfort she needed, but he couldn't. He had developed feelings for her that frightened him. He couldn't risk getting too close, especially after she'd dismissed the connection between them.

He opened the door. "Unless you want to talk about our investigation, I need to go."

"Avran, I can't tell you the truth."

Anger pumped through his body. He turned back to face her. "So you admit you lied about the woman you saw?"

"Yes. But I can't tell you who the woman is. If I did, it would put both of us in even more danger than we're in right now."

He knew she spoke the truth then. There were vampire secrets he could not risk telling her. Like what it would mean for him to Change a Deep Magician, or the true way a vampire could be killed. Such knowledge would be a death sentence.

But unreasonable as it was, he wanted to know who she'd seen. He wanted her to reveal the secrets she had locked in the most hidden part of her mind, the part he never dared draw near while they made love. "I'm willing to take that risk."

"I can't let you do that."

She looked so young, so vulnerable. She'd unbraided her hair, and it stretched across the pillows, making a curtain over her body. She was paler than normal, and he could feel chaos and unease all around her.

Should he give into his own desires and go to her? Would she permit him to touch her, or would she shut herself off completely as she'd threatened to do in her shop?

For hundreds of years he'd kept his heart out of his sexual relationships, but he feared he couldn't do that with Liz. She was right. It was impossible for them to be together. Ultimately, he would leave and hurt her. Yet he couldn't stop himself from wanting to experience all he could with her now.

He picked up the nearly empty tray and set it aside. Then he lay down next to her, nudging her so she would turn on her side and allow him to envelop her body with his. She melted against him, becoming one with him but in a much softer, sweeter way than their earlier joining.

He wrapped an arm around her waist and buried his face in her hair, inhaling her earthy, herbal scent. His hunger flared, but he'd fed enough from her earlier to keep himself under control.

"How did you become a vampire?" Her voice was soft, barely audible, as if her question was a thought that accidentally slipped out.

He hesitated. He'd never told his story to anyone. To explain his Change, he would have to talk about his human life, something he'd not spoken of in years. His life in Brittany was one of those things he kept locked deep inside. But lying there, wrapped around Liz, he felt like he was floating in a dream world where nothing would be remembered the next day.

"You don't have to tell me if you don't want to." The agitation in her tone told him she feared she'd made him angry.

"I want to tell you. But I must decide where to begin.

She sighed and pressed against him. "Take as long as you need. I don't ever want to get up."

He smiled and ran his hand along her side. She gave another contented sigh. He never wanted to get up either.

"I was born in 1390, in what would today be Northern France but was then the Duchy of Brittany. I was the son of a small landowner. With the land ravaged from the Black Death and so many landowners gone, my father was able to gain lands and establish himself as a member of the gentry. He pulled together enough coin to purchase me the training and equipment I needed to become a knight.

"He sent me to the household of a count, where I was constantly bullied and picked on. As self-defense against the treatment I received, I pushed myself to succeed, training for countless hours each day until I became a horseman and fighter of some skill.

"I was knighted in my twenty-first year, and I served as a knight on and off for a time, leading the feudal levy my father owed the Duke of Brittany. When I turned twenty-three, my father insisted I choose a wife.

"Nevena, a young woman whose family owned land near our village, was suspected of witchcraft. I wasn't in love with her, but we'd grown up as friends, and I felt a need to protect her. My mother was a healer, and she'd recognized the same talent in Nevena and began to teach her. I was well-respected, and I knew that if I married Nevena, no one would dare harm her. I had wanted to marry for love. But I knew that to be a foolish notion, so I resigned myself to make this sacrifice to help a friend.

"Our marriage was cordial, and she was protected, but try as I might, I could not love her. I was gone most of the two years we were married. During one of my absences, a traveling storyteller came to the village. At least, that was what he pretended to be. In truth, he was a vampire, and he seduced Nevena. She left me a note explaining that she'd gone to live with him. She wanted me to be free from my debt to her.

"I wanted to hate her, but I couldn't. I understood why she had left. What I did not yet know was the true nature of her lover or the fact that her inherited magical talents made her ripe for the Change."

Liz turned over and looked at him intently. "So it's true not everyone can be Changed?"

Avran propped himself up on his elbow and used his other hand to stroke her hair. "You are certainly very curious about our ways for someone who will reveal so little about her own gifts."

She smiled. "I can't help being curious."

"I'm sure you cannot, but the specifics of the Change are not something I should elaborate on. Simply telling you my own story is crossing a line I would be safer to stay on the other side of."

She nodded. "I understand."

Avran used his free arm to massage her neck as he continued his story. "A year later, I left for Agincourt. My company was part of the third charge in the battle fought there. By the time we took the field, the English had clearly won the day. Our charge was nothing short of suicide, but I went in anyway, hoping that one day bards in my village would tell of my heroics.

"I was wounded and left for dead. As I lay on the battlefield, slowly dying of blood loss and dehydration, a woman appeared next to me. I thought her an angel, coming to comfort me in my last hours, but it was Nevena. She had come to Change me.

"I was barely conscious when she explained what she was and told me how much my kindness had meant to her. She offered to give me the gift of eternal life. I don't think I truly believed her. I thought it was all a dream or a deluded vision, but I accepted her offer. No matter how brave I'd pretended to be, I feared death.

"She warned me that it might not work, but I was sure to die anyway if she didn't try. When I took her blood, sharp pain wracked my body. I thought surely I would die, but at least it would be quicker than the death that had awaited me. I was violently sick. All my muscles clenched and unclenched in horrible spasms. I gasped for air, but my lungs didn't work.

"Eventually I passed out. When I woke again, it was as if the whole world had changed. I could hear and see nuances that had never been present before. I felt drugged and unsteady, and I'd never been so hungry in my life. I knew instinctively that I must have blood."

Liz sat up and turned to face him. "So you were reunited with your wife?"

Avran didn't miss the pain on her face as she asked this. He smiled and reached for her hand. "There was no happy reunion following my Change. I looked around for Nevena, but she had vanished. She had given me her gift and then abandoned me. Most vampires stay with their fledglings for at least a year, teaching them our ways. It is forbidden to abandon one you have created. A new vampire lacks control or knowledge of what is and is not permitted.

"I saw her again, a few years later. She told me she'd left because Ivan, her lover, would have killed me. She could not let him know what she'd done. It was only then that I was able to hate her. As much as I reveled in my new life, I had been through hell that first year.

"I killed indiscriminately, unable to stop myself from drinking too much. Everywhere I went, I was threatened by other vampires. It was like living a nightmare."

Liz reached out a tentative hand and caressed his cheek. "I'm sorry. I was fortunate to have my mother and my mentor, Elspeth, to help me when my powers became active. It must have been awful to be alone."

"It was, but all that is in the past."

"You mentioned the need to learn the rules. Does that mean vampires have rules, organization?"

"Liz, you of all people should know I cannot answer that. It would be best for you to pretend you never heard a word I said tonight."

*****

Liz took a deep breath. She realized how terribly unfair she was being. She was not willing to tell him about the Synod, yet she expected him to reveal all his vampire secrets. Part of her wanted to see if they could strike a bargain, a trading of information, but she knew that too dangerous for both of them. She could not truly countenance such a betrayal of all she'd been taught.

She tried to absorb the fact that he'd lived through the Hundred Years' War. He'd been a knight. It was nearly impossible to accept. "So you're over six hundred years old?"

Avran laughed, but she thought there was a bitter tone to it. "I prefer to say that I'm still twenty-five. I've just been so for a very long time."

She laughed. "I really can't believe you've seen all the changes in the world since the 1400's."

"Sometimes I can't either. I try not to dwell on it too much. Those of us who don't change along with the world tend not to survive. We either go insane, commit suicide, or get ourselves killed."

Avran looked as though his thoughts had wandered far away. Perhaps he was thinking of another whose life had ended in such a way. She knew she shouldn't ask, but she did. "Where is Nevena now?"

A look of unbelievable anguish crossed his face. "Dead. She was too impetuous to survive long among our kind."

Avran turned away then. Liz wanted to do something to alleviate his pain, so she cupped his chin, lifting his head until their eyes locked. She pushed his soft hair from his face and bent to kiss him.

He responded with more hunger than she expected. Before she knew it, he'd rolled her under him. His hips thrust against hers. She felt his cock, hard and ready. Their tongues tangled, and his hand found one of her breasts, teasing her nipple until she thought she would die of the pleasure.

She responded with equal fierceness, nearly ripping his shirt in her effort to get to his bare skin. But when she felt him press against her shields, she hesitated to drop them. Her heart raced in panic. She wanted him, but this relationship was a risk to both their lives.

Avran pushed himself to his hands and knees and stood, his face hard and cold. "I'll be in my study. Let me know when you're ready to search your house." And then he was gone, instantly, as if he'd vanished into thin air.

Liz bent her knees, laid her head down on them, and let the tears come. Avran had every right to be angry. She'd been the one to kiss him. What was wrong with her? She had to get herself under better control.

She'd focus on searching her house. The sooner they found a way to stop Liftkin, the sooner Avran would be out of her life. She didn't want to admit it, even to herself, but she would miss him terribly. Still, the less contact they had, the easier the transition would be. Eventually she would be content on her own once again.

She looked down at her skirt and remembered his hands lifting it, gliding up her legs to the center of her need. After pushing it to the floor, she threw it across the room. She didn't need any reminders of their lovemaking while they worked tonight. Reaching into her bag, she grabbed the first outfit she could find, ending up with denim shorts and a tank top.

Standing in front of the bathroom mirror, she saw that her color was starting to return. Unbidden, her hand went to her neck, tracing the spot where his fangs had sunk deep. There was no trace of the bite, not even the tiniest reminder of what had happened. She should be grateful for that, but she wasn't. She didn't like the idea that something so monumental could happen and no evidence be left behind.

She brushed her long hair, braided it, and used a barrette to secure it in a knot. Taking a deep breath, she attempted to prepare herself to face Avran again. Tears threatened to spill once again, but she squeezed her hands into fists and successfully fought the tide of sorrow.

*****

Avran sat in his study, cursing both Liz and himself. Why the hell had she kissed him if she intended to shut him out again? And why couldn't he control himself? If he was sensible, he'd do what he must to see that she and the town were safe from Liftkin, and then he'd go spend a few years in one of his European residences.

But being sensible had not kept him alive for six hundred years. Following his instincts had. And his instincts told him to make the most of the time he and Liz had. He was closer than he'd ever come to falling in love with a woman. Walking away now would bring him nothing but regrets.

Never before had he been tempted to bring a woman over. He'd seen other vampires try, and always it had ended in disaster. Relationships could not last for eternity. Assuming the new vampire could handle what he or she became, eventually one member of the couple found a new lover and left, leaving the other to suffer year after year.

Once, a vampire of his acquaintance had tried to Change a woman he believed to be his true love. The woman hadn't survived the Change. Avran's friend started a backyard bonfire the next day and walked straight into it.

Avran wished no such end for himself or Liz. But if even that didn't hold him back, Changing a Deep Magician would be as fatal to them both as a raging inferno. He couldn't offer her the Change, but he could pursue her until she admitted how much she needed him. Then he could keep her for the time he'd been given.

Chapter 10

Rosalia had been here. Praying she was wrong, Liz rushed around the side of her house to back deck to test her wards from a different angle. Still reeling with shock, she forced herself to concentrate, closing her eyes and reaching for the magical barrier. She jerked away as if she'd been hit.

She couldn't deny it any longer. Rosalia had been at her house with Liftkin. Before, she'd only been able to pick out a faintly familiar essence. But seeing Rosalia had stirred her memories and the impression came through clearly. When she'd seen Rosalia in town, Liz had assumed a Synod member was in Granville to investigate Liftkin's actions, not to help him.

She wanted to believe Rosalia had come to her house looking for Liftkin, but their essences were too closely mixed. They'd been here together. Rosalia had avoided her in town, not because the Synod wanted to investigate behind Liz's back, but because Rosalia was working with Liftkin.

Liz let her shaky knees collapse, dumping her onto the steps of her deck. Fighting Liftkin was bad enough, but with Avran to help, she'd believed she could defeat him. Going up against a member of the Synod changed everything. Rosalia had powers Liz could only dream of.

"What's wrong?" Avran appeared before her. "I called, and you didn't respond."

Several seconds passed before she found her voice. She didn't stand a chance of defeating Rosalia on her own, but she was forbidden to tell Avran. She wasn't willing to risk his involvement in a fight with magicians from the Synod, so she lied. "I'm okay. I'm just trying to identify a presence I sensed when I touched my shields."

Avran took her arm and turned her to face him. "You're lying again." He was still angry with her, and his tone held none of its usual warmth, only cold assessment.

She stood abruptly, pushing him away. "I need to search for Liftkin's imprint inside."

He followed her in, saying nothing further. She walked from room to room, letting her hands brush walls and surfaces, but she found no impression of Liftkin.

She still didn't know how to deal with Avran, so she stalled, asking him to wait in the den while she checked her messages. There were six messages: three from Stephanie, all asking where the hell she was and telling her to call A.S.A.P.

The next message was from Cindy, explaining that a short dark-haired woman had been asking for her at the store but had refused to give her name. Liz's heart rate sped up. Rosalia. She was sure of it. The machine beeped and Rosalia's voice floated across Liz's kitchen.

"Ms. Carlson, this is Rosalia Bianchi. I need to talk to you about developments in the case you inquired about. Please call me as soon as possible. I can be reached at 828-555-2323."

Liz's head spun and she had to sit down. What the hell was Rosalia up to? She was the most dangerous woman Liz had ever met and one of the two most powerful Deep Magicians alive. Not to mention that she was beautiful, a skilled speaker, and a first class manipulator. She was the last woman on earth Liz wanted to confront alone, but did Liz dare bring Avran into this?

An image of Avran with a stake through his heart flashed into her mind. She grabbed the counter to steady herself. No, she would do this alone. She would likely die, but maybe she could take Liftkin and Rosalia out with her.

Taking a deep breath, she walked into the den where Avran waited. He was sitting on the couch, his feet stretched out in front of him, head tilted back, eyes closed. His jeans clung to the powerful muscles of his thighs, looking as if they might split at any moment. The planes of his chest were clearly visible under his black T-shirt. His silky, black hair fanned over the back of the couch. She wanted to climb on top of him, unzip his jeans, and take him inside her.

But that was a fantasy, and she had to exist in the real world. As she tried to make herself ask him to leave, a thought kept nagging her. The Lord and Lady had sent her to Avran. They'd told her he was the one who could help her. Would sending him away defy their wishes?

Follow what is in your soul. The Lady's words came back to her. Her soul cried out for union with Avran, but she could not see how the Mother of All would want her to risk Avran's existence by bringing him further in.

"Avran."

He opened his eyes. For a moment they blazed with hunger and desire. Then he quickly made his face more neutral.

"I need you to go." Not an auspicious beginning to the conversation.

"Go where?"

"Home. Away from me. Away from this investigation."

Avran stood, walking the few paces to place himself in front of her. "What's going on, Liz? What did you find?"

She shook her head. "We can't work together anymore."

He wrapped his hands around her arms. "Answer my question."

She tried to pull away, but he held her firm. "I can't do that. I need you to leave."

"I'm not leaving you here alone."

Liz didn't want to be alone. She almost weakened, but she clenched her fists in determination. "We can't work together anymore. I need you to leave, and I need to get my things from your house. I've got to do this alone now."

"No," Avran said, rage vibrating in his voice.

She fought to keep her tears from spilling. "Please, don't argue with me. This is how it's got to be."

A growl rumbled in his chest. "Tell me what you've found."

"No. Just leave. I'll get my things after you're asleep."

He let go, brushing past her and heading toward the kitchen.

Cold sweat broke out on the back of her neck. She couldn't let him hear the messages from Cindy or Rosalia. "Stay out of there."

He pressed the message button, and desperate to stop him, Liz threw out a bolt of energy.

Recovering quickly, he grabbed her wrist and stretched her arms upward, pinning her against the wall. She sent energy to her wrists where he held her. He jerked when he felt the jolt, but he absorbed it and never broke his hold on her. Rage made his eyes glow. And Liz was truly frightened of him for the first time.

"Never use your magic against me again, unless you're prepared to accept the consequences. I admit we are almost evenly matched, but you don't want to feel my full power. I will not hesitate to use it against you if you lose control again."

Stunned, Liz sagged against the wall. Avran released her and stepped back. "Gregory will bring Ares and Saffron, as well as your things. But don't delude yourself into thinking I won't continue this investigation on my own. I'll find out what has you so scared." He was halfway to the door when he turned around. "I hope you live long enough to regret this."

Before she could reply, he was gone. Damn his speed, his strength, his arrogance, and most especially, her feelings for him. Even as he'd held her down and threatened her, she'd wanted to lean forward and kiss his full lips. His anger would have changed to desire in an instant. She was sure of it.

Less than an hour later, Gregory appeared with her pets and her clothes. "I wish you'd reconsider your decision, Miss Carlson."

"Thank you for your concern, but I am making the only choice available to me."

He took a deep breath. She thought he intended to argue with her. Instead, he bent down and stroked Ares' back. "I'm going to miss my new friends."

"You could come visit them if you liked." Liz waited for a few seconds, thinking Gregory would say goodbye. When he didn't, she asked if he needed something else.

"Not exactly, I'm wrestling with my conscience. I don't want to call my loyalty to Mr. Niccolayic into question, but I must say this. Whatever appearances may indicate, he cares for you. Please don't abuse the power that gives you."

Liz felt as if the wind had been knocked from her. She knew Avran had inspired far more than lust in her, but she never considered she'd affected him that way too. She simply taken his concern for her safety as an inkling of the code of chivalry left over from his human life.

She realized Gregory was waiting for a response. "Thank you for telling me that. I can't let myself see Avran again though. I suppose if I'm not there, I can't hurt him."

Gregory shook his head. "I wish that were true."

*****

Butterflies danced in Liz's stomach as she punched the number Rosalia had left into her phone. She cleared her throat, praying she would be able to make her voice work if Rosalia answered.

"Hello." Rosalia's sexy, accented voice confronted her.

"Hello, this is Liz Carlson. I received your message."

"It is imperative that we meet. There are some urgent matters of business I need to discuss with you."

"I'm available for lunch tomorrow. Would that be convenient?"

"Yes. Meet at me at noon at Estephano's. I will reserve a private room, so we may speak without interruption."

Rosalia hung up before Liz could say anything else. Estephano's was a five star Spanish restaurant. It would be nearly impossible to get a table for lunch, let alone a private room. It was the height of the summer tourist season, and the town was chock-full of wealthy retirees taking in the cool temperatures and mountain scenery.

But Liz supposed if Rosalia was working with Liftkin then a little thing like using magical influence on the restaurant staff would be nothing. Although, knowing Rosalia, her foreign charm and stunning beauty might be all she would need.

Liz set the phone in its cradle and entered the extra bedroom, which she'd turned into a mediation room. She pulled out her directional candles and cast a circle. The Lord and Lady had been silent and elusive since leading her to ask Avran for help, but she wanted to attempt to contact them once again.

She lay on the floor and eased herself into a deep trance. She asked the Lord and Lady to speak to her, but all she heard was the Lady's injunction echoing in her mind. *Trust your deep instincts. Be led not by fear but by what resides within your soul.* Liz knew in her heart the message meant she should rethink her decision to push Avran away, but she chose to ignore the truth. She wouldn't put him at risk, no matter what she had to face.

*****

The maitre'd at Estephano's escorted Liz to table in a private upstairs room with tall windows overlooking the street below. He told Liz that Rosalia had stepped out to make a phone call and would return shortly.

Liz tried to look over the menu, but the words ran together. Her hands shook, and the butterflies she'd felt earlier had multiplied, making her stomach churn. Another headache pounded behind her eyes. She longed to go home, drink some fennel tea, and soak in a hot bath.

After a few minutes, Rosalia entered. She wore a black silk suit with a ridiculously short skirt. Her dark curly hair looked as if she just stepped out of a salon. "Hello, Liz. It's good to see you again." She grabbed Liz's hands and kissed her on both cheeks.

Liz did her best to appear pleased to see Rosalia, but she could not equal the other woman's animation.

Rosalia insisted on ordering for them, choosing the pear and gorgonzola salad. Then the petite woman took a sip of her wine and leaned forward as if about to impart a secret. "Liz, I want to tell you about some exciting changes happening within the Synod."

She had the overly perky tone one would expect from a religious zealot. Liz tried to suppress a shudder.

"There are, of course, a few stodgy old members who resist all but the smallest suggestion of change, but those of us who are young know we must adapt ourselves to the current culture."

Liz tensed as unease slithered along her spine. "What do you mean?"

"Surely you agree we cannot continue to use our powers so infrequently. Think of all we could accomplish if we used our powers as they were intended. If I had followed the rules of the old order, we would not have this nice room to eat in now. In fact, we likely wouldn't have gotten a table at all. Using my magic, I was able to arrange for us to dine in style, and we won't even have to pay for the meal."

"Neither of us are in need of money, and there are plenty of other good restaurants in town. There was no need to use magic this morning."

Rosalia gave an exasperated snort. "That's hardly the point. Why should we be satisfied living like normal humans, only using our powers to defend or heal? What is the point of being a Deep Magician if we cannot use our skills to our advantage?"

"The Lord and Lady gave us our powers so we could help others."

"So you've been taught. Think larger. Think of what you could be. Think of the kind of life you could lead if you unleashed yourself."

Fear clutched at Liz's heart. Rosalia and her allies had to be stopped, but she hadn't the power to do it on her own. "What you're suggesting goes against everything we believe."

"It goes against what the ancients believed and wanted to pass on. Why must we follow their lead? The world is a different place now. One gets ahead in life by acquiring power, and who is better suited to do so than a Deep Magician?"

Liz shook her head, "This is madness, Rosalia. Without restrictions on our powers, we would be free to harm others, to kill."

"Liz, you must forget what you've been taught. Think for yourself. How would you use your powers if you weren't bound by tradition?"

Anger flashed hot, overriding Liz's fear. "I will not use my powers for personal gain. My beliefs do not come from the ancients. They come from the words of the Lord and Lady themselves. I will not defy their wishes, no matter what the council decides."

Rosalia calmly took a sip of wine, but her eyes betrayed her anger. "There are those on the Synod who have made the same complaints. Rest assured those of us who believe change is imminent will quiet those voices however we need to. You can either join us or be eliminated."

The impact of the truth hit Liz with its full force. "Lord and Lady preserve us, Liftkin's working for you."

Rosalia's lips turned up in an evil smile. "He intended to kill you, but you are intelligent and unusually powerful. You would be an asset to our cause." She leaned forward and laid her hand over Liz's. Liz felt Rosalia's power buzz along her arm. "Join us, Liz. Help us create something new." Liz jerked away. The bitch was trying to influence her answer.

Liz grabbed her purse and stood. "I honor the vows that I took when my powers came to life."

Rosalia's face turned hard and cold. "You have twenty-four hours to change your mind. We will not offer again. We will simply eliminate you, as we would any other obstacle."

Careful to shield herself from attack, Liz turned and walked away.

Chapter 11

Liftkin and Rosalia sat on the balcony of his hotel room, sipping afternoon cocktails. He watched Rosalia carefully. He knew she was toying with her thoughts, trying to determine how best to manipulate him. How he wished he could reach out, wrap his hands around her neck, and squeeze until the little bitch ceased to breathe. One day soon he would have her in his power.

She sat her drink down and turned to him. "Didn't you have a run-in with Avran Niccolayic?"

"Yes, he's evidentially a witch who thinks far too highly of himself."

"No. He's a vampire."

"That's a popular rumor in town, but I've felt his mind. He's nowhere near that powerful."

Rosalia gripped his arm with her hand, not bothering to stop her wicked nails from digging into his skin. "Do you think I'm stupid enough to have believed some rumor? He's obviously powerful enough to have fooled you, even when you touched his thoughts."

"What makes you so certain he's a vampire?"

"When I met with Liz today, she smelled of vampire. The fool allowed me to kiss her cheek. I got a clear picture of her in a rather compromising position with our Mr. Niccolayic. Our innocent little Ms. Carlson likes to feel his fangs buried in her throat."

Liftkin shook his head. "My God, you're serious."

"Yes, I am. See that he does not wake tonight."

"You expect me to destroy a vampire."

"Yes." The bitch looked at him as if he were a simpleton. "They're rather vulnerable when they sleep."

He wanted to tell her to do it herself if it was so easy, but he didn't dare. She still held the key to the thing he wanted most.

"Are you certain we should interfere with him? What if there are other vampires in the area?"

"There are not," she said as if her words could make it so. "If Liz is spending time in his bed, then she's certain to tell him what she knows about us." Rosalia slammed her hand down on the table. "The self-righteous little prig. She doesn't deserve a man with his obvious attributes." Rosalia twirled a strand of her hair around her finger and smiled like a devious cat. "Too bad there isn't time for me to have a taste of him."

Liftkin snorted with disgust. "I'll arrange it, as long as you promise me I can destroy Liz if she interferes again." He rubbed his thigh as he spoke, looking down at the wound, which still ached despite multiple applications of his strongest poultices.

"You may do with her as you like once she's had time to consider our offer. I fear there's little hope she'll come to see things our way."

Rosalia stood to leave. Liftkin was glad to be rid of her for a few hours. He would indeed arrange for Avran's demise, but he would call in a few favors and send someone else to do Rosalia's dirty work this time.

*****

As Liz drove to the meeting of the downtown business association, she rehearsed what she would say when asked about Avran. She was so rattled from her talk with Rosalia she was afraid she wouldn't be able to string two words together. She'd gone straight home after leaving the restaurant, telling Cindy she had a migraine and wouldn't be able to come back to the store.

She'd flung herself on the couch and let the tears that welled inside spill out. Her long cry had worn her out, and she'd fallen asleep. But she'd dreamed vividly. She stood standing in a stone circle with Avran. Fairy-like creatures danced around them. They kneeled and were blessed by the Lord and Lady. Avran was dressed as the knight he'd been in life, and though no words were spoken, she knew the Lord and Lady had assigned them a quest.

Liz blinked trying to clear her mind of the vision and focus on the road in front of her. She had no energy for dealing with her confused feelings for Avran. Thwarting Rosalia and Liftkin would take every ounce of strength she had.

The business association leaders had reserved a meeting room at the library, and Liz had difficulty finding a space in the tiny parking lot. As she turned off the car, she took a deep breath and rehearsed what she would say when asked about her talk with Avran. Then, double checking to see that her keys were in her purse, she shut the car door and walked inside.

When she entered the meeting room, she could tell something either exciting, disastrous, or both had happened. Tension, agitation, and concern were thick in the air.

Mrs. Eccles entered right behind her and grabbed her arm. "Did you get in touch with Mr. Niccolayic again?"

She started to give her planned response, but before she could, Dorothy Cumberland joined them. "You've heard, haven't you?"

"Heard what?" Liz asked, fearing Dorothy would say her mother had passed away.

"There was a fire at Mr. Niccolayic's house."

Liz grabbed the back of a nearby chair to steady herself. "What happened? Was he hurt?" The thought of Avran burnt to ashes made bile rise in her throat.

"No. Apparently his valet got it put out before much damage was done. It started in an outbuilding. I heard the building was mostly destroyed, but the house itself wasn't harmed. No injuries were reported."

Could Liz be sure this was the truth? Would anyone know if Avran had perished? "Has anyone seen Mr. Niccolayic?" She was afraid of the answer.

Kathryn Beecham, the manager of a jewelry store, joined them and answered Liz's question. "He's fine. Ricky, my husband, he's a firefighter. He talked to Mr. Niccolayic when he went out on the call. He said it might've been arson, but Mr. Niccolayic was most insistent that he'd simply been careless with a can of kerosene."

"So there won't be an investigation?" Liz asked.

"No. It's Mr. Niccolayic's property, so it's his call."

Liz was thankful for that. She could easily guess who'd started the fire, and it wasn't a matter for the police. Before she could ask Kathryn her next question, a commotion near the room's entrance drew their attention.

Too many people crowded near for her to see what was going on. But she heard the whisper of Avran's name and she felt a change in the room's energy. She elbowed her way past a few people she knew only by name, finally getting a clear view. Avran stood in the doorway, introducing himself to people and looking as attractive as ever.

He was obviously unharmed, and the dark gray suit he wore added to his usual air of power and authority. Confidence poured off him, but he acted as if he didn't realize that every female eye in the room, including those of seventy-eight-year-old Mrs. Eccles, was glued to him.

Dorothy and Mrs. Eccles had followed Liz toward the door, and Avran began walking toward their little group. Liz introduced him to her friends. Dorothy smiled at him dreamily, like a sixteen-year-old girl meeting a movie star. "We were discussing the fire at your house. We're so glad to see you weren't hurt."

"Thank you. I feel quite fortunate." His voice was smooth and silky, but Liz could see his tension in the way he held himself.

He caught Liz's eye despite her attempt to avoid his gaze. "Ms. Carlson, I would like to speak to you after the meeting."

"I'm sorry. I have to go home as soon as the meeting ends. I have a lot of business to catch up on tonight."

"What I have to say won't take long." He walked off before she could protest.

"What was that about?" Dorothy asked.

"He probably has a question about speaking at Liftkin's hearing. I've spoken with him several times about supporting our cause."

"If you ask me, he looked like he was interested in far more than business. He couldn't keep his eyes off you."

"He might've been surprised that I declined to do his bidding. I don't think he's used to being rejected."

"I can see why he wouldn't be," Dorothy said, throwing another appreciative glance in his direction.

"You got that right dear." Mrs. Eccles actually giggled.

Mr. Brown, a middle-aged man who ran the old-style drug store across the square from Liz's store, served as head of the merchant council. He whistled loudly and asked for everyone to be seated.

The chairs were arranged in a circle. Liz waited until Avran found a chair near Mr. Brown. Then, she strategically seated herself a quarter of the way around the circle, so she neither had to sit beside him nor make eye contact with him. She needed time to re-think her strategy before being confronted by him again.

The meeting began, and Mr. Brown called on Avran first. When he began to speak, everyone locked their gazes on him. Not so much as a whisper was heard. Liz felt no disturbance of the energy in the room, but it was hard to believe he wasn't using magic to garner such attention.

"After Ms. Carlson approached me and explained your dilemma," he paused to lean forward and make eye contact with her. "I agreed to support your cause without hesitation. I have no intention of letting Max Liftkin, a man who has apparently little experience in the realm of city planning, destroy such a fine area as Granville's city square. I wholeheartedly support your efforts, and I will be glad to contribute to your cause in any way, including speaking on your behalf at the public hearing."

When he sat down, clapping erupted all around the circle. Mr. Brown stood again, shook Avran's hand and thanked him for his support. The rest of the meeting consisted of a discussion of who would speak to which topic at the upcoming hearing and the continuing call for everyone to look for new ways to explain the importance of the Mercer building, both aesthetically and historically.

When the meeting adjourned, Mr. Brown pulled Avran aside, and Liz saw her chance to escape. After inquiring as quickly as she could about Mrs. Cumberland's mother's condition, Liz slipped out the door and headed for her Jeep.

She'd reached for the handle of her door when Avran appeared at her side. "Surely you didn't think to get away from me that easily?" His seductive voice rushed over her.

"There's no need to continue your seductive act. It worked quite successfully on all the women in the meeting, but I can't allow myself to be charmed by you again."

"I'm not sure you have a choice." His breath was warm against her ear, and he pressed his body firmly against her back. "I feel the tension in you." He inhaled deeply. "And I smell your desire."

She whirled to face him. "Stop it, Avran. This is not a game."

"You're damned right it's not. Someone was hoping I never woke up again. I assume it was Liftkin. What I still don't know is what you found out yesterday and whether you had anything to do with it."

Liz gasped. "I would never truly harm you. I lashed out at you yesterday, but I didn't hurt you. I couldn't have. Harming others goes against everything I believe in."

His face softened. She realized he'd never really thought she'd betrayed him. He was only trying to provoke her. "Liz, tell me why someone tried to kill me."

"I'm certain Liftkin started the fire. He must have discovered your true identity, but we can't talk here." The time had come to tell him. The dictates of the Synod no longer mattered. "Get in. We'll go back to my house."

He didn't move. "How did they find out what I am?"

"I don't know." She paused for a moment and then it hit her. "Oh gods, the kiss."

He gripped her arm and pulled her tight against him. "Who have you kissed, Liz?" He went utterly still, but Liz felt the venom inside him, ready to come pouring out. His voice had changed from satin to stabbing ice.

"Back off. I met with the woman I was searching for. She kissed my cheeks in greeting." Avran released her and relaxed visibly. "She would have been able to pick up my surface thoughts from the contact. I can't believe I'm such a fool."

"I was part of your surface thoughts?"

"Yes." Her cheeks heated. "When her hair tickled my cheek as she embraced me, I thought about how much I enjoyed the feel of your hair flowing over my face as you fed from me." Liz leaned her head against the car and squeezed her eyes shut to keep the tears inside. "Avran, I'm so sorry. It's all my fault."

He wrapped his arms around her. She stiffened. She'd just humiliated herself. The last thing she needed was for him to see how quickly he could seduce her. She pushed away from the car and opened her door. "Let's get out of here."

"You sent me away yesterday. What makes you think I want to go with you now?"

"Damn it, Avran. Stop this. Either you want in or not. Choose and don't play with me."

He reached out and caressed her cheek. "Your heart beating fast, darling Liz. Anger and passion complement each other so well. Your blood would taste like the finest wine were I to taste you now." He leaned over and skimmed his lips over neck, barely touching the skin with his tongue. "Admit it. There's an inferno of desire blazing inside you. Then I will come with you as you ask."

"My desire for you has nothing to do with the fact that someone wants you dead. You're wasting precious time."

He sighed. "To my shame, I can no more walk away from you than I could drive a stake through my own heart. Damn you, Liz. You're the one who's playing a game."

She would've rather he'd hit her than cut right to her heart with such cold words, words she could not deny. The heat of his body disappeared, and he reappeared by the passenger door. She unlocked it, and he got in.

An uneasy silence pervaded the car during the drive to Liz's house. Avran was so still and quiet that even though he'd told her he couldn't literally disappear, she had to keep glancing at the passenger seat to make sure he was still there. When they went inside, she fed Ares and Saffron and made herself busy getting a glass of water and making coffee, anything to delay another confrontation with Avran.

She felt rather than heard him enter the kitchen. "Would you like some coffee?"

"Stop trying to run away, Liz." His voice caressed her.

"How do you do that?"

"Do what?" The words floated around her, brushing against her skin like silk.

She refused to give him the satisfaction of explaining, so she turned to face him. "If I tell you what you want to know, you will be in even greater danger. Are you sure that is what you want?

"Yes. For you, Liz, I would risk everything." The words swirled around her breasts, making her nipples tighten.

She was so aroused she wanted to scream. Concentrating on what she had to say was a struggle. "You are about to hear things no vampire and few normal humans have ever heard. If another Deep Magician finds out what I've told you, we'll certainly be killed. Of course, Liftkin's already trying to kill us anyway, so I suppose at this point it doesn't much matter."

"I have no intention of giving that bastard the satisfaction of seeing me die."

She followed Avran to the den, carrying their cups of coffee. He took off his jacket and tie, and her breath caught as she watched him move. Why did he have the ability to make her so weak?

They sat down on the leather sofa in her den, and she began her tale. "The powers of a Deep Magician are inherited, and the strength of one's power depends on the power of one's ancestors. The first people to manifest such power were born over a thousand years ago. There were ten of them, belonging to ten different families. The representatives of these families comprise what we call the Synod. The woman I saw in town is a member of the Synod. Her name is Rosalia, and Liftkin is working for her."

"What's she got that he wants?"

Liz took a sip of her coffee before she spoke. "The simplest answer to that question would be power, but the real answer is far more complicated. Knowing about the Synod could get you killed; knowing what I'm telling you now could get you killed in a vicious painful way as a message to all who would dare interfere with her."

"And I suppose an even more torturous fate awaits you."

Liz had known that was true, but hearing him say it made her shiver. She'd let herself give into anger, despair, feelings of loneliness, but fear was the one emotion she'd kept locked away. If she let it near the surface, she might fall apart and never recover.

Avran leaned forward and skimmed her hair with the back of his hand. "I won't let that happen. I'm not as easy to kill as they may think. I will see that you're protected no matter what I have to do."

She looked up at him. "I wish I had your confidence. I guess there are moments when I do, when I know what I'm doing is right. But most of the time, I doubt I have the strength to fight them."

"Between the two of us, we will find the strength." He covered her hand with his. "Tell me what Liftkin wants."

"The Synod is responsible for creating and upholding the rules Deep Magicians live by. We're taught these rules by our mentors when we come into our power. The most important rule is that our magic is never used to harm others or to increase our personal power or wealth. We don't even use it to make our lives easier. Minor infractions are usually overlooked. Most of us are guilty of things like using our power to unlock our doors when our hands are full or shifting the energy around us to make ourselves warm on a cold night, but serious infractions are investigated and punished. In rare, extreme cases, that punishment is execution.

"Rosalia and, if she's to be believed, several of the younger members of the Synod, want to change that. They think we've been hiding our powers for too long. She said we have a right to use our magic for gain and that we're cheating ourselves by not getting what we want out of life."

"Most vampires would agree with them."

Cold fear rushed from Liz's toes up through her body.

Avran smiled. "I'm not one of them. I'm perfectly happy to have Deep Magicians governed by their moral impulses. And no matter what their personal philosophy, I want to see Liftkin and Rosalia and anyone else who's helped them die a painful death."

"As much as it goes against what I am supposed to wish for, so do I."

"Liz, I know you don't approve of killing, but in this case, you are defending yourself and the thousands of innocents Liftkin and Rosalia may harm. You don't have to like violence, but I need to know that if the time comes and you need to, you can kill Liftkin. Otherwise, you're far more vulnerable than you think."

Liz took a long deep breath, closed her eyes, and exhaled slowly. "I can do it."

Avran nodded, obviously believing her. "Tell me more about Rosalia's plans."

She recounted what Rosalia had said, adding her speculation that Liftkin was retrieving the coins for Rosalia, rather than himself.

"Is there anyone on the Synod that you trust, anyone you know wouldn't side with Rosalia?"

"No, I don't know any of them well enough to bring them into my confidence. Duncan is the oldest member of the Synod and I cannot imagine him betraying our ideals, but I don't know him well enough to be certain."

"Do you think Rosalia is the mastermind behind this scheme?"

"Yes. She was only nineteen when her mother died and she took her place on the Synod, but she's been a dominant force ever since. Her powers are unusually strong, even for a Synod family, and she is dangerously intelligent. Her mind sees all the threads of an idea at once and fits them together seamlessly.

"A dangerous woman."

"And a beautiful one. She'll spin her web around you, hoping to have you begging for a taste of her. She uses men. She always has. But Liftkin doesn't seem like the type to be anyone's stooge. He's too powerful in his own right. I think we are missing something, something she's offering him beyond the opportunity to be a part of her scheme."

"What do you suggest for our first move?"

"We need to go back to your house. I want to see if I pick up any energies from the area around the fire. I doubt Liftkin himself was there, and Rosalia's not the type of woman who gets her hands dirty, but I want to see if I can pick up the essence of anyone I recognize."

"Very good, but there's something we need to take care of first." Raw sexuality was back in his voice, and Liz felt his words sliding over her torso and slipping into the vee between her legs.

"No, we're working together, but that's it. I'm not having sex with you again."

"I'm hungry, and I need to be at my peak strength in order to protect you."

"You're not hungry. Your skin is pink and your body is warm. You fed before coming to the meeting. You don't need my blood when you've already—" Damn it. The thought of him feeding from another brought jealousy boiling up in her.

Avran smiled, obviously following her thoughts. "Darling Liz, you needn't worry about me taking blood from another. It was meaningless. Sex need not be involved in our feedings, but they're just better if it is."

"It doesn't matter where you get blood as long as you don't harm anyone."

He slid toward her on the sofa and reached out to caress her cheek. "You can't deny the fact that the thought of my taking blood from another woman disturbs you."

"It doesn't disturb me in the least. Stop playing with me. Lives are in danger here, ours as well as others. We need to get to work."

"My desire for you is not a game. It's deadly serious. I'm not going anywhere until I've had another taste of you." He leaned forward, pressing her back. She wiggled her hips, trying to slide off the couch so she could stand, but he used his weight to trap her.

"Avran, I—"

"Liz," he purred her name, stretching it out, bringing her desire roaring to life.

"What are you doing to me?"

"Forcing you to admit what you want. You have the strength to push me away if that's what you truly desire, but wouldn't you rather give in?"

"You told me never to use my magic against you again." Her voice came out breathy and forced.

"I was angry. I wouldn't hurt you unless you had truly turned against me. Besides you would ignore my threats if you were truly frightened."

He let the full weight of his hips rest against hers and levered himself up over her. His tongue licked her lips and ran over her chin, under it, and along the curve of her neck. "Open to me," he whispered against her ear.

Chapter 12

His voice was velvet sin, the strongest temptation Liz had ever faced. She wasn't equal to the test. Her shields slid down, and she felt the rush of his thoughts as he came into her mind. Images of their naked forms embracing swirled around her. He'd thought of taking her in every conceivable way, of drinking from her, of bringing her to climax an impossible number of times. His fierce primitive hunger thoroughly seduced her.

She could no longer remember why she needed to resist him. She gave herself up to the painful pleasure he stirred in her. He pushed up her tank top and bent to work her nipples with his mouth, sucking, biting, but not yet drawing blood.

Without lifting his mouth from her breasts, Avran reached behind her to unzip her skirt. He shoved the waistband down, and she lifted her hips so he could slip the skirt and her panties off in one swift motion.

Then he returned his attention to her lips. Their tongues tangled. He licked long, slow strokes across the roof of her mouth. The heat of him made her wild. Her hips pumped against him, stroking up and down along the hard ridge of his erection.

She worked at the buttons on his shirt. When she got it open, she pushed it over his shoulders. Then she grasped the sides of his undershirt, pulling it up and over his head. The feel of his perfect skin nearly drove her mad. Their time apart had strengthened her need, and his tongue rasping over her nipples raised it to a fevered pitch.

Her strength was not equal to that of a vampire, but she was far stronger than a normal human. In the grip of need, she feared she would rip Avran's back apart if she touched him. So she reached her arms over her head and gripped the arm of the sofa, breathing in the rich scent of the leather, a smell she'd always connected with primitive males.

"Don't worry about hurting me," he gasped as he licked a line of fire across her belly. "Go ahead. Sink your claws in me. I want to know how wild I've made you."

He lifted his mouth a mere fraction of an inch from her skin and scooted further down, settling between her legs. She thought he was going to use his tongue on her as he had in her store. Instead, without warning, he sank his fangs deep into her thigh near where her leg joined her body.

She cried out, at first from pain and then from indescribable ecstasy sizzling like lightning from his fangs to her swollen clit. She arched her hips, and her hands came down against his shoulders, holding him to her leg.

She couldn't hold back. She let her nails sink deep into his skin, ripping and tearing at him, knowing she was drawing blood. She felt the echo of slight pain in their joined minds and then nothing but pleasure.

One of Avran's hands was locked around her leg, but the other crept up to tease her clit. His fingers brushed lightly against her, the fluttering touch making her insane. She grabbed his wrist and pushed his hand down until several of his fingers plunged inside her. She held tightly to his wrist, thursting her hips against him.

The intensity of her building climax terrified her. For a split second, she hung on the precipice, fearing her heart would stop if she went over. Then Avran wiggled his fingers inside her, and she couldn't stop herself. She tumbled into oblivion.

*****

Avran's head swam with pleasure as her blood rushed into him. She tasted rich and velvety like dark chocolate or dry red wine. She was so delicious he could easily drink too much. Reluctantly, he pulled his lips off the wound he'd made and began to lick it closed.

Liz lay limp and spent under him, but he knew it would take little to revive her. Her passion was nowhere near quenched.

As Avran attempted to slow the pace of his desire, he delved into her mind, searching for her most potent fantasy. Her physical release had opened her mind completely. Pressing into the substance of her thoughts was like swimming through warm butter. Flashes of her fantasies passed before his eyes. Then he saw what he sought, her desire to truly let go. It called to the animal in him.

Thankful for the ease with which he could lift her, he flipped her onto her stomach. She sighed and he smiled. Soon she would be screaming. "Lift your knees," he said, his voice soft and sensuous.

"I can't move. I think you broke me." Her voice was barely audible.

"Darling Liz, I haven't even started yet." He lifted her hips and pushed her legs under her until she knelt on the couch with her head and arms hung over the side. The position would allow him to sink deep inside her. It also kept his fangs safely away from her. He knew he shouldn't drink from her again, but he wasn't sure he could stop himself once he was surrounded by her burning flesh.

"What are you doing?"

"Readying you for the ride of your life." He let the words swirl over her skin, brushing against her nipples and her clit.

"Avran, I—" He cut off her words by reaching between her open legs and gripping her clit between his fingers. He teased her and then pushed a few fingers deep inside. She pressed herself against the arm of the couch, needing the friction and crying out from the pleasure.

Avran continued to squeeze her clit while using his other hand to unzip his pants. Leaning forward, he nipped the smooth skin of her back while he rid himself of the last of his clothes.

Liz wiggled violently, trying to press back to feel more of his fangs while simultaneously rubbing her pubic bone against his hand. He straightened up and grabbed her hips, digging his fingers into her skin and pulling her back against him.

"Give me everything this time. Let yourself fall apart. Become the most primitive part of yourself."

She moaned and struggled against his hands, but he held her fast. "Please."

"Tell me what you want."

She growled. "Damn it, Avran."

"Tell me."

"I want you inside me.

"Tell me more."

"I want you fuck me as hard as you can."

He slid into her in one fast stroke. She whimpered. His hands on her hips forced her to remain still while he pulled out inch by inch.

"More, give me more!"

"That's it. Embrace what you need."

She clenched her inner muscles, shattering his perfect control. He thrust against her so hard her knees slipped. She fell forward against the arm of the couch, her hands going to the floor to support her.

He couldn't slow the rapid pace he'd begun, but he detected no hint of distress in her mind. She panted and whimpered, but her body bucked under him, enveloping his whole length with each stroke.

"Tell me...if I...hurt you." He choked out the words as he slammed himself against her, feeling his balls slap against her pussy.

"More. Goddess. More."

Her hot words almost threw him over the edge, but he was determined to bring her to a searing orgasm first. "I'm going to...give you more than you...ever dreamed of." He reached his hand under her and stroked her clit.

She said his name over and over with growing desperation.

"Let go. Scream for me!"

Her cries echoed around the room and in his mind, and the spasms of her body broke him. He exploded against her, pumping every last drop of himself into her. He barely managed to pull her back onto the couch before he collapsed.

Liz emerged first from the haze of passion. She was lying on her side, tucked against Avran. She stretched out her hand, reaching for her top, which lay on the floor, but Avran grabbed her arm and pulled it back against their bodies.

"I'm not done with you yet," he said.

"Goddess, Avran. I can't possibly take any more."

His hand slid up from her waist and cupped her breast. When his thumb brushed her nipple, it tightened instantly. She tensed.

"Your passion is boundless. "You could go on all night."

"I can hardly move."

"You don't have to move. Lay back and let me worship you."

Never had she dreamed of finding a man who fulfilled her every desire. Pain stabbed through her heart when she remembered why this couldn't last. She tried to ignore the sensations his exploring hands created and began to rebuild her shields.

Avran sat up abruptly, pushing her over on her back. "No, don't close yourself off. Don't analyze this, or you'll deny yourself a chance to truly live."

She realized the will to resist no longer existed within her. She would regret it later, but she had to cherish this moment.

She looked into his silvery eyes. "I want to touch you."

He understood what she needed without her having to say more. He allowed her to sit up and shift her position, so he was lying under her. As she let her eyes trace all the lines of his body, he lay completely still in the way that only his kind could, holding his breath and slowing his pulse.

His skin was smoother, warmer, and more supple than it had been before he'd fed from her. His well-sculpted body fascinated her. Starting at his feet, she ran her hands up his legs, stopping to rub and massage the firm muscles of his calves and thighs. Her fingers brushed across his lower abdomen, teasingly close to his shaft. She watched it begin to stiffen again.

When she reached his flat nipples, she pinched them gently, watching them pucker. Then she rested her hands against his slim hips and bent over so she could taste as well as touch. His light covering of hair tickled her tongue as she made teasing licks on his chest and across his abdomen.

She sucked his shaft inside her mouth. His gasp made her smile. She traced the length of him with her tongue, and his hips lifted, urging her to take him deeper. She swallowed as much of him as she could, pulling him against the back of her throat and flicking her tongue along the underside of his shaft.

She looked up, so she could watch his reaction. His eyes flew open and locked with hers. They'd darkened almost to black. The intensity of the hunger he poured into her mind frightened her, and she pulled back.

He sat up, grabbing her around the waist and flipping her onto her back. She supposed her exploration was over. His eyes remained locked with hers as he held himself over her, thrusting deep in a single stroke.

She moaned, gripping his hips to hold him against her. He grabbed her hands and pushed them over her head, pinning her wrists in one of his hands. He drove into her in slow, shallow strokes. She bit her lip to keep from begging him to go deeper. She turned her head to the side, in clear invitation, but he shook his head. "No now. I'll take too much."

She gasped as drew his cock from her ever so slowly, as if he were caressing her insides. "Please, I want to feel your fangs while you ride me."

"I'll take too much and make you sick again."

"This time I'm prepared. I can take precautions when we're done."

She squeezed her inner muscles against him as she tilted her head back, offering herself again.

He ignored her and increased the pace of his thrusts. But when he had her riding the edge of orgasm. He leaned forward and bit her viciously. Their minds merged and his pleasure screamed through her, forcing her to climax. The waves of pleasure threatened to crush her.

Chapter 13

Liz woke with Avran's head resting on her chest. She curled her head up to kiss Avran's silky hair. Shaking him gently to wake him, she whispered, "I hope you're done now. I don't think I could live through anymore."

He lifted his head and smiled. "I think I can wait a few hours while you recover."

She pushed lightly at his shoulder. "It's not fair that you gain strength and nourishment while I get exhausted."

He smiled. "One of the many advantages to the vampire lifestyle. We never have to stop having sex, not even to eat."

"It's a shame you can't give some of that strength back to me."

"I could, but . . . "

"You could what?"

"Technically, I could revive you. If you drank from me, your powers would be augmented temporarily, at least a normal human's would. I can only assume your powers would increase as well."

"You said 'I could, but'. What's holding you back?"

"Our blood is like a drug to humans, addictive and dangerous. When the effects wear off, you crash hard and want more. The first time it's not so bad. Vampires have successfully shared their blood with human lovers when it's reserved as a special treat, but if given too often, a physical addiction develops. Ultimately, the human must either be brought over or killed. The stories of vampires enslaving humans came from our blood's intoxicating qualities."

"I think I'll stick with the traditional remedy of sleep and human food." But part of her was curious. She wanted to know how it would feel to drink from him. Suddenly, she realized their minds were still linked. Mortified, she threw up her shields, disentangled herself, and rushed to the kitchen.

Avran followed her. "It's natural to be curious. I'm told it tastes and feels delightful, much like what we experience drinking human blood. If the exchange is done during sex, it is the most intimate experience we're capable of."

"If it feels better than what we did just now, I don't think I would survive the experience."

He gave her a wicked smile. "Yes, you could And tonight was merely an introduction to what you can experience as my lover."

Liz's heart pounded and her body already wanted more of him. "Avran, will you promise me something?"

He took one of her hands in his and brought it to his lips. "As long as you don't ask me not to touch you again."

"No, I've accepted that our relationshipor whatever you want to call this—is inevitable. I want you. I'm not going to stop wanting you. But promise me that when the time comes for you to leave, you won't come back until I'mgone. I couldn't bear you coming back to find me old and helpless."

"As you wish."

Liz couldn't help but turn away from the sadness in his eyes.

*****

A few hours later, stomach full of ham sandwich, chocolate cake and juice, Liz combed through the ashes left from the fire at Avran's house as she listened to his explanation of what had happened.

"I don't think they realized Gregory lives here with me. Apparently, they were making no effort to be quiet."

"They? How many were there?"

"Three. All male, but only two escaped."

Liz dropped the ashes she held in her hand and turned to him, fearing she knew what had happened to the other one. "Where's the third man?"

"Dead." Avran answered too quickly, too calmly.

"Everyone was talking about the fire before the meeting, but nobody said anything about a death. In fact, the police seem to have dropped the matter entirely, assuming it was an accident."

"Liz, I think you understand quite clearly why the police can't be involved."

"Gods, Avran, what did you do?"

"Something you would not approve of, I'm sure. Just let me finish explaining what happened."

"You killed him, didn't you?"

Avran sighed and pushed back the strands of hair that had come loose from the tie at his neck. "I did, and I would have killed the other two bastards if they hadn't run into the sunlight."

Liz felt all the heat drain from her face. She knew what he was. Most vampires killed regularly, even got off on it. He didn't. Sill, facing the reality of how easily he could kill when he needed to shook her up.

"Where's the body?"

"Gregory took it away. He wouldn't approve of my killing indiscriminately. I was defending my home. If the police had come they would have viewed the killing as self-defense."

"But it would have been hard for you to explain why the body was drained of blood."

"No."

"Most people killed in self-defense bear gun-shot wounds, not fang marks."

"I killed him, but I didn't drink from him. It's been hundreds of years since I've drained anyone, including those who've deserved it. It's too addictive, too dangerous."

She'd pulled her hair into two braids, and he took one in each of his hands, running his fingers over them all the way to the ends, which reached her waist. She felt his touch as if it were on her skin. "I may not revere life the way you do, and I feel no remorse for killing a man sent to burn me to ashes. But I think that deep inside, you know I'm not evil."

When Liz looked up and met his gaze, she saw anguish and love in his silvery eyes. She stepped back from him, afraid of the emotions he kindled in her heart. "Please tell me the rest of what happened."

Pain flashed in his eyes, but he stepped away. "Gregory heard a noise outside and went to investigate. He saw Liftkin's men spreading kerosene around the side of the shed. I can only assume their orders were to torch the house itself, but the protection I have around it wouldn't let them approach.

"Gregory didn't know how to get rid of them without using a gun, but he knew firing shots would alert the neighbors and one would likely call the police. So he tried to waken me. The hour was earlier than I'd ever risen but I heard his call.

"By the time I reached the shed, the men had already set the blaze. When they saw me, they freaked. I wanted to convince myself they didn't really know what I was. If I hadn't seen the look of horror their faces, I might've succeeded, but they knew. The choice of a daytime fire was no accident. Two of them ran quickly and were careful to keep themselves in the direct sun. The third was too slow."

"Did you learn anything from his thoughts?"

"I wish I had. I was angry, barely controlled. I wanted to rip him apart, not finesse my way through the channels of his mind. He was well-blocked and with so little sleep, I didn't have the patience or skill to learn much. The only thing I can tell you is that he had little or no magical ability. He couldn't have set the shields himself. Rosalia or Liftkin must have done it. I sorry I didn't learn more, but I couldn't think straight."

"No, it's fine. I'm glad you're alive."

Avran smiled but it didn't reach his eyes. "Yeah, so am I. Gregory put out the fire while I dealt with the men, but before we could clean up, a fire truck and a police car came flying up the street."

"How did you get rid of them?"

"I broke more of your rules."

His voice was bitter and cold. Liz knew she'd hurt him, so she tried to keep her voice calm. "You invaded their minds?"

"Yes, I did. I believe in using my powers to protect myself and those I love. If that makes me a manipulative bastard then so be it."

He turned away from her and leaned against the rock wall that ran around the side of the outbuilding. The wind tossed his long black hair. As Liz watched him silhouetted in the moonlight, she thought he looked as dangerous as he was. Passion, anger, and uncertainty swirled in the air around him, wafting to her on the breeze.

She dropped the pile of ash she'd been examining and approached him, tentatively laying a hand on his shoulder. He flinched but didn't pull away. "I believe in rules. I've tried to live by the ones created for Deep Magicians, but I understand that there are times when we have to break the rules for the good of others."

He sighed and placed his hand on top of hers. "I lived a life based on killing and power when I was human. I tried to enjoy it as a vampire, but I couldn't. I enjoy drinking warm blood laced with passion, the incredible sex, the pure sensual awareness that I have now, but I try to keep the beast at bay. Sometimes, though, it can't be done. If I see Liftkin or Rosalia, I won't try to stop myself from killing them."

Liz nodded and with a silent agreement to end the conversation, they returned to their search of the rubble that had been Avran's storage shed.

When Liz had combed the entire area, she stretched her back and sighed in disgust.

"Nothing?"

"No, and the strangest thing is that I get no sense of magical presence. Why would Liftkin or Rosalia send people who had no power, especially if they've realize who you really are? And if the men knew you were a vampire, what could Rosalia or Liftkin have offered them to make them risk coming here?"

Avran shrugged. "Drugs? A vulgar amount of money? The assurance that I could not wake until dark?"

"Possibly all of the above, but what really worries me is that if these men knew about you then they probably also know about Liftkin, Rosalia, and me. The most sacred of all our rules is that we never reveal our true nature to anyone. I never even told my father."

"Surely there are people out there who know or at least suspect."

"Suspicion is one thing. Confirmation is another. The women in my Goddess Circle know I have very special gifts, but they cannot put a name to them. The only ones who can are other paranormals like you. These men cannot be allowed to reveal our secrets. We must find them."

"And kill them?"

"No!"

"Then what do you propose we do? Ask them nicely not to tell anyone the truth?"

"Can't you erase their memories?"

"Ahh, yes, but that would be altering their minds without their permission."

"Avran, why are you making this so hard on me?"

"Because I want you to admit that part of fighting for the system you believe in involves breaking the very rules you're trying to protect."

"So you our rules are pointless? Should I just let Rosalia win then?"

"No." Avran approached her and turned her so he could massage away some of the tension she was holding in her neck and shoulders. "What you're doing is most certainly right. What isn't right is the way you've locked yourself away. You've hidden behind your rules and not allowed yourself to really live."

"I suppose you're an expert on all my faults after knowing me for less than a week?" She pulled away from him, fighting the urge to run.

Avran grabbed her and pulled her to face him, gripping her chin in one hand so she was forced to meet his eyes. "I might as well have known you all your life. I've seen inside you. I've been inside you. I've felt your hopes and fears and—"

"No more, please. I can't think about that. I..."

"Liz, I won't betray you. I won't use the things I know to hurt you. You're beautiful inside, and you could share so much more of that beauty with everyone. Don't let the burden of your powers keep you from that."

Her shoulders began to shake. Avran tried to read her thoughts, but here shields were tightly closed. Even so, her sadness poured through.

"Don't do this, Avran. Don't make me lose my control. I don't know if I'll ever get it back again."

He pulled her to him, rubbing his hands along her back. "I want you to lose control. I want you to give yourself permission to be who you truly are."

She sobbed against his chest, soaking the front of his shirt. "I can't. I just can't."

When the tears had run out, Liz continued to rest against his chest in silence for a few more minutes. Then she pushed away from him. "I need to go back upstairs now." Her voice and her body shook. He started to speak but she held up her hand. "Alone. I think I've had all the emotional, philosophical, and personal revelations I can take for tonight."

Avran wanted to stop her, to call her back and convince her to let him make love to her again, but instead, he stood in silence and let her go.

Chapter 14

The next morning, Liz arrived at the store an hour before opening. She and Avran had argued about her leaving his house while he slept, but she'd pointed out that his house wasn't safe now. She was more worried about him being there defenseless. Rosalia had promised her a day's reprieve, and she intended to make the best of it.

So with the constant threat of attack and her fear for Avran and Gregory marring her concentration, she tried to make a list of things for Cindy to do at the shop that day. She intended to leave the store once they'd opened and try once more to find a document in the library or the Native American Cultural Center that would reveal the location of the silver.

A knock on the shop's front door of the shop made her jump, but when she looked up she saw it was her friend, Stephanie.

Stephanie started talking before Liz could get the door unlocked. "Olivia Cumberland's awake. I wanted to let you know. I also wanted to talk to you about last night."

"That's great! Is she allowed visitors?"

"Not yet, but maybe tomorrow," Stephanie said, dropping into one of the reading chairs.

Liz grabbed her water bottle from the counter and joined her. "What'd you want to ask about last night? The meeting went well, if that's it."

"No, I ran into Dorothy, and she mentioned that she'd followed you out to your car to tell you something and saw you with Mr. Niccolayic."

"He needed to ask me something about the public hearing."

"It didn't look like business talk to her. She said she was afraid to interrupt, because she thought he was about to kiss you."

Damn, she hadn't thought anyone had seen them. "It was dark out. She must've been mistaken."

"Liz, you've hardly been home at all for the last few days. You've been acting distracted and strange. I've known something was up. Now I think I know what's going on."

Liz shook her head. "No, you don't. You definitely don't."

"Come on, Liz. What's up with you two?"

Liz figured a partial truth would dispel Stephanie's curiosity better than a lie. "All right. Avran and I have been on a few dates. I met him, because I went to ask him to support the merchant's council. He asked me out, and I accepted."

"So is he really a vampire like the gossips say?" Stephanie asked, giggling.

Liz cursed the sudden flush she knew had come to her face. Of all the things for Stephanie to say. "A...a vampire?" She forced a laugh. "Of course not."

"I bet he's a wonderful kisser though, seductive vampire or not. Or have you sampled far more than his kisses?"

The fire in Liz's cheeks only grew hotter. "I don't want to talk about this," she said, getting up and walking to the counter.

"Fine, you don't have to share all the juicy bits, though it would be so much more fun that way, but in all seriousness, I'm concerned about you."

"I'm fine."

"Liz, you don't look fine. You look tired, and you're as jittery as I am after my third cappuccino."

Not wanting to meet her friend's eyes, Liz played with a strand of her hair and looked at some papers lying on the counter. "I've been working really hard doing research on the Mercer Building. I'm trying to find some new evidence to share with—"

"Liz, there's more than that. I can tell." Liz felt Stephanie's hands on her shoulder, urging her to turn around. Reluctantly she did so. "No one really knows much about Avran. There've been all kinds of nasty rumors about him, most far more unsettling than the ridiculous vampire thing. I don't want you to get hurt."

"Look, we've had a few dates, that's all." Liz ducked out of her friend's arms and turned away again.

"Then why can't you look at me and say that?" Stephanie walked up and down one of the aisles while Liz settled back into a chair. "He's gorgeous. There's no denying that. And according to Dorothy, he's oh so charming, but you need to be sure you know what he's after."

"Oh, I know what he's after all right."

"Do you mean what I think you mean?" Stephanie walked back toward Liz, her eyes wide.

"Yes, he wants what all men want, but I'm taking care of myself. Don't worry."

"Don't get me wrong. I'm thrilled you're going out with someone. God knows I've been trying to send you on a date for...what has it been, years?"

"Stephanie, as I've told you before, dating is not a priority for me. I'm not going to let a few evenings with Avran change that."

"I know that defensive tone far too well. You've really fallen for him, haven't you?"

"Please drop it, okay. I'm telling you I'm fine. I'm going into this with my eyes open."

"All right." Stephanie looked down at her watch. "I've got to run. Just remember I'm here to listen if you want to talk, and if he tries to hurt you, dangerous man or not, I'll make sure he suffers."

Liz had to smile as she shut the door behind Stephanie. If only her friend knew what she was saying.

After locking up again, the shakiness in her legs forced her to sit back down. Her friend's words had hit her with brutal force. Why was she being so defensive? Was it only because Avran was a vampire? She wanted that to be the case, but she knew it wasn't. The real answer was much scarier. Stephanie was right. She was in love with Avran.

She'd fought her feelings, first by trying to ignore him, then by trying to build a wall around herself that he couldn't penetrate. But when she'd let herself go the night before, her last defenses had been whisked away.

She'd known him such a short time, but already, deep in her soul, she knew he was everything she wanted or needed in a partner. Except of course for that one insurmountable problem—he *was* a vampire. Of course, there were some advantages to this—his ability to understand the part of her life she kept hidden from everyone else, his ability to block her magic and to be a true equal. And sex with a vampire certainly had its advantages—the mind tricks, the biting, his six hundred years of experience.

Liz couldn't convince herself what she felt was only lust. When she dropped her shields and let his mind flow into hers, she felt as much in her heart as she did between her legs. Still, she couldn't allow herself to dream about a future with him. Why couldn't she have fallen for a normal man?

Because a normal man would not understand you. The musical tones of the Lady's voice echoed in her head and the energy of the room shivered. Liz turned to see the Lady appear behind her. She was as real and solid as any human would be. Such clear manifestations of the Divine forces were quite rare. Liz had only experienced such a presence once, when her powers first began to manifest.

"My child, you're greatly troubled. I thought perhaps if I advised you in person you would take what I say to heart and stop draining your energy with worry. You'll need all your strength to endure the battle that lies ahead."

"I'm trying, my Lady, but I—I feel so helpless. I don't understand what I am supposed to do."

"Stop trying to understand. Listen instead. Listen to your deepest, truest feelings."

"But I have to do more than that. The whole system I live by is in danger."

"If you allow yourself to become overwhelmed by your problem, you will never find the solution."

"What should I do? What is the solution?"

"You know I cannot solve your problems for you. I can only tell you as I did before that your instincts are right. Follow what your soul knows to be the truth."

"But what I want...it can never happen."

"Sometimes your deeper instincts conflict with what your head says is right or what you've been taught to do. They can even lead you away from your most tightly held convictions, but still, you must trust yourself to know what is right."

"What about Avran? Was I right to tell him?"

"What does your innermost self say?"

"Yes."

"Then you were right."

"I dreamed that you and the Lord blessed me and Avran and sent us out together. Can he hear you? Do you speak to him too?"

"We would speak to him if he would listen. He does not hold your faith in us or any higher power, but that does not mean he cannot teach you about yourself and your path."

"Was this a vision of our future?"

"As to your future, you know I cannot tell you what will be, only that what you saw is one of numerous possibilities."

"Was it wrong of me to give into my desire for him? Can you at least tell me that?"

"Did it feel right?"

"It felt more right than anything I've ever done, but it terrified me."

"That which is right is not always easy, but you must embrace it anyway. I fear you've forgotten how to drink in life, how to fully live. Don't throw away opportunities that could help you learn how.

The Lady's form began to fade. "Don't go. I have so many more questions."

She smiled, disappearing completely, but Liz heard her voice in her head. *I have said all I can. A time will come when you must call on me. You will know when it arrives*

"Wait, please. What do you mean?"

There was no response.

*****

When Liz entered the Native American Cultural Center, she was greeted by a very young Cherokee woman dressed in traditional clothing. "Can I help you?"

"Yes, I'm looking for information about a legendary treasure, one that might be buried under the Mercer Building.

I've found some correspondence between a woman named Flowing River and a Mrs. Ida Lu Mazey. One of the letters was dated 1886, and the treasure was referred to as Red Bird's treasure."

The young woman frowned. "I'm afraid I've never heard anything about it. Let me go ask Lenora. If anyone can help you, she can."

"Okay. I'll wait here." Liz sat down on a sofa and picked up one of the pamphlets describing the center.

After five or ten minutes, a tall large-boned woman with gray streaks in her long black braid came out of the door behind the counter. "Hello, I'm Lenora. I understand you're interested in reading about Red Bird's treasure."

Liz stood and walked toward her. "Yes, I'm doing some research on the Mercer building. I'm hoping to connect it with some interesting local legends. According to some documents I've read, I believe this treasure may have been buried on the spot where the building stands."

"I would love to help you. But I'm afraid we recently loaned out the documents you would be interested in." Liz took note that the woman's smile didn't reach her eyes. Unease shimmered in the energy around her.

Damn. Liftkin, or more likely Rosalia, had beaten Liz here. "There are a few other people in town working on the same project. Perhaps one of them came by without telling me. Could you tell me the name of the person you loaned the materials to?"

The woman shook her head. "I'm sorry. I can't give out that information."

"This is really very important. We don't have much time left before a decision will be made about the building. I really need to know."

"No matter your circumstances, I can't discuss other patrons' business with you." The woman's voice had lost its overly friendly tone. Liz decided she'd do best to leave and regroup.

"All right. Could you at least tell me when the materials will be returned?"

"Yes, they should be back in a week."

"Thank you. I will inquire with my friends and return later."

The woman didn't say anything else as Liz left the center.

Liz knew she had to get her hands on that information and the sooner the better. It would be easy enough to find out where Liftkin was staying and she was willing to risk a search of his room. But before doing so, she needed to know whether he or Rosalia had what she needed. She only knew of only one way to force the cultural center curator to tell her who had the papers—Avran.

He could easily extract the information from Lenora's mind, but how could Liz ask that of him? That type of manipulation was exactly what she told him she disapproved of. The Lady had warned her she might have to go against her own principles. But encouraging Avran to read someone's mind?

Chapter 15

A file folder hit the wall and papers scattered everywhere. "These are completely useless," Rosalia yelled, gesturing toward the mess she'd made.

Liftkin barely resisted the urge to throw the papers back at her. "I told you there was something funny about that woman at the museum. I knew she was lying to me."

"You can't handle a vampire, but I thought you could at least extract information from a museum employee."

"What did you want me to do? Hold a knife to her throat? Threaten her with torture? I thought you wanted us to keep a low profile."

"Yes, I do. But since you fucked this up, we're going to have to break into the center to see what they're hiding."

Liftkin wanted to slap her pert little face. God he was going to mess her up when he'd gotten what he wanted. "Not a problem. I'll take care of it tonight."

"Fine. I also want twenty-four hour surveillance on Liz and Avran. Since you botched the attempt to kill him, maybe we can use them to lead us straight to the treasure and then eliminate them. Successfully this time."

"Vicious bitch," Liftkin muttered as Rosalia slammed the door behind her.

*****

Avran woke in the middle of a dream. His body had tangled with Liz's as her blood flowed into him. She was near. From his dark resting place deep below the house, he could feel the heat and energy of her body.

He followed the call of her body and found her in the greenhouse, studying the night-blooming plants, which still slept in the late-afternoon sun. He paused, watching her from the doorway.

Her beauty hit him like a tangible thing. She bent over an evening primrose, holding the stem gently in her hand and studying the closed blossom. Her unbound hair lay across her back, giving tantalizing glimpses of skin and the velvet of her tank top. Her firm behind tilted up, begging him to come and cup his hands around it. A long, satiny black skirt swirled around her legs. She was a delectable study in textures. He longed to strip off his own clothes and rub his naked body against her, feeling the smoothness of her skin mixed with velvet and satin.

He wondered that she could be unaware of the vibrations of his lust. It pleased him that she was so comfortable in his house, but night now, she needed to surround herself with the strongest protection possible.

"Good afternoon, Liz."

She jumped, almost breaking the stem of the primrose. "You startled me," she said, turning to face him.

"I wasn't masking my presence. If you'd been paying attention, you would have felt me."

"I'm sorry. I was...thinking. I suppose I let myself get distracted."

Avran gripped her shoulder and struggled to keep fear out of her voice. "You can't afford to let your guard down. I have to know that you are watching out for yourself while I sleep."

"I am, when I'm not here, that is. I know I shouldn't, but I let myself feel safe here."

"You know how close Liftkin's agents came to torching the place. I've put up a strong protection, but you can't take such risks."

Liz nodded. "You're right. I'm sorry."

The fact that she didn't argue brought Avran's defenses up. "What's wrong?"

She frowned. "Nothing. I came here early, because I need to ask you a favor. If you agree, we must act within the next hour."

"You should have called to me, and I would have wakened sooner."

"I didn't want to prevent you fully restoring yourself. Who knows what we might face today?"

"The older my kind get, the less sleep we need. You can always call if you need me." Placing his hand on her back, he gently moved her toward the door. "Come with me. If we are to talk, I must find a darker room."

When they were seated in tall leather wing chairs by the fireplace in his study, Avran waited for her to ask her favor. He watched her take several deep breaths and wondered why she was stalling. What was it she didn't want to say?

Finally, she spoke. "I went to the Native American Cultural Center today, hoping to find more documents about the treasure. The woman I spoke with told me someone else had borrowed the materials I needed. I asked her to tell me who had the documents, but she refused, saying only that they would be due back in a week. I'm assuming Liftkin and Rosalia have them, but we need to know for sure. I..."

Her voice trailed off. She looked down. Her hands played with her skirt.

Avran didn't move. He wanted to prod her, but he knew she would eventually come to her point.

After a long silence, she looked up at him, holding his gaze with hers. "I'm sorry. This is really hard for me to ask, but I need you to come back with me. I need you to encourage Lenora to tell me who has those documents and find out if she's hiding anything else."

"Ahh, now I know why you were reluctant to speak."

"Yes, my asking goes against everything I said last night. Will you do this for me anyway?"

"Liz, I would do far more than this for you. You don't have to explain yourself." He stood and held out his hand to her. "Let's go."

She eyed him warily. "You aren't going to taunt me?"

"No, my darling. I'm thrilled you asked immediately, instead of wasting time trying to find a more palatable solution. I wouldn't dare discourage you."

Liz took his hand and allowed him to pull her to her feet. Stretching up on her tiptoes, she kissed his lips gently. "Thank you."

He couldn't resist pulling her back, deepening the kiss. He wrapped his arms around her and kneaded the firm cheeks of her ass, which he had so admired earlier. His tongue pressed into her mouth to tangle with hers, and she moaned softly. He loved that she rarely wore a bra. It allowed him to feel the hard buds of her breasts through the thin linen of his shirt. He brought his hands around to tease them further.

Pulling away from her questing tongue, he kissed the column of her throat and felt his heartbeat and hers accelerate. His mouth watered. He longed to pierce the tender juncture of her neck and shoulder, but he pushed her back from him. "I can't drink from you again this soon. We should...go." His shaft throbbed, begging him to rethink his decision to stop.

Liz's eyes were glazed. She stumbled back from him as though drunk. "How do you manage to sap my control so quickly? I only meant to give you a brief kiss of thanks."

He smiled and caressed her cheek. "I am as much a slave to our desire as you."

She squeezed her eyes shut for a moment before looking at him again with wide eyes. "I think I actually believe you."

"How could you doubt your effect on me?" He let his voice turn soft, husky, let it curl around her.

He watched her shiver from the effect of his voice. "I think we better go now, or we won't make it in time," she said, nearly running for the door.

"As you wish," he said, still letting his voice play over her. He wanted to keep her aroused, because once their errand was done, he intended to bring her back and teach her more about letting go.

*****

When Liz and Avran arrived at the museum, a couple stood at the counter, and a few students sat working in the reading room. Liz and Avran looked around, pretending to be engrossed in the small museum that occupied the larger room of the first floor. When the couple exited with an armload of books, Avran caught Liz's eye. She nodded. It was time for him to work his magic.

She sat on a bench and watched while he approached the counter. He looked like a large dangerous cat, moving soundlessly across the room. She couldn't hear what he said to the younger woman whose name she'd never learned, but soon the woman went through the door to the back room and reappeared with Lenora.

Avran spoke with her and gestured toward Liz. Lenora held her back straight and stiff, and while Liz could not make out the words Lenora was saying, the tone of her voice made it clear she was angry. Avran's responded with words meant to lull her into doing exactly as he said. Liz let his words flow over her. She felt peace soaking into her muscles.

Lenora's tension oozed out of her, and she leaned against the counter. Then, as if time had stopped for everyone except Avran and Liz—Lenora, the younger woman, and the students froze. For a few seconds, Avran held Lenora's hands, stroking the back of it slowly as though soothing her. Without warning, everyone came back to life, and Lenora disappeared into the back room.

Avran walked toward Liz as if nothing strange had occurred. "They have the documents we need." He smiled at her and took her hand.

When they got back to the counter, Lenora came through the door, carrying two large folders and a few books. "These are all the documents we have that might mention Red Bird's treasure. I'm sorry. I got confused when you were in earlier today, ma'am. I could have sworn they'd been loaned out, but they were here all the time."

"That's quite all right," Liz said, smiling to reassure her.

Liz bent to fill out the card that would allow her to take the materials, but Avran took Lenora's hand and began rubbing it again. He locked his gaze with Lenora's and took the card from Liz with his free hand, pushing it into the pocket of his jeans.

After a few seconds, he dropped Lenora's hand. Then he scooped up the stack of documents and handed them to Liz. He put his hand against Liz's lower back and ushered her out of the center.

"What did you do to Lenora?" Liz asked when they were a block down the street.

"Exactly what you asked me to."

Liz snorted in exasperation. "I mean right before we left. She looked right through us when we turned to go, like she couldn't see us."

"I made sure she wouldn't remember us. She didn't see us as we left, because in her mind, we'd never come in."

Liz shuddered at the thought of someone taking her own memories away, even the bad ones. At least she was well protected against such invasion. "I never told you to mess with her like that, to erase her memory. I only wanted you to find out who had the information."

"Well, as you can see, no one had the real information. Do you want Liftkin or Rosalia to come in there and sense our presence from her thoughts?"

"No...I...this is just hard for me."

"Well, if you're over being squeamish, perhaps you'd be interested to learn why the documents were actually there."

"Damn it, Avran! Can't you have a little respect for my convictions?"

"Not when they put our lives on the line."

They walked the rest of the way to the car in silence. Avran opened her door for her then got in himself. Instead of starting the car, he tucked a few errant strands of hair behind his ears and turned to face her. "I'm trying to see that we're protected and that we have a chance in hell of stopping Rosalia before she turns the world upside down. I'm sorry more of your rules got broken today, but if you ask me for a favor, I'm going to do it my way."

Liz knew she was in the wrong and part of her really wanted to apologize, but her pride kept her from it. "Tell me what you learned or take me home, so I can study these." She tapped the stack of folders on her lap.

Avran's hands gripped the steering wheel so tightly Liz was sure it would break, but he started the car and backed out of the parking space.

They rode in silence for several blocks. When he finally spoke, his voice startled her. "Rosalia came into the center and requested information about the treasure. She was given some documents, but they will tell her nothing more than what we already know."

Avran's voice was cold as ice, and instead of caressing Liz, it stabbed at her skin. She simply waited, hoping he would continue, embarrassed by the way she was acting, but unable to make herself stop.

"The real documents about the treasure are never given out. They are kept in a safe, preserved so a few people in each generation can pass along the information and the necessity of keeping it hidden. Lenora and the few others who know about it fear what would happen if anyone else found out the truth. So if someone asks for such information, they pretend they don't know much about it and only give out minimal information."

Liz couldn't help but be amazed. "You learned all that in less than a minute?"

"Thoughts about the cover up were in Lenora's active mind, so I had no trouble seeing them. Six hundred years of practice has made me rather proficient at picking out what I need."

His voice took on a bitter edge, and Liz knew he was taunting her, throwing his age and his use of techniques she shunned in her face. What could she say to clear the air between them, to make him understand that she appreciated his help?

Avran turned into his driveway and cut the engine. He leaned back against the seat and closed his eyes as though was exhausted by the tension swirling between them. As Liz watched him, feelings of lust overpowered her anger and confusion.

She unhooked her seatbelt and pulled her knees up into her seat so she could lean toward him. He didn't move, so she reached one hand across him to rest on his door. Holding herself above him, she whispered, "Thank you."

He opened his eyes, and she fell into the deep smoky pools. She lowered herself more and let her lips brush his, pulling back quickly before passion trapped her.

"I have to trust you while I watch you do the very things I'm fighting against. Please try to understand how hard that is for me."

"Later tonight, I intend to teach you more about how to let go, about how to give yourself over and savor the experience. You did an exemplary job of that last night, by the way."

His voice was once again a caress. Goosebumps rose across her torso as his words floated around her. Heat rose into her cheeks. *You have forgotten how to drink in life.* The Lady's words echoed around her.

He lowered his seat back with one hand while he slid the other through the curtain of her hair to the back of her neck. One finger drew a line along the top of her spine, the nail grazing her lightly. The passion she'd been holding at bay broke. Without conscious thought, she shifted position until she straddled Avran. Her skirt bunched up around her thighs, and his hard cock pressed into her. Only the fabric of his jeans and the thin satin of her underwear separated them.

Needing more, she sank down against him, rubbing herself back and forth, slowly experiencing the full length of him. He groaned and closed his eyes once again, and his hands moved up to cup her breasts, his thumbs brushing her nipples. She increased her pace, reveling in the feel of him against her pussy.

He moved no part of himself besides his hands. He let her enjoy him as she wanted to. She relished the opportunity to immerse herself in the wonder of his body. Slowing her pace again, she pressed down as hard as she could and slid herself along him one centimeter at a time. Her hands fondled the muscles of his chest, drinking in his strength and the energy of his power.

She sat up, ignoring the steering wheel, which jabbed her back. Her hands dropped to the snap on his jeans. He opened his eyes and took hold of her wrists.

She glanced up. "What's wrong?"

Passion burned in his eyes, and she felt the tension in his thighs. "Nothing. This is delightful, but we need to read over those documents. They must be returned first thing in the morning or someone might miss them. Then I would have to alter the thoughts of others."

Ignoring his words, she slid herself against him. "How can you think about reading now?"

He smiled. "Because I know waiting will only make us hotter."

She pressed down and rocked from side to side. "I don't want to wait."

His hands clamped down on her hips, forcing her to still. "I have many plans for you tonight, but I will not be rushed. We will read first. I promise to make the wait worth while."

Liz drug air into her constricted lungs. "I don't think I can stop."

"You can." He smiled wickedly. "I every confidence in your powers." He lifted her and sat her down in the passenger seat.

Chapter 16

Despite Lenora's fear of releasing the documents about the treasure, several hours of reading had revealed only a few small clues. A few references to a secret underground room located beneath the basement of the Mercer building convinced Liz and Avran that the treasure would be found when they'd located this room. This was good news since it meant they wouldn't have to blast through the buildings foundation to get to the coins. But they had only a vague idea of where to find it.

Another of Mrs. Mazey's journal entries mentioned a rumor that the treasure could be found by moving toward the building from the statue in the town square, but no specific number of paces was mentioned. Since the building was several rooms wide, this could still involve a lot of searching.

Exasperated, Liz laid the stack of letters she was reading beside her on the sofa. Folding her legs under herself, she reached for one of her dinner plates. Gregory had brought her a hamburger, fries, and a special iron and protein rich smoothie he'd made. She finished off the last of the fries while she took a break from reading.

The thought of why she needed extra protein made her mind stray. She turned to watch Avran as he sat at his desk, silently reading. The sight of him sent raw lust coursing through her body. The force of it was almost frightening.

He looked up and smiled. "Liz, darling, you don't look like a woman contemplating old dusty documents."

His velvet voice stroked her. She wanted him sharply, but instead she picked up the letters and settled back onto the couch. "I haven't the slightest idea what you mean." She tried to pull off a stern tone, but her voice sounded more strangled.

"If we were finished, I would come and show you exactly what I mean."

She sighed. "I'm nearly done with my stack, but I haven't found anything else useful."

"Neither have I." He stood and walked toward her. Every move he made was fluid and graceful, and she couldn't take her eyes off him. He'd released his hair from the rubber band that had held it back. She longed to run her hands through it and feel it brush across her body.

He sat down beside her but didn't touch her. Instead, he spoke in a sharp, serious voice. "There is one option I haven't discussed with you yet."

"Option for what?"

"For finding the treasure's hiding place."

A cold rush of fear ran through her stomach. "What have you been hiding from me?"

"It's not that I've been hiding it, it's just...I didn't want to mention it unless it was absolutely necessary. It will put you at risk."

Anger threatened to overwhelm her. She had to work to keep her voice steady. "How dare you make that choice for me? I deserve to know any options we have no matter how risky they are. It's not only me who'll be at risk if Rosalia gets her way. She will be a danger to all humans and possibly other magical creatures as well."

"I know. That's why I'm telling you now." He took a deep breath. "I might be able to track the silver."

"Track it how?"

"Vampires are, for lack of a better term, allergic to silver."

"So that's one legend that is true?"

"Partially. Being around a large quantity of silver weakens us and makes us feel nauseous and dizzy. The properties of the silver interfere with our powers. In great enough quantity, it can even render one of us unconscious. But a small amount of silver, such as handcuffs or a silver bullet would have no serious effect except on a fledgling."

"Do you think Rosalia and Liftkin know this?"

"I don't know, but if they suspect we're going after the treasure, they will surely try to find out more about the truth of vampire legends. I'm old enough and strong enough to partially block the effects with my shields, but I'll need to be fully open to track it. My powers are certain to be at least partially diminished, and you'll be left vulnerable."

"Could you rebuild your shields if we were attacked?"

"Not if the force from the silver is strong. And I can't be sure how the silver's magic will affect me until I am near it. The magical properties could lessen the effect of the silver itself, or it could make it worse. I cannot assume I'll have the strength to shield myself once I've opened up."

The thought of Avran, weak and vulnerable, made her heart flutter. "I don't want to ask this of you, but if it becomes our only option, I will do all I can to protect you."

"Liz, I'm not worried about me. I'm worried about what will happen to you, if I'm too weak to fight off Liftkin or Rosalia's magic."

"The faster we act, the less chance they'll know we're going after the treasure."

"But they likely have underlings watching the building. If we're seen going into the building, Liftkin will surely be contacted."

Liz let her head rest in her hands. While she dismissed the threat to herself, she hated the idea of risking Avran or causing him pain. He said he'd feel discomfort, but something about the tone of his voice made her wonder if it might not be worse than that.

She could use a strengthening spell, and she had an invigoration tincture, which boosted her energy levels. But neither of those would give her the strength to fight Liftkin and Rosalia simultaneously.

Drinking his blood would make her stronger. Something in her mind clicked then and she knew that was what she would have to do. "I know how I can protect us both."

Avran eyed her suspiciously.

She took a deep breath. He'd said that blood sharing was the most intimate experience a vampire could have. She wasn't sure she could live through anything more intimate than what they'd done last night, but she had to try. "If I drink some of your blood before we start our search, I should be strong enough to defend us both."

"No." Avran was suddenly on the far side of the room, arms stretched to brace himself on the window sill. It sounded as though he were breathing hard. For a man who could hold his breath for several minutes at a time, that was quite a reaction.

"You said it would strengthen me."

A few seconds of silence. "I also said it could be addictive and that the effects on Deep Magicians were unknown." Avran's voice shook. Liz had never seen him so agitated.

"You said addiction happens when a human drinks too frequently. I only need to drink once."

"It's not safe."

"Then I'll have to go after the treasure alone and pray I'm strong enough as I am."

"You're not going alone."

"I'm not going with you unless I can defend us both."

Avran whirled to face her, his eyes glowing. "Damn it! Don't you understand? I can't be sure what will happen if you drink from me. You aren't like other humans. What if you become addicted with only a taste? You'll hate me and yourself, because your body will be enslaved to me."

Liz stood and approached him. "I can accept the risk. I can't accept harming you or doing nothing."

*****

Avran turned back toward the window, unable even to look at Liz with temptation riding him. Imagining her lips clasped to his wrist, her eyes wide and dark, locked with his as she drank down raw power, made his cock harden painfully. He clenched his hands against the window to anchor himself, lest he turn around and pull her against him.

He knew how desperately they needed to improve their strength. But the thought of what could happen to Liz terrified him as nothing had in hundreds of years. What if his magic and hers were incompatible? He could end up killing her.

"Avran, please. We have to go after the silver as soon as possible. There are only two days before Liftkin's hearing." Her soft voice cut through him like the sharpest sword. How could he do what she asked? Yet how could he deny her?

Avran's heart pounded in his chest. A true sign of his anxiety. "We will have until tomorrow to go after the silver. The strengthening doesn't take effect right away."

"Does that mean you agree to my plan?"

He wanted to refuse her, but he couldn't. "Yes."

He turned to look at her and sucked in his breath. She fastened her gaze to his and began to strip for him. With aching slowness, she inched the hem of her tank top up her ribs, finally lifting it over her head and baring her breasts. Her nipples were already puckered in anticipation of what was to come.

Earlier she'd braided her hair to keep it out of her face while she read. Now, she pulled the braid over her shoulder, unraveling it twist by twist. When her hair was loose, she shook her head, letting it fall all around her. Avran longed to rub it over his face and breathe in the earthy scent of her, but he didn't dare stop her performance.

Reaching behind her, careful not to get her hands tangled in her hair, she released the zipper of her skirt and pushed the slippery satin over her hips. The sight of her standing there in nothing but lacy black panties made his fangs and his cock ache with need. But he was determined to let her continue her role as the aggressor so he leaned into the wall, forcing himself to remain still.

After slipping her panties down her legs and kicking them off to join her other clothes, Liz walked toward Avran. When she stood inches from him, she reached for the buttons of his shirt. He concentrated on keeping his hands off her and letting her take him where she would. As she pushed the two sides of his shirt apart, her tongue followed the path her fingers had taken. The hot, moist contact made his knees buckle.

*****

Liz dropped to her knees in front of Avran, breathing deeply of his primal scent. As she unzipped his pants, she anticipated getting her hands around the velvety skin of his shaft. Her pussy was so wet her cream had dampened her inner thighs. She'd never relished her own sensuality in quite this way, but desire for Avran overpowered her. She'd spent the whole night hungry for him. Now she intended to enjoy every inch.

She pushed his pants over his hips and wrapped one of her hands around his cock. His deep groan made her smile. As her hand slid up and down, his shaft pulsed against her fingers. She cupped his balls and lifted each one, testing its weight in her hands. Releasing his sac, she ran her hands over his powerful thighs, feeling the tension in them. Knowing she had power over this magnificent man made her feel vital and alive. Was this what the Lady meant about embracing life? If so, then she could get used to it.

Returning her attention to Avran's shaft, she wrapped one hand around the base and drew it into her mouth. The salty taste of him and the mix of textures she could explore with her tongue made her dizzy with pleasure.

Avran made a strangled noise, and she tilted her head to look up at him. His eyes had turned a deep gray, and he gazed at her as though she were a seductive siren. Keeping her eyes locked with his, she pushed his hips against the wall and drew as much of his cock as she could into her mouth. He fought her hold on him, trying to thrust deeper into her.

His obvious ecstasy empowered her. She slid her mouth up and down, increasing the strength of her sucking. She was determined to drive him wild.

He fisted his hands in her hair, tugging hard, but she wouldn't let him gain control. Summoning energy from the center of her body, she drew strength into her hands so she could keep hips trapped against the wall.

He gasped and struggled beneath her hands, making desperate, strangled sounds as she ran her tongue ever so slowly up and down his cock.

"Liz, please!" His voice shook.

His power burst from him and ran along her arms. Liz's lost her ability to hold him. With a fierce growl, he scooped her up. His hands came under her bottom and forced her legs apart.

Then he reversed their positions, pressing her into the wall. He entered her in one savage thrust. The pleasure/pain made her scream.

He started out fast and hard and never let up. Each stroke forced her against the wall. He pushed past her mental shields with equal force. She opened to him, and he sank his fangs into her neck, eliciting another scream.

Her body began the long crescendo to climax. She panted and pleaded. Telling him to give her more, to never stop. Then her words turned to moans. She couldn't breathe, couldn't move. All she could do was feel. Her whole world disintegrated as she came. She heard her screams as if they came from someone else.

She'd just begun to recover when he jerked her head to the side, sinking his fangs deeper. He thrust so deep inside her she could feel it in her chest. The hot explosion of his seed pushed her over the edge again. She sagged against the wall, barely conscious.

*****

When Avran could think again, he tested Liz's thoughts, making sure he hadn't hurt her. He'd never meant to take her so fiercely, but she'd taken away all his defenses with her aggression and the delight she took in going down on him. Thankfully, no fear or pain echoed in her mind, only pleasure and exhaustion. He'd only frightened her enough to give an edge to her satisfaction.

He pulled her close to him, letting her body drape over his chest. She sighed, but otherwise, she didn't stir. He knew exactly how to wake her up and prime her for drinking from him.

Keeping her cradled against him, he knelt by the sofa and laid her back against the soft, velvet cushions. He unhooked her legs from his waist, letting one rest on the floor and pushing the other up so she was fully exposed to him. His eyes feasted on the plump pink folds still dripping with cream.

He ran his hand over her belly, across her pubic bone, and let a finger slide inside her. She moaned and stirred, but her eyes remained closed. Slipping another finger inside, he reveled in the heat and tightness of her while he teased her clit with his tongue.

He drew his fingers out and slid his hands under her ass, lifting her slightly so he could look at her face while he tasted her. Her cream was as intoxicating as her blood, and he never wanted to stop drinking her down.

Liz arched up, pressing herself against his mouth and spearing her hands into his hair. He called to her mentally, telling her to look at him. She opened her catlike green eyes. Her face showed traces of panic. He felt her nearing sensory overload.

"Please...I..."

He flicked his tongue along the side of her clit, effectively silencing her protest. Her head fell back against the sofa.

She moaned and whimpered. Her hips pumped rhythmically against his mouth. He listened in on her thoughts, but all coherency had left him. He gave one last tug with his mouth and let his teeth scrape her gently. Then he released her, and sat up.

Her eyes flew open. "No!"

He smiled. "I have other plans for you."

She gripped his arms, nails biting into his skin. "Make me come." Her voice came out as a husky growl.

"Oh, you will, but I want you drinking from me when you do." He lightly scored her stomach with the nails of his free hand. "You do want to taste me, don't you?"

"Gods, yes!" She released his arms and dug her fingers into the sofa cushions.

Avran cupped her face in his hands. "Look at me."

Her eyes opened. He felt her trying to slow her breathing. He lifted his wrist to his mouth and pierced the skin with his fangs. Her eyes widened. He deepened their mental connection, monitoring her response. She was afraid and slightly disturbed, but desire overrode everything else.

He offered his arm to her. "Drink."

*****

A drop of blood fell from the wound on Avran's wrist as Liz pulled his arm closer to her mouth. Her heart pounded so hard she thought it might give out. She glanced up at his face. The pure raw heat in his eyes gave her the courage she needed. She brought his wrist to her mouth and ran her tongue across it.

The taste of him inflamed her. She locked her lips to his wrist, letting his power flood her body. His blood wasn't like anything she'd ever tasted. The closest thing she could compare it to was melted chocolate, but it was more intoxicating, more enticing, more potent.

Avran pulled free of her mouth and licked his wrist to staunch the flow of blood. Then he lifted her, bringing her astride his lap. Without warning, he shoved himself deep inside her. She screamed, the wonderful fullness almost more than she could take.

He lifted her only to bring her sliding back down his length. He repeated the motion over and over, using more force each time. Liz's whole world narrowed to the sensations between her legs and the blood she could still taste on her tongue. Orgasm crashed over her. Her head fell back. She cried out and then the world went black.

When she awoke, her first realization was that Avran's cock was still buried in her, hard as a rock. She sat back. Before she could speak, Avran reached up and stroked the side of her face, concern evident in his eyes. "How do you feel?"

Liz took a deep breath and concentrated on her body. Was she feeling any effect from his blood? Not yet. "I'm fine. I..." Oh Goddess. Heat slammed through her. Suddenly she couldn't breathe, couldn't think.

She thrust her hips, bringing her clit against Avran's pubic bone and bearing down as hard as she could. She was desperate for relief. All she wanted was to ride Avran's cock until they both exploded. She'd thought letting Avran drink from her had made her lust-crazed, but she'd never felt anything like this.

"Liz?"

She needed a deeper angle and more room to move. She twisted her hips and pushed at his shoulders until he lay back on the couch. He groaned when she pressed back taking him deep.

"Liz, are you sure you're okay?"

She struggled to gather enough breath to speak. "Shut...up...and fuck me."

She thought she heard him laugh but the sound was drowned out by her moan as he thrust against her with brutal force.

She pushed back against him. He met her every stroke, but still it wasn't enough. "More. I need more."

He flipped them over so he was on top. She clawed at his back, trying to pull him down on top of her, needing to make contact with his entire body. But he sat back and pushed at her legs until they were doubled on her chest. Then he leaned forward, supporting himself on his hands and ground himself into her.

Lord and Lady, he felt even thicker and longer in this position. Goddess, he was deep inside her.

He bucked against her, slamming into her until his balls slapped against her ass. "Is this what you need? Is this how hard you need me to fuck you?"

"Yes. Yes, please." She tried to meet his thrusts, but he held her legs, immobilizing her. Her head thrashed against the sofa cushions. She dug her fingers into the fabric, certain it would rip.

Her clit tightened, and her pleasure reached the point of pain. She knew she'd go over any second.

"I've got to come, are you with me?" Avran's voice came out as a growl but his punishing rhythm never faltered.

Liz tried to say she was on the edge, but she crested before she could. Her entire body dissolved into pulsing sparks. She thought she screamed, but she'd lost contact with reality.

The aftershocks of her orgasm continued to rock her for many long minutes. Continuing to breathe as her body spasmed was almost more than she could do. When she was certain every ounce of pleasure has pulsed out of her, she forced herself to open her eyes.

Avran was propped on his elbow, staring down at her.

She tried to smile but even her facial muscles were exhausted. "Is *that* as good as it gets?"

He laughed softly. "If I drank from you while you drank from me, our minds would meld completely. We would each feel what the other felt so we could double our pleasure. My climax would be your climax."

Liz shook her head, but immediately regretted it. Her head felt like someone was hammering on the inside of her skull. Her stomach gave a sickening lurch. Apparently one could get a hangover from vampire blood. "I don't think my heart could handle anything more spectacular than what I just felt."

Avran smiled again. "I imagine you would survive, but it will be a long time before we can consider testing the theory. We can't risk you drinking my blood anytime soon."

Liz wanted to respond, but she felt her eyelids drooping. Avran's voice seemed to come from far away. "It's all right, darling. Take some time to sleep. Let the blood work its magic. I'll be right here when you wake."

Chapter 17

Avran's world was spinning out of control. Once again, he stood at the window where Liz had approached him earlier, where she'd blown his mind with her openness and her hunger for him. He glanced over his shoulder, making sure she was still resting peacefully.

He'd covered her with a soft blanket, but as his eyes traveled over her body, his mind filled in every luscious inch he couldn't see. She'd automatically rebuilt her shields as she'd fallen asleep, a natural defense he was glad she had. Yet he wished to know how her drowsy mind was processing her experience.

Her hair spilled across her body, nearly touching the floor. It obscured part of her face, but he could see that her full lips were slightly stained with his blood.

He'd been afraid her body wouldn't be able to accept his gift or that she would be repulsed when the time came for her to drink from him. In the midst of these concerns, he'd dismissed the impact their sharing of blood would have on his emotions. When he'd watched her and felt the wild pleasure that crashed through her, he'd considered risking it all—death, torture, his freedom—for the chance to keep her.

He couldn't deny it any longer. After six hundred years of existence, he'd finally fallen in love. The thought of Liz finding someone else, someone she would grow old with, someone she could have children with made him ache deep inside.

Maybe it would be best for both of them if he left Granville as soon as Liz was safe again. Of course, even if they succeeded in destroying Liftkin and Rosalia, Rosalia had allies who were sure to come after Liz eventually. Who would help her if he were gone? And who would force her to stop closing herself off from the world? But if he stayed, he doubted he could resist the temptation to Change her? That could prove more dangerous to her than any of Rosalia's allies.

He knelt beside her, pushing the hair out of her face and taking in her beauty. He loved her. He really did love her, but now he realized she'd been right. They would have been better off not getting involved. If he made love to her again, he didn't think he'd be able to leave her, ever. After tonight, he would have to keep his distance when they weren't working. He leaned down and kissed her gently. "Goodbye, my darling," he said. "I must say it now, because I might not be able to later."

*****

Liz's eyes flew open. Never had she jolted awake so fully or so quickly. It was night. Only a few candles burned in the room to give it light, yet she could see as if it were midday. Sounds flooded her ears—the creaks and groans of an old house that were usually too soft to be heard, insects buzzing and chirping all around, and even, she thought, the rustle of carpet fibers as a breeze blew across the room.

And the smells. Flowers and grass that grew outside the open window, spicy, rich red wine left in a glass on the table beside her, and the unique scent that was Avran.

She sat up and looked over the back of the sofa. He was at his desk, writing. She could hear the pen scratching over the page, hear the paper moving ever so slightly and see all the lines of worry on his face despite the dim light. She wondered what he was thinking about.

"Avran, I'm awake and I think...I think it worked."

He looked up. For just a moment, she felt intense pain radiating from him. He covered it quickly, broadcasting concern for her instead. "Are you okay?"

"I feel wonderful. I can see and hear and smell things I never noticed before. I must have gained the type of senses you have."

Moving with vampire speed, he appeared beside her. "Tell me more about what you're feeling."

"I don't know how to describe it really. I can see as if it were day. I can hear things I didn't hear before. I can smell things without having to bring them to my nose. I could smell you as soon as I woke."

"I've heard of this happening before, but usually it's only after a human has drunk from one of us several times, and then the enhancements are much more subtle. Do you feel...different in any other way?"

She smiled. "I don't feel the need to drink more if that's what you're worried about. And I think I've gained more control over myself." She felt heat creep into her cheeks and she knew they were turning red.

Avran smiled. She reached out for his hand, but suddenly, he pulled away and stood. "We should talk about our preparations for tomorrow night. Then you should test yourself, see if your magic feels stronger.

His business-like manner stung. She'd shared the most amazing moment of her life with him. But now he was acting like he was annoyed with her. "Is something wrong?"

"I'm fine." His voice held no emotion at all, none of his usual sensuality. But when he'd been angry before, his voice turned to ice, raising chill bumps on her skin. But she felt nothing. He might as well have been human. Why was he working so hard to mask what he felt?

"Avran, we just shared the most wonderfully intimate experience I've ever had, and you're suddenly all business. How am I supposed to believe nothing is wrong?"

He refused to meet her eyes. "I'm concerned about finding the silver. I can't help but be a little distracted."

"Distracted yes, but cold? I've never known you to so thoroughly erase all the passion from yourself."

"Then maybe you don't really know me as well as you think you do."

Liz felt like she'd been hit. She'd done what Avran asked. She'd opened herself to him, let him see deep down inside her, allowed herself to feel, and now dared to shut himself off from her. The hell with him. If he could truly be such an asshole, then she'd find the treasure on her own.

Gathering her clothes from the floor, she yanked them back on, not caring when she put her top on inside out. "When you decide to be honest with me, let me know."

"Liz, wait!" She heard him call, but she was already out the door and down the hall. Apparently, she'd gained some of his speed as well. She was certain he could catch her if he wanted to, but he didn't bother.

She forgot that her car sat in his driveway, she just started to run and didn't stop until she was home. Usually pushing her body physically helped her pound out all the feelings of despair that were never far beneath the surface. But curse Avran and his vampire powers, she was now too strong to be winded after her two mile run.

She knew she needed to test her powers as Avran had suggested, but she'd never be able to concentrate in her current state. All she could focus on was the big hole Avran's had left in her heart. Ares sensed her mood and joined her on the couch, snuggling tight against her side. Even Saffron padded over and plopped her warm weight now on Liz's feet. Their obvious affection helped allowed her to sink into the tension and let some of the tension drain from her muscles. She'd thought once she relaxed, she would fall apart, but no tears would come. Her entire body felt numb.

*****

Liz woke as quickly and fully as she had at Avran's house. She'd only slept a few hours, but physically, she felt perfectly revived. Emotionally, she was still a wreck. She forced herself to get up so she could feed Ares and Saffron. As she searched for a new bag of cat food, all she could think of was whether she'd misjudged Avran. Did she truly not know him as well as she'd thought?

Had he regretted letting her drink from him? If so, why? Because she was stronger now? Because she would have a better chance of challenging him? He must know she wouldn't attack him, no matter how much their opinions differed on the issue of mind control.

She might never find an answer to all her questions, but the one thing she knew for certain was that she had to find Red Bird's treasure before Liftkin did. Therefore, the first thing she needed to do was determine how her powers had altered and how much physical strength she'd gained. Luckily she had a couple of hours before she needed to open her shop.

The threat of attack from Liftkin or Rosalia hung over her, and she had to keep at least part of her mind alert for any sign that they were approaching. But even so, she discovered she could lift at least ten times the load she'd been able to before. Her energy pooled faster and made a far more lethal strike. She felt confident she could now defend herself against either Liftkin or Rosalia, but if they both showed up...well, she'd just have to do the best she could.

As soon as she could get the shop opened and brief Cindy on the day, she intended to go look at the courthouse records and the documents at the library one last time, hoping to uncover something they'd missed.

The thought of research made her remember the documents she'd left at Avran's. They had to be returned to the center before it opened and the earlier the better. She'd hoped to put off going back to Avran's to retrieve her car until the sun was high in the sky. But she had no choice. She'd just have to hope he'd gone to bed as soon as the sun began to rise.

When she arrived Avran was nowhere in sight, but Gregory met her at the door.

"I'm here to pick up some papers that must be returned today."

Gregory nodded and ushered her inside. "Avran thought you might come by. He wanted me to tell you he has taken care of it."

Liz couldn't help feeling relieved that she wouldn't have to return to the center. "Thanks. I'll go then."

"Ms. Carlson," Gregory called, stopping her with a hand on her arm. "I'd really like to talk with you."

"I've told you to call me Liz, but I don't have time to talk now. I need to get to work."

"It will only take a moment." He pulled gently on her arm to pull her back to him. "I know you were upset when you left last night, and I just want to make sure you're all right."

"No, you want to make sure I haven't hurt Avran, but let me inform you that you were wrong before. He doesn't care enough about me to be bothered."

"Then why did I find him crying in his study after you left?"

Liz's heartbeat accelerated. "You...you must be mistaken. He..."

Gregory exhaled sharply. "Liz, I know what I saw."

"Did you ask him what happened?"

"No, I left as soon as I realized I was intruding. I knew he'd find me if he wanted to talk."

Liz tried to slow her breathing. She didn't want Gregory to know how deeply his words affected her. "Then maybe you were wrong about what you saw."

Gregory shook his head. "No, I wasn't. If you are honest with yourself, you know he cares deeply for you, no matter what he might have said or done."

"I really have to go." This time, Gregory didn't stop her as she fled across the porch and down the steps to her car.

Her heart thudded against her chest, and her improved hearing allowed her to discern every nuance in her ragged breathing.

Gregory must have been mistaken. Avran couldn't have been crying over her. He was the one who'd dismissive her. If he truly cared for her, he wouldn't have been so cold.

Follow what is deep in your soul. A reminder of the Lady's words rang in her head.

But there were things deep in her soul that were better left uncovered. It was easier to dismiss what Gregory had seen and to stay angry than to analyze her true feelings for Avran or his for her.

*****

Liz didn't find any new information, so she went to a hardware store and purchased the tools she would need for digging. Of course she had to find her way into the chamber below the basement first. But she was determined she *would* find it, and it *would* have a dirt floor, one that would require nothing more than a shovel and her superhuman strength to penetrate.

She carried her shovel, pick, flashlight, and lantern out to her Jeep, hoping none of her neighbors were watching and wondering what she was up to. As she stretched up to shut the rear door, she felt the air stir behind her. Avran's scent assaulted her, instantly making her knees weaken. She refused to turn around. She didn't even want to acknowledge his presence.

"Where the hell do you think you're going?" Chilling frost blew over her as he spoke, but she stayed perfectly still, nearly as still as Avran could make himself. "I hope you don't think you're going after that treasure alone."

For several seconds, they both stood, silent, hardly breathing. Liz's patience ran out first, and she turned around. "That is exactly what I'm doing. Please move out of my way. I need to get going."

Avran grabbed both her arms, and she struggled to get out of his hold. His voice remained soft and dangerous as he tightened his grip even more. "Don't. I'm still stronger than you, and I don't want to hurt you."

She gathered her energy, too angry to think what she was doing. His eyes narrowed, but he abruptly let her go.

She moved around the vehicle and pulled the driver's door open. Climbing in, she realized her keys were still inside the house.

He came around to the door. "Please stay and listen to me."

His words were still cold, not painfully so, but they held none of the passion she'd felt from him before. His attitude hurt her so much that she broke one of her own rules by starting the car with magic.

She slammed her foot on the accelerator and jolted out of her driveway. A thump shook the car. She looked in the rearview mirror. Avran's legs dangled down from where he'd apparently taken hold of the luggage rack.

She thought seriously about popping the rear door. It would serve him right. She doubted he'd be seriously hurt, but she couldn't do it, nor could she continue to drive down the street with him hanging off her car. The last thing she wanted to do was attract attention.

She slowed the car and pulled over though she couldn't resist jamming the brake in as she came to a full stop. When she looked up, he'd disappeared.

Slowly, she opened her door. He grabbed her. This time she felt power radiating from him. She didn't know what he was capable of, as insistent as he'd been that she be completely open with him he'd never fully explained what his powers could do. But the rage in his eyes kept her from using her own magic. She stayed perfectly still.

"Avran. Let me go. I don't want to fight with you, but I'm going after that treasure."

"Not without me."

She knew they had a much better chance of success if he came with her. Could she put her own feelings out of the way for the next few hours? Could she be around him without blowing up? She exhaled all the air she'd been holding. "Fine, get in the car."

His jaw tensed. Liz thought he was going to say something else, but he let her go and walked at a regular human pace to the passenger door.

She stood still for a few moments, fighting back tears. What had she expected? That he would suddenly apologize, sweep her up and carry her back to her house. Did she think things would suddenly be as they had before...before what? She didn't know what had happened to change his attitude.

When she had enough control to know she wouldn't cry, she settled into the driver's seat and quickly started the car with her magic, praying Avran wouldn't notice.

She was not so lucky. "No keys?"

"You're the one who attacked me in front of my house. It's not my fault. I'd been planning to go back inside."

He didn't say anything else, but she glanced over at him and he was smiling.

"Don't you dare make fun of me about this." Oh gods, she was going to cry.

Maybe he sensed it and knew he'd pushed her as far as she could go. "Liz, I admire you for always doing what must be done, no matter how hard it is for you. I would never mock that."

The words would have been comforting if his tone hadn't been so flat.

Chapter 18

Liz tugged on the grate she and Avran were trying to loosen. Even with her augmented strength, they'd yet to make it budge. And worse, they weren't even sure it led to the secret room reported to exist below the basement level.

Letting themselves in by magically undoing the locked doors had been amazingly easy. Once inside, they'd quickly found their way into the storage area of the basement, located directly across from the statue in the square. After a thorough search, the drain grate was the only access point they could find that would lead further underground.

Liz was convinced they were at the correct point. If she walked straight from it to the wall and stood on one of chairs stored beneath the high, narrow windows, she could see the statue directly ahead. Why would there be a drain here anyway? There were no pipes or faucets in the room to indicate it had ever been used for anything other than the storage of office furniture and boxes.

They stood up to take a break, and Liz made a suggestion. "Why don't I try heating the metal? Normally, I wouldn't have enough power to heat it to the point of flexibility, but tonight, I might."

"All right, but be careful. Could there be a spell on it that you can't sense?"

His voice still held no emotion. He'd been painfully polite since they'd gotten to the building. His anger appeared to have dissolved, but he was treating her like an acquaintance, not a lover. She struggled to keep him from knowing how much he was hurting her, but her own voice shook every time she spoke. "Why? Do you feel something unusual?"

"No, but I still think I should be able to lift it on my own."

Liz kneeled by the grate and gripped the metal in her hand. She opened her mind slowly and cautiously. The force of the spell hit her like a slap. She threw up her shields, preventing herself from being truly hurt. Despite her efforts, she was knocked back against the concrete floor.

"Liz! Are you all right?" Avran rushed over to her. His face and his voice belying the coolness he'd been showing her all night.

She shook her head to clear it. "I'm fine. I shielded myself from the full force of it." Touching his hand sent shivers through her, but she allowed him to help her up. When she looked into his eyes, she saw all of the concern she would have expected from him a day ago.

She sensed both desire and tenderness, but he broke the contact and stepped back from her before she could grab any more impressions of his feelings. Once they got out of this mess, she was determined to figure out what he was up to.

*****

Avran watched Liz as she lifted the grate without any help from him. She'd broken a spell so strong she hadn't sensed its magic until her shields were down. She didn't recognize the personality of the spell but she'd said the Magician who set it must have been as powerful as Rosalia. If Liz could conquer such magic after a few sips of his blood, what would she be capable of if he Changed her?

Now he understood why changing a Deep Magician was so forbidden by his kind. A woman like Rosalia, whose motives were nowhere near as pure as Liz's, could destroy the world if given such power.

Avran's night vision allowed him to see the dirt floor below the grate. It was a straight drop of about fifteen feet. His senses didn't indicate anything harmful down there, but he still insisted he should go first.

"Avran. I can see in the dark now too. There's no need for you to protect me."

He pulled her back. "I'm going down first. When I've checked it out, I'll help you down.

Without giving her a chance to protest further, he lowered himself into the hole until he hung by his hands. Then he dropped to the floor.

He wanted time to look around before Liz came down, but as soon as he hit the ground, she started lowering the tools, the light, and then herself through the hole. Swearing, he laid the tools on the floor. Then he reached up and wrapped his arms around her legs as she swung down. He caught her and lowered her slowly to the floor.

With her increased strength, she could have taken the fall easily, but he couldn't suppress his need to protect her. He meant to release her as soon as she steadied herself, but as he lowered her to the ground, their bodies touched. The spark of desire that always smoldered under the surface caught flame, arousing him in a way he'd meant to avoid.

Instead of releasing her, he searched her face for her reaction. He knew how much he'd hurt her the night before. Now he was making things worse by letting his passion control him once again. He wished he knew what she was thinking, but he realized he would probably never get to touch her open mind again.

That thought sent pain shooting through him, jarring him from his frozen state. He let go of her and stepped back. His body cooled almost instantly, but he had to dig his nails into his palms, stabbing himself, to keep from grabbing her again.

Her face showed disbelief. Certainly she must be angry, but more than anything she seemed unable to comprehend his wildly oscillating behavior toward her. He wasn't surprised. He could barely comprehend it himself.

She turned away from him, switched on the battery-powered lantern and set it on the floor. With the room illuminated, she turned back and gave him a scrutinizing once over. "Avran, what the hell is going on?"

He felt the surge of power from her that indicated strong emotions. This wasn't the place to have this discussion. Not that he relished the thought of having it anywhere, but they had to stay calm and focused. He knew the silver nearby. He was already feeling its effects though his shields were still up. They needed to get it and get out quickly.

"After we've gotten the treasure neutralized, I'll...try to explain."

"Fine," she snapped, obviously displeased but thankfully willing to accept that they couldn't waste any time.

"I can feel the silver. It's here and there's a lot of it, so much we may have trouble getting it out."

"We'll worry about that when we've found it. What do you need to do to pinpoint its location?"

"I'll lower my shields. Then I'll walk around until I find the place where the effect is strongest, but Liz, as much as it's affecting me already, I'm going to be fairly incapacitated when I find it. You may have to help me move away and do the digging on your own. Can you handle that?"

"I'll be fine. Don't...please be careful."

The raw concern on her face almost did him in. He came dangerously close to pulling her into his arms, begging her forgiveness and confessing his feelings. Instead, he took a deep breath and slowly began letting down his shields. Intense shooting pains ransacked his body, and his head reeled. He fought to stay upright.

"Avran stop! Build them back!"

He heard Liz's voice as if it came from the end of a long tunnel. He'd never experienced anything like this. Either there was enough silver to fill the entire room, or the magic it held increased its effect on him.

He prayed he was on the spot right over the treasure. If the pain got worse, he might pass out.

"Avran! Can you hear me? Don't hurt yourself!"

He didn't have the strength to respond, so he ignored her words and took a few steps forward. The agony intensified. Nausea curled in his stomach. He felt like all his muscles were being ripped from his bones. The sensation brought him to his knees. He had to brace himself on his hands to keep from falling over completely.

*****

Liz could hardly breathe. Panic gripped her as she tried to figure out how to help Avran. She'd known he was hiding how badly he would be affected, trying to pretend he would only be a little dizzy.

He was whiter than a picket fence and blood-tinged sweat poured from his skin. He looked like he might pass out at any moment. She'd tried to send energy to him with her mind, but it hadn't worked. She walked toward him, intending to try giving him energy with her touch when she heard a thump overhead.

She froze. Avran jerked, looking up. He must have heard it as well. At least he was aware of his surroundings. She lowered her shields enough to project her mind into the room above, questing for the source of the noise.

She sensed two men, neither of them were Deep Magicians, but she sensed Liftkin's power riding them. He'd evidently set some type of spell to enhance their natural strength. Before she could learn more, one of them dropped through the ceiling.

He pointed a gun at her. She reacted without thinking. A bolt of energy flew from her hand and slammed against his wrist. He dropped his gun, and she grabbed it before he had a chance to react.

Another man entered the room. Avran pulled himself from the floor and tried to move forward. The man aimed his gun at Avran. "Drop it or I'll shoot him." The man looked pointedly at the gun in Liz's hand.

Before she could think, Liz fired her gun, hitting the man who'd threatened Avran.

She wasn't fast enough. He got off a shot before he went down. It hit Avran in the upper chest, knocking him to the ground.

Liz prayed he could survive.

She turned her gun back on the first man who clung to the wall, apparently scared to death of her. "Take him," she gestured toward the man she'd shot, "and get out of here."

He looked around, frantically trying to figure out how to get back out of the hole in the ceiling. She pointed to a ladder leaning against the wall closest to the entrance.

As scared as he was, he made one last foolish effort to use his magic against her. She intercepted his hit and knocked him to the ground. "Do what I said if you want to get out of here alive."

He got the ladder from the corner of the room, and with obvious difficulty, lifted the other man over his shoulder and climbed up.

Liz waited until she knew they'd left the building before going to Avran. She'd wanted to check his wound immediately, but he would be worse off if the men came back, and she was unprepared.

He lay on his back. As far as she knew, he hadn't moved after being shot. She bent over him and examined the wound. Lifting his shoulder carefully, she noted that there was both an entrance and an exit wound. At least she didn't have to remove the bullet.

His loss of blood wasn't as great as a human's would have been. The flow had slowed considerably, but he was still losing some. If he'd been at full strength, the wound would already have closed.

Would he be able to heal it? Gods, she hoped so. First, she needed to get him away from the silver so he could get his power back. The only way to do that was to carry him. Hopefully, her added strength would allow her to do it.

She didn't want to try picking him up while he was still bleeding, so she ripped two pieces of her T-shirt and pressed them to both sides of his shoulder, applying steady pressure, cursing herself for not bringing her emergency kit down into the hole with her.

She forced herself to focus on the mechanics of what she was doing, knowing if she allowed her emotions to take over she would break down. She'd been angry with him, even wished she never had to see him again, but she knew she still loved him whether he wanted her or not.

When she'd shot the man who threatened him, she hadn't stopped to worry about her personal rules against violence. She'd acted to defend herself and him, despite the breech in her ethics. And she wasn't sorry she'd done it. She would've killed both men to protect him.

When the bleeding had nearly stopped, she ripped another longer strip from her T-shirt and wrapped it under his arm and back around his shoulder, knotting it tightly to keep pressure on his wound.

It took all the power she possessed, but she managed to lift his body and cradle him in her arms. Carefully, she struggled up the ladder. She'd hoped he'd wake up after they moved away from the silver, but he remained unconscious.

Once they reached the top, she sat him down while she replaced the grate and put a spell on it. Working on nothing but adrenaline and the remaining boost from Avran's blood, she got him into the passenger seat. Once she was inside the car with him, she shook him gently and called his name, trying to wake him. He didn't respond.

What could she do? She had to revive him herself. It wasn't like she could take him to an emergency room.

Blood. That should help. He'd lost a lot, and he was always strongest right after he fed.

Not knowing what she might need to get to the treasure, she'd put her father's pocket knife in her pocket. Pulling it out, she opened it and stared at the blade. Then she looked at her arm. Could she really do this? She simply didn't have a choice. No matter how scared she was, giving Avran some of her blood was the only thing she knew to do.

Before she could change her mind, she used the blade to slice her wrist, not deep enough to do herself serious injury but enough to allow blood to flow easily. Pain seared her, but she ignored both it and the swimmy feeling in her head.

She held her wrist over Avran's mouth, trying to pry his lips open so the blood would go in.

For several seconds, nothing happened. Then his lips pressed against her, and his hands gripped her arms. His fangs sunk into her skin, and he began to suck. The pull against her wrist was excruciating and the antiseptic in his saliva stung like salt rubbed into her wound.

She dropped her shields, remembering that he'd warned her he could not make his bite pleasurable if she closed herself off, but she felt none of the warm flood of sensation that usually accompanied his feeding. Steeling herself to endure the pain, she continued to let him drink for several long moments.

She tried to pull her arm away, but couldn't free herself. Panic beat at her. He was going to drain her. But just as she began to see spots, Avran opened his eyes and pulled away.

She slumped back against the seat as he took her wrist once more, licking this time to close the wound. He reached out with soothing thoughts that lessened the pain. "Liz? Are you all right?"

She tried to answer but she didn't have the strength to even open her mouth. The effect of his blood had worn off, and she was more exhausted that she'd ever been.

"Liz, what have I done?"

He pushed her hair off her face, and she managed to smile at him. She gathered the last of her energy. "I saved you." Then she let the blackness take her.

*****

Avran laid his fingers against Liz's neck. Her pulse was slow but clear, and she was breathing normally. He prayed she had not let him drink too much. His shoulder twinged when he picked her up, but it was already healing, thanks to her.

How could he have been so cold to her? How could he have thought he could leave her? Looking down into her face, he knew he wouldn't back away again. He loved her, and he couldn't live without her.

He drove them to his house and took her to the room she'd used before, careful to be attentive to any signs of attack. If his memory of what happened in the chamber was correct, then

Liftkin and Rosalia had once again sent someone else to do their dirty work. That meant the two Magicians could be lurking anywhere.

Liz's bed was made up with dark blue sheets, and she looked so pale next to them that Avran feared for her. What could he do? If he took her to a hospital, he would have to explain how she'd lost so much blood when she had no visible wounds.

If Liz were conscious, she could probably recommend one of her own preparations, but when he tried to wake her he had no success. He knew she'd been teaching her healing techniques to her friend Stephanie. According to Liz, Stephanie had some magical abilities. He might be able to add his strength to hers, so they could heal Liz together. Did he dare call on her?

By doing so, he would break the biggest prohibition of all for both Deep Magicians and his own kind. But he wasn't going to let Liz die. He would break whatever rules necessary to see that she survived.

He lifted Liz's wrist and turned it over. The cut she'd made was nearly healed, but the pulse below felt shallower than it had earlier. She was fading. He called for Gregory and told him to watch over Liz and to call him if her condition changed.

Chapter 19

Avran let himself into Liz's house, found her address book, and quickly located a listing for Stephanie. He wanted to talk to her in person instead of calling. This wasn't something he could explain over the phone.

He doubled-checked her address and ran back to his BMW. He could travel faster on foot, but Stephanie would be leaving with him. He had plenty of outrageous things to tell her. He didn't need to add the experience of being carried while he ran faster than most cars could go.

As he approached Stephanie's door, his heart beat faster than normal. Willing to call on anyone who might help, he spoke to the Lord and Lady to whom Liz prayed, asking them to help Stephanie understand what he had to say and to accept it. If at all possible, he intended to convince Stephanie to follow him without violating her privacy or her free will by delving into her mind. But he would do whatever was necessary to save Liz.

As he heard Stephanie approach her door, he thought he heard a soft female voice say, "We are with you. All will be well." Perhaps he had lost his mind along with his heart.

He heard Stephanie breathing on the other side of the door. Her heart raced and he smelled her fear. "Stephanie, it's Avran Niccolayic. Liz is in trouble. She needs your help. Please let me in."

Stephanie continued to stand still for several seconds. Avran feared he would have to breech her defenses, but finally she opened the door an inch or two and peeked through the crack.

"What's happened?"

"Liz was injured. I need you to help me heal her."

Stephanie's hand flew to her chest. "Heal her?"

Avran nodded, trying to keep his features neutral. "Yes, she told me she's been teaching you her techniques."

"She has but, but I'm just starting out."

"I know, but I'm hoping you'll know enough to help her."

"Surely she can tell you how to make any of her preparations."

"No, she can't." Avran paused, pushing his hair back from his face. "She's . . . unconscious."

"What have you done to her?" Stephanie stepped back from the door.

Avran heard her heartbeat accelerate. He fought against his own anger, knowing it was crucial not to frighten her more. "I would never harm her. She was hurt defending me."

Stephanie's eyes widened ever more. "Defending you from what? What's going on?"

"She's only getting worse while we stand here talking. I'll explain on the way to her house."

Stephanie turned and picked up her phone. "If she's unconscious, then she needs to go to a hospital."

"No." Avran grabbed her arm and forced a command into his tone that could not be obeyed.

Stephanie set the phone down. "What are you?"

She stared at him as though she could see inside him, and he almost flinched. Her determination screamed at him. "I will explain as we drive. Please trust me."

Stephanie narrowed her eyes, but finally she agreed to do as he asked.

As they drove to Liz's house, Avran explained about the treasure and how he and Liz had gone to look for it. He gave as few details as possible saying only that the silver coins held magical properties and Liftkin wanted to use them for his own profit.

"So Liz was hurt while you were looking for the treasure?"

Avran hesitated for a moment. Then he nodded.

"Why can't she go to the hospital?"

"Liz shot one of our attackers after he shot me, and—"

Stephanie gasped. "You were shot? Don't *you* need attention?"

"No, I'm fine. It was a very minor wound, but if Liz goes to the hospital the police will be called."

"Surely you could explain or you could make something up about how she was injured."

"No." Avran parked his car in front of Liz's house.

"I'm not leaving this car until you tell me exactly what's going on."

Avran knew he had two choices. He could go on leading Stephanie in circles and ultimately give in to the need to use mind control, or he could tell her the truth. From what he could read of her on a surface scan, she was strong and intelligent and resilient. Not many people would be able to accept what he was. Still, he could always resort to mind control if she freaked out on him.

"Some of this is going to be hard to believe, but I need you to try for Liz's sake."

"I just want to know the truth."

"When I was shot, I was already weak. The properties of the magic in the silver coins had made me sick. Liz knew she had to do something drastic to help me, so she gave me some of her blood."

Stephanie paled and scooted toward the passenger door. "What do you mean she gave you blood? Liz isn't a doctor. She would never risk trying something like that on her own."

"You're right. She wouldn't."

He was trying to decide how to tell her the truth when she figured it out on her own. Pressing herself against the far side of the car, her eyes wide, she said, "You...the rumors...you really are a vampire."

"Yes."

Her breath came in pants, and she shook her head violently. "No...no, that's ridiculous. You're only trying to scare me."

He smiled at her, letting his fangs show, and then, using his most seductive voice tricks, he said, "Stephanie, you know it's true."

She blinked and looked down at his hands, making sure they weren't touching her. "How did you do that?"

"With magic."

"I asked Liz about the vampire rumors and she laughed at me...oh God, this is really happening isn't it."

"Yes, it's really happening."

Stephanie's was close to hyperventilating, and she was very pale. Avran attempted to calm her. "I'm not going to hurt you, and I haven't intentionally hurt Liz. I was unconscious when she started giving me blood. Without being aware of it, I took too much. Now-"

"So you are the one who hurt her."

"No, I—"

"You son of a bitch." Stephanie intended to slap him, but he grabbed her wrist.

He knew his arm had moved so fast she couldn't see it, and he felt the fear rise in her again. He'd been right to tell her though. If she had the courage to fight with him, then she could come to terms with his existence. He hated to threaten her, but he had to get her focused on Liz. "Don't try that again. I can snap your arm in two before you see me move."

She began to struggle, but he held her tight enough to keep her from getting away. "I have no desire to hurt you, but I need your help. You're going to come inside with me and determine what preparations Liz might have to strengthen her and improve her body's production of blood. We can't waste any more time."

Stephanie followed him inside, but she kept questioning him as she walked. "Why should I trust you? How do I know you're telling the truth about how she was hurt?"

"Because I'm in love with her." Stephanie's eyes widened. "I haven't told her yet, because...well, because I was trying to fight my feelings, but I can't anymore."

Stephanie continued to stare at him for a few seconds. Then she smiled. "I knew she was in love with you when I asked her what was going on between you. She wouldn't say it, but she loves you too. I will help you, but if I find out you're lying to me, I will find a way to hurt you, vampire or not."

Avran smiled. "I believe you."

Stephanie quickly found what she thought they needed in Liz's workroom, and they headed back to Avran's house.

"Liz is more than she seems just like you are, isn't she?"

"Yes, but I'm going to let her tell you the details."

"I'm guessing since I see her in the daylight that she's not a vampire."

Avran laughed, but then pain gripped his heart. "No...no, she's definitely not."

*****

Avran quickly came to understand why Liz liked Stephanie so much. She'd protested that she didn't know enough to help Liz, and she kept trying to convince him to concoct a story that would allow them to take Liz to the hospital. But once she saw her friend, she worked quickly and efficiently to help her.

After Stephanie had decided Avran's love for Liz was real, she seemed to have forgotten the fact that he was a vampire. She showed less fear of him than younger ones of his own kind did. He imagined she treated him no differently than she would any man Liz was going out with. She was slightly wary, but not fearful.

Once she'd examined Liz, she cast a circle and blessed the preparations she'd acquired at Liz's house. Then she rubbed her friend down with an oil, which would increase the activity of her blood cells and placed drops of an invigorating tincture on her tongue. Every few minutes, one of them checked her pulse. Each time it was stronger, and Liz's color was gradually coming back. Stephanie prepared a blood enriching tea to give Liz as soon as she was aware enough to drink.

For hours, Avran and Stephanie sat by Liz's bed in companionable silence, both praying for Liz in their own way. When dawn came, Avran fought his need to go to sleep, but even as strong as he was, he could only put off sleep for a few hours after the sun came up. While Liz's pulse was close to normal, and her skin was once again warm and pink, he didn't want to leave her until she woke.

Stephanie's hand on his arm startled him from his thoughts. Concern showed on her face. "Avran, she's going to be all right. I may not have her powers, but I can feel your fatigue. You need to go wherever it is vampires go in the day." A look of distress came over her face. "You don't really sleep in a coffin, do you?"

As worried as he was, he couldn't help but smile. It wasn't the first time her straightforward words had cheered him during the night. "No, I don't. My daytime accommodations are quite comfortable."

"Good. I promise I'll stay with her. She'll be right here when you wake."

"Knowing her, she'll want to head to that damn store as soon as she's able to get out of bed."

"I'll call Cindy, the young woman who works for her, and make sure she has everything taken care of."

"Ask Gregory for anything you might need. Everything I have is at your disposal."

Stephanie nodded. "When Liz told me she was going out with you, I was convinced you'd end up breaking her heart, but now I see how much you care for her and—"

"Stephanie, by falling in love with her, I've already hurt her. Relationships with mortals are impossible. I...it just can't work out. I'm going to leave town after we've gotten the treasure."

Horror crossed Stephanie's face. "You can't."

"Stephanie, please...I can't argue about this right now."

"I'm not going to let you leave. You're her soul mate. I can see it. You don't leave someone you love that much."

He shook his head, gripping the door frame for support in his exhausted state. "Stephanie, you don't understand. I will end up hurting her more if I stay."

"No, nothing could hurt her more than your leaving."

"I'm six hundred years old. I look exactly the same as I did when I was Changed in 1415. Eventually people will notice I haven't aged, and I will have to leave Granville."

"Then take her with you."

"Stephanie—"

"Why don't you...make her like you are?"

"No!"

"Why not?"

"It is forbidden."

"Why?"

"I will not continue this conversation." He felt himself growing weaker. The curtains closed, but the sun still burned his eyes. "I must go now. Please take care of her and trust me to know what is best for us."

"I promise the first, but I can't watch you both give up something like this. The love I feel in you doesn't happen every day. Sometimes you must dare to do the forbidden. It may be exactly what you need."

Chapter 20

When Liz woke, her mouth felt as if she'd drunk a glass of sand. Her head throbbed as if the blood had to force its way through constricted vessels. She feared that the slightest movement would cause her to be sick.

Slowly pulling the covers off her head, she opened her eyes to slits. She was facing a window. Sunlight streamed in with a painful fury. She wished someone would close the curtains.

Closing her eyes, she tried to think. Where was she? Peeking at the window again, she noted the heavy dark curtains, the kind designed to keep out all the light. She must be at Avran's house, but how had she gotten here?

At first, all she could remember was being angry with him. Then slowly the events of the night began to knit themselves together in her mind. Avran had insisted on going after the treasure with her. She saw him weakened and gasping on the floor of the secret room. Then she relived the moment when she'd shot the man who'd surely been sent by Liftkin. Was Avran all right? She took a deep breath and stopped all thought for a moment while she fought to still her roiling stomach.

When she had her body under control, she let the rest of the evening play in her mind—carrying Avran, offering him her blood, seeing his face alive with the love she thought never to see again. And then nothing, until now.

She realized someone was sitting at the end of her bed, surely not Avran in sun so bright. Gregory? She had to make herself look. With desperate caution, she raised her head slightly and opened her eyes. "Stephanie?"

"Yes, it's me. Lie back down. I'm going to bring you some tea."

"How did you get here? What happened?"

"Shh! I will tell you everything, but I want you to lie down. You scared us last night. I wasn't sure if I could save you."

"Us?"

"Avran and me."

"But you don't even know Avran."

"I do now."

Liz ignored the pounding in her head as best she could and struggled to sit up. She watched as Stephanie turned on a hotpot and put an herbal mixture in a tea ball. The table where she worked was covered with bottles and bags of herbs.

"Where did you get all those things?"

"Most of them came from your house."

"My house?"

Stephanie turned back around and sighed. "I told you to lie down. Avran was right. You're a terrible patient." She moved to Liz's side and propped pillows against the head of the bed. "Would you at least lean back?"

"Stephanie, what the hell is going on?"

"If I tell you the whole story, will you promise to lie still while talk"

"Yes," Liz said, realizing she did feel quite tired and her throat begged for water. "Before you start could I have some water?"

Stephanie nodded.

"Why am I so thirsty?"

Stephanie rolled her eyes. "You really don't remember what happened, do you?"

The blood. She remembered giving Avran blood, a lot of it. He must've taken too much. But she couldn't tell Stephanie that, could she? What had Avran told her to get her here? "No, I don't suppose I do."

"Well I don't know all the details either, but Avran showed up at my house late last night insisting I come help you, saying you needed medical attention but he couldn't take you to the hospital. I got angry. I thought he'd hurt you, and I refused to help until he told me what had happened. And...well, he told me."

Liz sunk deeper into the pillows, unable to hold herself up as shock coursed through her. Surely he hadn't risked his very existence for her. "What exactly did he tell you?"

"That he was a vampire and that you'd saved his—would you call it life? I guess so, he assured me he wasn't dead. He said you'd given him too much blood and weakened yourself. Do you remember now?"

Trust Stephanie to make it sound so normal. You'd think Avran had told her he was an accountant or a banker. She didn't seem the least bit disturbed.

Liz took a deep breath, trying to absorb her shock. "How did you take this news? Did you believe him?"

"I tried not to at first, but somehow, I knew he was telling the truth. He showed me his fangs. They could have been fake, but then he did something with his voice. There was no way to fake that."

Liz sat up higher. "Did he hurt you?"

"No, it was very...pleasant, actually." Stephanie looked terribly embarrassed.

"Yes, I know what you mean." Liz smiled. She didn't like the idea of Avran caressing Stephanie with his words, but it had been an easy, painless way to make his point.

Liz could hear water boiling, and Stephanie turned back to the table to pour the tea. "Don't worry. I don't mind that you enjoyed it. You'd have to be crazy not to get turned on by him."

As Stephanie handed Liz her mug, she smiled, all trace of worry or embarrassment gone from her face. "I think that's the most complimentary thing I've heard you say about a man in ages." Her expression turned more serious. "How do you feel about him?"

"Let's not talk about that. I want to know what else he told you. You promised me the whole story."

"I'm not going to let you get out of answering me, but I suppose I'll let you postpone the inevitable for a bit."

Liz started to protest, but Stephanie gave her a look that drew an exasperated sigh from her. She took a sip of tea. "Fine. Just tell me what else Avran told you."

"As if discovering the existence of vampires isn't enough." Stephanie snorted.

Liz lifted her brows but declined to respond.

"He admitted that you were more than human in some way, but he wouldn't give me details. He told me to ask you."

"Can you accept that I can't explain more, at least not now? Knowing what you do could already put you in danger. I don't want to add to that."

Stephanie sighed and nodded her head. "I won't press you now, but you have to know I'm curious as hell. And by the way I haven't forgotten how quickly you laughed off the idea of Avran being a vampire."

Liz smiled. "I did, but I almost choked when you asked me. But I could hardly tell you. You'd have thought I was crazy."

"No, not you. You'd never say such a thing if it wasn't true. You take the supernatural very seriously."

Liz was thinking about how to respond to that when she remembered she was supposed to be at the store. "What time is it?"

"It's nine o'clock, but you're not going to the store. Cindy can handle it."

Scowling at how easily her friend followed her train of thought, Liz said, "Cindy's been working too hard this week. I don't want to leave her on her own."

"Then I will go help her. Under no circumstances are you leaving that bed. I wasn't kidding when I said you nearly died last night."

"I hardly think I was that bad off. I was only a little weak from loss of blood and all I'd been through."

"When I arrived with Avran, your pulse was barely there. You shouldn't have been able to survive after he drank as much as he did."

Liz froze and felt the color drain from her face. "You're not exaggerating, are you?"

"No, Avran considered giving you some of his blood. He said it would make you better but that it was risky. He didn't elaborate, but he wanted me to try and save you first, so I did."

Liz fought back tears. "What did you do?"

"I asked the Lord and Lady for help. Then I rubbed you down with the blood enriching oil you showed me how to make and fed you some red clover tincture. I couldn't think of anything else to do but pray…"

Stephanie's voice trailed off, and she began to cry. Liz sat up and they held each other for several minutes until their sniffles quieted.

"Promise me you won't leave the bed if I go."

"I promise."

"Good. Avran will track me down if he thinks I took less than perfect care of you."

"I thought you'd be the one after him, since he let me risk my life."

"I hated him, until I realized how much he loves you."

"Steph, he doesn't—" Stephanie's raised brow made her stop her protests. "Fine, just go on to the store. I will rest and be a good girl."

Stephanie started to leave, but she turned back toward Liz. "Avran stayed up through the dawn trying to wait for you to wake. I had to force him to go sleep." Liz scowled at her. "Oh, do forgive me, I won't mention anything else that might force you to admit how much he cares for you. I'll tell Gregory to bring you some food."

Stephanie opened the door, but still she didn't leave. "One more thing before I go?"

"Okay, what?"

"Is he as good in bed as I think he would be?"

Liz couldn't help but laugh at her friend. She threw one of her pillows toward the door. "He's a hundred times better. Now get out of here."

*****

Liz set her lunch tray on a table. Gregory had insisted she call him if she needed anything, but she could certainly make her own tea. Walking into the bathroom to fill the hotpot with water did tire her more than she liked, but she couldn't afford to spend the whole day in bed.

Now that Liftkin and Rosalia knew she and Avran had tried to get the treasure, they would surely come out that night to get it themselves. After their minions had failed so miserably, they wouldn't trust anyone else to do it. Liz wished she could trust the spell she'd put on the grate, but it would be foolish to think

Rosalia wouldn't be able to break it. The best she could hope for was to delay them.

Somehow, she had to go back and get the treasure before they did. She didn't want to involve Avran again, not after what had happened last night. She both longed to see him and dreaded it. What would his attitude be? He obviously did care for her or he would never have revealed himself to Stephanie. He'd taken a huge risk to save her.

She hoped his bullet wound had healed properly and that he'd fully recovered from the effects of the silver. He must have since Stephanie hadn't mentioned any weakness. But, no matter what condition he was in, he wasn't going to let her go after the treasure alone. She was sure of that, but she couldn't bear to see him in pain again.

Was this the time of crisis the Lady had alluded to? She desperately needed Divine counsel. She used the phone beside her bed to page Gregory and request the items she would need for her ritual.

When he got to her room with four white candles, a bowl of water, a bowl of salt, and the other things she'd asked for, he looked none too pleased. "You're supposed to be resting."

"I feel fine. I'm only going to meditate. It's not like I'm proposing to go for a run."

"Meditating takes energy and performing magic takes more. I would guess you're going to do a bit of both."

"Only enough magic to cast my circle. Please don't fuss at me, Gregory. I really have to do this. I promise it won't drain my energy too much. When I'm done, I'll rest until Avran wakes."

"Very well. Promise you'll call if you feel weak. Ms. Nelson asked that I make sure you drank some more of the tea she made for you this morning."

"I just made myself a cup. I'll drink it before I begin."

For a moment after Gregory left, Liz worried he might try to call Avran from his sleep. She hoped he knew Avran needed rest as much as she did.

She often did rituals while soaking in a hot bath. Since her whole body ached liked she'd just finished a killer workout she decided the huge sunken tub in her bathroom would be the perfect place to let herself relax and listen for the answers she desperately needed. The water would soothe her and help her focus on the peace she sought rather than on what was around her.

As she ran the water, she positioned a candle at each of the four corners of the tub. She placed the other things she would need along the wide rim. Adding a few drops of the oil Stephanie had used to revive her, she climbed into the water.

She breathed deeply, letting her body adjust to the heat. She'd been careful not to make the bath as hot as she usually liked it since she didn't want to risk getting lightheaded. But it was still warm enough to soothe her.

When she felt centered, she turned to the candle aligned most closely to the east. Lighting it, she acknowledged the powers of air and visualized herself standing on a beach, buffeted by the strong wind rolling off the sea. Turning her body ninety degrees, she lit the candle for fire and thought of the powerful heat of the sun's rays warming her on a chilly morning.

Turning again, she stopped to contemplate the essence of water. Then finally she acknowledged the earth as she faced north. When all the elements had been named, she visualized a circle of soft violet light floating around her and sank down in the water, leaning back against the side of the tub.

Taking a few moments to enjoy the safe sacred space she had created, she thought to herself that it had been far too long since she'd allowed herself such comfort. She needed to take more time for contemplation and for communing with the Lord and Lady and the elements.

When she had slowed her body to a point less than full consciousness, she closed her eyes and let her limbs float to the surface of the water. The gentle waves moved her from side to side. She felt the core of her true self being pulled from her body. She floated out of reality and into the astral realm where she could sit in the grove of the Lord and Lady and ask their aid.

"Welcome, my child," they said in unison as she felt herself descend to the dewy ground of the forest.

"I need help." The words were simple, but she didn't know what else to say.

The Lord spoke first. "You fear that the balance of your world will be undone and that it is up to you to save it."

Liz frowned. "When you put it like that, it sounds as though I ask the impossible."

"Perhaps you do," he said, his expression grave.

"I will not accept that. There must be something I can do."

The Lady responded. "You cannot do it alone."

"How can I ask others to put themselves at risk?"

"How can you expect to work in isolation?"

"But I was gifted with power so I could help others not put them in danger."

"You were not given enough power to control the world on your own," the Lord told her, his voice soothing yet commanding at the same time.

"I can't ask Avran to return with me to the treasure, not when it affects him so badly."

The Lady laid her hand on Liz's bowed head. "If you open yourself to him, you can find a way to strengthen yourself. He can help you find the power you need to defeat one as strong as Rosalia."

"Should I drink from him again? I'm willing, but I don't think he'll allow it."

"What you suggest is only one of your options," the Lady responded.

"What do you mean? What else can I do?"

"When the time comes, you will know and the choice will be yours."

Desperation closed around Liz's heart. Why wouldn't they give her a straight answer? "Please. I need to know what to do to defeat Rosalia."

The Lord approached her and drew her into his strong arms. "You know we cannot, we can only tell you that you do have the power within you to do what you seek. It only needs to be released."

"How do I release it?" Her voice shook, and tears ran down her cheeks.

"Trust those who touch your soul and follow your deepest instincts." The Lady hugged her from behind, closing her in a protective circle.

"That is what you said before, but it nearly got Avran and I killed." Her tears continued to flow. She tried to draw strength from the Lord and Lady's bodies.

"Did you trust him with all your heart? Did you open yourself to him completely?" the Lady asked.

"I have given him all I can without falling apart. I love him. But I can't have him and every time I think of it, it kills me a little more. I can't open to him any more, or I won't survive when he leaves."

The Lady sighed. "Liz, take a few deep breaths and lay down."

Liz did as she was asked. The ground was cool and soft. She wanted to sink into it, but her body was tense and rigid.

"Relax," the Lord and Lady said together.

The Lady stroked her hair back from her face. "Remember the vision of you and Avran that you asked me about?"

"Yes."

"See it again."

Liz recalled it easily. She'd thought of it often, thinking how thoroughly united she and Avran seemed in that circle, and how good it would feel to be protected, to have him as her champion.

"Now, study it. What do you see?"

"Avran dressed as a knight. Me, in a white dress. Both of you blessing Avran with a sword."

"Look beyond the physical. Look with your inner sight."

Liz concentrated. "Protection. Love. Union."

"Good. Focus on this vision. Let it speak to you and tell you what must be."

Liz continued to take deep breaths. Slowly, the tension left her body, and she sank into the earth, letting it support her. She studied the vision as she breathed, searching for something new.

"Listen to your soul." The Lady's soft words echoed in her head. Then Liz opened her eyes and was once again soaking in the bath.

Frustration instantly returned. The Lord and Lady had always been cryptic in her conversations with them, but lately when she'd needed them more than ever, they'd become impossible to understand. How could she follow her soul when it was telling her she could never leave Avran?

Gripping the sides of the tub, she repressed a scream of frustration. She needed answers. She was tired of being told to follow her own instincts. Her instincts wouldn't tell her what she needed to do. Of course if she wanted any chance of hearing something, she had to be quiet and listen.

Once again she allowed her limbs to float in the water and dismissed all thoughts except those connected with her body.

Floating and listening to her inner self, she heard nothing but a jumble of confusion and chaos at first. All her inner voices were giving conflicting messages. *Don't risk it. Run. Avran has stolen your heart. Stay with him. Drink from him.* But the clearest voice of all, the one that remained when the others faded, said, *Share with him.*

She knew that was what she would do. It went against all logic, all desire for preservation, but she would do it. She would experience the final, deepest level of intimacy with him. In doing so, she would risk putting herself completely in his hands. She could have the chance to be with him once more and the strength to take the treasure.

If only there could be more. But no, this would be the last time they would make love. She hoped he would agree to leave town afterwards. It would be too painful to risk seeing him again.

*****

In the late afternoon, Liz woke, groggy and confused. She'd lain down on her bed after her ritual but she hadn't thought she would fall asleep. When she'd oriented herself, she looked at the clock. It was after four. Why wasn't Avran awake? She wasn't sure exactly when he woke but he'd always been awake by now when she'd needed him. Was something wrong? Had he not recovered properly or did he need extra sleep to restore himself?

She was about to page Gregory when the door began to open. Avran peeked in. "Ahh, you're awake now. How are you feeling?"

"I'm fine. I was wondering why you hadn't been up here yet."

"I had. You were sound asleep. I wasn't going to wake you."

"I didn't mean to fall asleep again."

"Liz, you need rest."

The pain emanating from him made Liz's heart ache. "Stephanie told me what happened last night. Thank you."

His face reflected the pain she felt radiating from him. "When my kind are unconscious or weak, we don't realize how much we're drinking. We can't stop ourselves. Our bodies take over. I'm sorry. I never wanted to hurt you."

"I know that. I didn't think about the danger. I couldn't let you die."

"Do you know how much that means to me that you would make such a sacrifice?"

Neither of them had made a move to touch the other. Liz felt a strange tension in the air as if after all that had happened, after their true concern for each other had been shown so plainly, they no longer knew how to relate to each other.

After several long seconds of silence, she asked the question that had eaten at her since she'd drunk from him. "Why did you pretend you no longer wanted me?"

Avran walked to the window and looked out. Tension and despair rolled off him. Liz had to fight to keep from crying.

"I thought it was the best way to keep from hurting you more. I decided that if I got any closer, I would never leave. The more time we spent together, the harder it got to think of saying good-bye, so...I backed away. I'd planned to leave after we got the treasure and got rid of Liftkin and Rosalia."

Liz waited for a few moments to make sure he didn't have anything else to say. "I understand. I do think that would be best, but—"

"No!" His vehement response made her jump. "I realized when I saw you lying there, pale and barely breathing that I wouldn't be able to do it."

"Avran, you have to. Neither of us will survive the separation if we let this go on."

Avran shook his head. "Liz, I can't leave. I won't."

Silence reverberated off the walls. Liz wiped at the tears in her eyes and thought she saw Avran do the same though his face was turned toward the window.

She was the first to speak. "Avran...we'll talk about that later. First, I...I need to ask you a favor."

He turned to face her. "How can I help you? "

"I need more of your blood."

"No."

"It's the only way we're going to defeat Liftkin and Rosalia. They'll be back for the treasure tonight. I'm sure of it. I have to increase my strength to defeat them."

Avran continued to face away from her. His back was rigid and she'd never felt such anguish coming from him. She said the only thing she thought might change his mind. "I don't just want to drink. I want to do what you described before—drinking while you drink from me. I want it all, Avran. All the intimacy you can give."

He turned to her. She saw the spark of desire in his eyes. "There is another way. A way you can be strong, and we can be intimate beyond your wildest dreams."

His voice was silk and velvet and as sexy as it had been days ago. What was he up to? "What do you mean?"

"Let me Change you."

Chapter 21

Liz's mouth fell open, and she could do nothing but stare. Her heartbeat accelerated, and her breath caught in her lungs. She felt as though her chest might burst. She'd tried not to think about the possibility of becoming a vampire, and yet she'd almost wished he'd ask because it was so tempting.

How could she even contemplate it? If she became a vampire, she wouldn't be able to interact with humans or use her healing gifts. She might not even have the gift of healing anymore. As much as she used to long for her powers to go away, she knew the Lord and Lady had given them to her for a purpose. She had to remain human to fulfill her own destiny.

"Avran, I can't."

"Liz, before you answer, there are things you don't know. Things I need to explain. I shouldn't have spoken so quickly. I meant to explain everything first, but I had to ask before I talked myself out of it."

"Avran-"

"Liz, please. Changing you will put us both in danger, but—"

"Why? What makes it dangerous?"

"Changing a Deep Magician is forbidden."

"Some magicians say we can't become vampire or werewolves or anything else that would alter our genetic structure."

"They're wrong. My kind would like you to believe that, but it's not true."

"Why didn't you offer this to me before instead of deciding to leave?"

He knelt before her, his eyes full of love and pain. "I was afraid to offer and afraid of what the consequences would be. I promised myself that no matter how much I wanted you with me, I would not risk you this way."

"Why are you offering now?"

"I realized that being apart would be worse than anything else that could happen. Please give me a chance to explain."

She almost told him she couldn't allow herself to be tempted, but a part of her did want to hear his words—the same part that believed there was a way for them to stay together. "I'll listen."

He lifted the covers and slid into bed with her. He wanted her to rest her head on his chest, but she feared she would be more easily persuaded if he were holding her. She needed to be on equal ground. So she turned on her side and supported herself on her elbow.

He frowned at her, but he started his explanation without further comment. "It is believed that if a Deep Magician is Changed, he or she will become the most powerful of all vampires. Our kind believes the Magician would retain all his or her powers and gain none of the undesirable characteristics of my kind. According to our legends, a Deep Magician vampire would be able to walk in the sunlight, consume food, stay awake through the dawn, and survive for weeks on a few sips of blood."

Liz couldn't believe what she was hearing. If she could have all of this and spend eternity with Avran, how could she say no? Yet saying yes would put them both in great danger.

After pausing to push his silky hair back from his face, Avran captured her gaze and continued. Liz had to concentrate to hear what he said while staring into his silvery eyes.

"I don't know how much of this is true, nor do any of the vampires I've met. It's one of the legends we all learn as fledglings. But my kind live in fear of such a creature. Someone who could have all our power and none of our weakness would have the power to destroy us all. Changing Deep Magicians is prohibited, and the penalty for doing so is death.

Liz's heart raced. If Avran changed her, she could stay with him and continue to use her powers for good, but would she be strong enough to protect him and would he be willing to be ostracized by his own kind?

As if he were listening to her thoughts, Avran answered her questions. "If I Change you, especially if the legends are true, and you do keep all your powers, we will be hunted. As other vampires hear of what I've done, our execution will be called for. If you were truly as powerful as they fear, then you could defeat them, but I don't know if we could survive indefinitely."

"Then why—"

"Because I'm a fool and Changing you is the only hope we have of staying together."

Liz's heart sank. For a moment she had been truly tempted, but she would never consent to anything that would put Avran in danger. "You know I couldn't do something that would risk your life. I love you too much."

*****

Avran watched as the tears that had been shimmering in Liz's eyes spilled over in huge drops. He pulled her into his arms and stroked her hair while she cried.

"I love you, too. That's why I can't leave you. But I can't ask you to risk yourself for me." Her voice was still choked with tears.

Avran felt like his heart would break in two. There had to be something he could do, some way he could keep from losing her. But he would never force the Change on her, even if he could. "You aren't asking. I'm offering. It goes against what I've been taught but I've lost all control, all discipline, when it comes to you. I've already broken so many rules, personal ones and vampire ones, and I want desperately to break this one to."

She looked at him and the sadness in her eyes hurt worse than the bullet he'd taken the night before. "Avran, can we just have tonight? Can we not think about the future and concentrate on what we have right now? I need to drink from you again. I have to if I'm going to defeat Liftkin and Rosalia. Let me share that with you without pain or sadness. Drink from me while I drink from you. Show me what it's like to be as completely one as we can be."

Avran knew her request held danger. His desire to be inside her, to keep her with him, to make her what he was threatened to explode. He wasn't sure he could restrain himself enough to keep from hurting her. Blood sharing was what led to a Change. Would he have enough control to stop before it was too late?

But when Liz pulled his head down to hers and took his mouth in a fierce kiss, he forgot all his doubts. Desire engulfed him. He slipped his tongue between her lips and lapped at the inside of her mouth. She moaned softly and pulled him more tightly against her, entwining her tongue with his.

Avran felt his hunger rise, but he didn't want this coupling to be fast and furious like their last. He wanted to draw it out, to enjoy her for hours, to touch her and kiss her, and seduce her all over again.

He reached behind his head and took hold of her hands as he stepped back. He moved her hands until they were clasped against his heart. "The blood magic affected you quickly before, so we don't have to rush. We have hours yet before it's dark enough to get the treasure. I want to savor every moment."

"But I need you now." She struggled to free her hands from his.

He smiled. "It will be all the sweeter if we let our need simmer." He made sure his voice reached out, caressing her in the places where she felt her need most fiercely, and he watched her shudder.

"Wait here." He gestured to the sofa while he went to the phone to page Gregory and request some wine and the treats he'd ordered from Eccles Bakery.

✦✦✦✦✦

Liz watched Avran. He wore black jeans and one of his favorite white linen shirts. His feet were bare, and he flexed his toes as he talked to Gregory, scrunching them into the thick carpet. She marveled at how his feet were as strong and perfectly shaped as the rest of him.

Her eyes swept back up to his handsome face, nearly hidden by his hair as he leaned forward to hang up the phone. For a second, her earlier sadness returned. He was everything she'd ever longed for, and he'd offered her the chance to have him for all eternity. But even such a prize as that was not worth reducing his chance of survival.

She forced herself to relinquish her thoughts of the future and concentrate on the next few hours. Her desire for him already burned her. How could she wait much longer?

He walked toward her and held out his hand. "Gregory will be bringing some treats to the master bedroom. I have a fireplace, velvet floor pillows, and most importantly..." He paused to look pointedly over his shoulder at the bed. "A bigger bed." The look on his face reminded her of a panther stalking its prey, but she took his hand and let him help her up.

When they entered his suite, she saw he did indeed have the largest bed she'd ever seen. She thought he must have had it custom made. "Do you really sleep here? I thought you had a secure place to go during the day."

"I do. I use this room for more recreational activities." Liz shivered as his voice caressed her.

They walked though the bedroom into a small sitting room, which Liz thought must have been a dressing room when the house was first built. He picked up a remote, which lay on the low table and pressed a button. Gas logs blazed to life. His hands caressed her back. "I like to watch the flames. Let me know if it gets too warm."

His sensuous voice nearly over-powered her, and she had to swallow before she could speak. "I like them too," was all she could manage to say.

He arranged some pillows on the floor by the fire and asked Liz to make herself comfortable while he turned on the stereo. She sank down into them. There were several pillows large enough for her to curl her whole body onto. The fabric was dark and rich. Some were made from black or brown velvet and the others were fake fur in leopard or tiger print. She couldn't resist bringing one up to her face, so she could feel its softness on her cheek.

Exotic Eastern music floated from the speakers. Combined with the sensuous feel of the fabric, it made Liz feel as if she were in a forbidden pleasure chamber.

A knock at the door signaled Gregory's arrival and Avran went to open it. She continued to look around and take in the atmosphere, she couldn't help but think this was the first time they'd experienced anything like a date. She supposed if she'd given in to Avran's obvious desire for her the night they met, he might have brought her here and lulled her senses with an evening like this, but all their times together had been spontaneous, usually with one of them resisting at first. Now when they had so little time left, they were both ready to admit how much they needed the other.

Avran set a tray on the low table by the pillows and joined her, leaning over to brush the back of his hand across her cheek and helping her banish her disturbing thoughts. "Would you like some wine, darling?"

"Yes, please." She looked down at the tray Gregory had brought them. It contained a bottle of Cabernet—a vintage she recognized as one of her favorites—two glasses, and a plate of assorted items from Eccles Bakery including sausage balls, broiled buttery shrimp, cheese twists, stuffed mushrooms. There was also a plate of desserts: brownies, cream puffs and a few chocolate cupcakes.

Avran handed her a glass of wine, and she took a sip. "Mmmm, that's nice."

He smiled. "Would you like to dance before we eat?"

Liz wasn't sure what to say. She hadn't danced with a man in years. Yet the thought of Avran's firm body pressed against her made her want to purr with delight. "I'm not much of a dancer."

"You always move perfectly when you're in my arms."

She blushed, thinking of the ways he'd made her move for him, but she stood to join him as he moved away from the pillow pile.

The music was slow and sensuous. He pulled her fully against him, the way she used to dance with boys in high school except there was no awkwardness about feeling the hard length of him pressed against her. She lifted the hem of his shirt and slid her hands up to touch his back, desperate to feel his skin.

He reached around her to cup her behind, kneading her and pressing her more fully against his erection. She couldn't resist tilting her hips and sliding up and down as he rocked her. "Avran?"

"Hmmm," he murmured against her ear, letting his tongue snake out to lick its outer edge.

She moaned softly. "Let's forget about eating. I want to try out your enormous bed."

He laughed and pulled back to look at her. "No, darling. I'm determined to stretch this out and heat you up to scorching."

She rubbed her hips against him again, letting her hands come down against his firm ass. "I'm already scorching."

"Oh, no. If you think you're hot now, just wait. I'm going to work you until you beg for ice to cool you down."

She gasped as his words floated around her, caressing her nipples where they poked at the fabric of her T-shirt. She wished she'd put on something sexier than the T-shirt and shorts she'd been sleeping in, but Avran didn't seem to care. His gaze ran over her as though she was naked, and lust was plainly visible in his eyes.

He took her hand and drew her toward the pillows. "Come, Liz, let me feed you."

She didn't say a word. She followed simply followed him, wishing he was naked so she could watch the thick muscles of his thighs and calves as he moved.

They settled on floor by the table and he reached out and picked up a shrimp. Butter ran across his fingers and dripped onto the platter. Liz reached out to take it, but he shook his head. "Open your mouth."

She obeyed, and he placed the shrimp on her tongue. She sucked the butter from it and couldn't resist running her tongue up and down the length of Avran's finger, cleaning it for him.

He pulled away before she could suck his finger all the way into her mouth, so she chewed the succulent shrimp and waited to see what was next.

He selected a spicy cheese twist. But before he put it in her mouth, he caressed her lower lip with it. The pepper gave made her tender skin tingle.

She took a sip of wine to temper the pepper, and then Avran fed her a stuffed mushroom, affording her another chance to lick warm butter from his fingers. After a few more savory treats, she noticed his hand moving toward the dessert plate, but instead of picking anything up, he ran his finger through the chocolate icing on one of the cupcakes.

"Take off your shirt."

The command sent a lightening bolt streaking down her body. She could have sworn that velvet-covered hands had slid over her breasts.

When she was naked from the waist up, Avran painted one of her nipples with the icing. She sucked in her breath, shocked by his action and the cool, sticky sensation.

Avran bent his head and swiped his tongue across her. She jerked and thrust herself toward him. He licked her again, another hard fast stroke. "More."

He laughed. "More what?"

"Suck me. Please." She captured his gaze with hers, hoping he could see her desire like she saw his.

He growled and seized her nipple with his teeth, licking roughly at the chocolate then tugging fiercely.

Liz whimpered and begged him to stop and then not to stop ever, but he pulled away right when she thought he would bring her to climax without ever touching her below the waist.

She had to gasp to pull in air. Her chest rose and fell rapidly. She glanced down and noted Avran had been very thorough. All the chocolate was gone. She couldn't decide what she wanted more—for him to begin the process with her other nipple or to allow her to put chocolate on him and see how it tasted with his spicy skin.

She decided on the latter and reached out to begin unbuttoning his shirt. He caught her wrists. "Not yet."

He lifted one wrist toward his mouth. Her heart pounded. Was he going to bite her? She let her shields down in anticipation. He inhaled deeply with his nose pressed to the tender skin of her inner wrist. Then he ran his tongue slowly over the veins there. Liz could barely breathe. She was so wet she feared her shorts were soaked.

Avran's tongue flicked rapidly over her wrist, back and forth several times. Then he stopped, turning her arm over and placing a delicate kiss to the back of her hand. "Your smell intoxicates me, and the throb of your heart calls to me so loudly I can hardly think."

"Then take me." She lifted her arms to his neck.

"All in good time. We have hours yet to play."

"Avran, I—"

"Eat some more, and then I'm going to give you a massage. I imagine you're sore after last night?"

"Yes, but-"

"As the effects of the blood wear off, you begin to feel all the ways you exerted your body. I want to relieve that tension before I make you sore all over again." His devilish smile dizzied her. And the thought of his strong hands massaging her body nearly undid her, but he was right, she did need to eat. Not all of her weakness was coming from her desire for him.

Avran watched her, his hunger radiating from him as she sipped her wine and ate more of the savories.

"I can have Gregory bring you something more substantial if you need it," he said, tender concern mixing with his desire.

"I'm fine. I'm already getting full, and I haven't started on dessert yet. I guess you can't eat any of this?"

"No, unfortunately I haven't been able to enjoy food since roast boar was the height of fine cuisine. I can taste things like I did with the chocolate, but I can't really eat. My body won't digest it."

"That's too bad. I can't imagine giving up chocolate cake." He looked stricken, and she realized immediately what she'd said. "I'm sorry. I didn't mean it like that. I wasn't thinking, and you said I probably wouldn't have to if I—"

He put a finger against her lips. "Let's not think about it anymore."

She ate the cupcake he'd used in his play and every taste of chocolate icing made her want him more. She looked up at him as she licked the last of the icing from her lips. The look on his face as he followed the movements of her tongue indicated his need for her was growing harder to ignore.

She took a cream puff from the tray and scooped out a tiny bit of cream with her finger. She held it up to Avran's lips. "Taste."

He did, but instead of taking the cream from her fingertip, he licked the whole length of her finger and then sucked on it, making her feel his attention all the way to her clit.

When he let her go, she recovered her composure and ate the rest of the cream puff. "Do you want to taste anything else?"

"Only you." He smiled. "Are you ready to let me massage you?"

She swallowed and tried to find her voice. "Yes."

"Good. Take off the rest of your clothes. I'll get some towels."

Liz didn't trust herself to say anything else. She did as he asked, and when he came back carrying thick black towels and a bottle of oil, she was stretched out naked among the pillows.

"Mmmmmm. You're exquisite."

She smiled at the compliment. "I want you to take your clothes off too. I want to see you."

"As much as I revel in your appreciation, I don't trust myself to do this naked."

"At least take off your shirt, so I can feel your skin against me as you work."

He complied with her wish and asked her to lie down on one of the towels he'd spread on the thick carpet.

She lowered herself to the floor and sighed. It was warm and soft. She couldn't keep from wiggling against it as she adjusted herself. He opened the bottle of oil, and its multi-layered smell floated to her. First the bright smell of lemons assaulted her nose, so strong she could almost taste fresh lemonade. Next she smelled crisp mint and then the sharpness of licorice.

He started the massage at her feet, rubbing gently at first and then more firmly. By the time he reached her calves, she already felt more relaxed, almost as if she floated in warm water. But with each touch of his hands, each brush of his body against hers, the tension in her body moved between her legs where she could feel every beat of her heart.

The warm slickness of his hands as they moved over her body made her feel like she would melt into the towels, becoming one fiery puddle of need. She couldn't help but move her hips when his hands reached between her legs to manipulate her thigh muscles. How would she ever last until he finished with her?

*****

Avran watched Liz as she squirmed while he poured more oil on his hands. All the herbs in the oil were used to increase lust and, from the way she was pressing her pelvis into the floor, they seemed to be working well. He could imagine how the thick towel tickled her between her legs and how his touch deepened her need for him.

He pressed against her shields, encouraging her to open to him. When she did, he began to send soothing, intoxicating energy into her with each touch of his hands. She tensed at first but then relaxed and let him use his mind to move her into a place where she was aware of nothing but his touch and her need.

He wanted her desperately. Every time he felt her desire spike higher, he wanted to turn her over and plunge into her, but he had more planned. Even as she writhed on the floor, he knew he could make her hotter still.

By the time he reached her neck and shoulders, Liz was moaning and seemed to be on another level of consciousness between sleep and waking. He had to call her name three times before she answered him.

"Mmmm, what?" Her words were slurred as if her passion had confused her senses.

"I take it you feel sufficiently relaxed?" He couldn't help but smile as he watched her slither against the towel.

"What was in that oil?"

"Nothing to truly drug you, just some herbs to heighten your desire."

"I feel like I'm floating."

"I'm going to help you float to the shower. We need to wash the oil off you, so it won't get all over the sheets or all over my tongue."

She turned over and opened her eyes wide, locking her gaze with his. "Avran, don't make me wait anymore. I need you." She bent her knees and opened her legs.

He had to turn away to keep from ripping off his pants. His cock was so hard it hurt, but he had to make this last. If this was to be their last time together, he was damn well going to make sure she had a lot to remember.

He scooped her up and carried her to the bathroom, sitting her down on the fluffy rug while he let the water heat. Once the shower was going full blast, he made sure she could stand before sending her in ahead of him.

When he got his jeans off, he pulled open the curtain to step in. She stood with her head tilted back, wetting her hair. The smooth line of her neck was prominently displayed, and he could smell the rich, dizzying scent of her blood. His gums ached, and his fangs pulsed. Just a taste. That's all he would take for now, but he had to have it. His tongue was tracing her pulse before he stopped himself.

He jerked back, and his sudden movement brought her head up. She opened her eyes. He could imagine what she saw. His intense hunger, both for her body and her blood, would make him look feral. It would frighten most women, but she only smiled. As if it happened in slow motion, he watched her lift her hand and run her index finger down the line of her throat, lightly scoring it with her nail.

"Don't you want to taste me?"

"Yes." He gasped for air and leaned heavily against the wall. "But not now."

*****

Liz's head swirled with the strange sensations Avran had created while massaging her. She knew he'd used his mind to affect her. It had frightened her at first but then she'd given in. It had been so delicious. She felt out of control. She was willing and ready to do anything he suggested, and she had some rather wild suggestions herself.

"Turn around," he commanded, his voice still choked with need.

He soaped her hair and began scrubbing her scalp. His fingers kneaded deeply. She sighed, almost falling forward under the pressure and dizziness of her delight. When he turned her around so she could rinse, he began washing her with his hands. The feel of his soap slicked fingers sliding over her wet body made her moan.

He knelt and started at her feet, as he had with the massage. As his hands crossed her belly, she sucked in her breath. Her breasts ached for him, and her nipples thrust out. When his slippery fingers slid over those peaks, it was as if a switch had been flipped. She instantly lost all her control. The languor that had overcome her body disappeared.

She grabbed his hair and pulled his face toward her as she came up on her tiptoes. Dropping her shields, she pressed into his mind, letting him feel her ferocity as she seized his mouth.

She felt his shock as her mind merged with his. His hand reached between her thighs, and his fingers plunged inside her as she surged against him, begging him with mind and body to quench the fire he'd set.

His shields slammed shut, closing her off from his thoughts, and he grabbed her hands, trapping them behind her back with one of his hands. He brought the fingers that had been inside her to his mouth and slowly licked them clean, closing his eyes as if to savor her more. She moaned and laid her head against the wall.

Using his vampire speed, he turned the water off and scooped her up, taking her out of the shower before she could blink. He dropped her on the bed and stepped back. "*Now* you're scorching. I think it's time for the ice."

Chapter 22

"W-what ice?"

"The ice you need to cool you off." His words did the opposite of cooling. They felt like warm fingers trailing down her sides.

He stepped away from the bed, and she started to get up. "Lie still. I'm coming right back."

She couldn't possibly be still. Fire raged in her body, but she didn't want to cool down, she wanted to explode with Avran's shaft thrusting into her and his fangs buried in her neck.

He came back carrying an ice bucket. A feeling of apprehension came over her. "Avran, what are you doing? I thought you were kidding about the ice."

He crunched down on the piece of ice he was sucking on and chewed it up. "Relax."

"Avran—"

"Lay back and close your eyes."

She hesitated.

"Trust me."

As soon as her eyes were closed, Avran pressed her arms into the mattress and brought his mouth over her nipple. The shock of his freezing cold mouth made her jerk. Yet the feeling was exquisite as if lightning bolts were shooting through her belly straight to the pulsing center of her need.

He shifted his hold on her. He now held both her wrists in one hand, and he reached for another piece of ice. Her mind raced with the possibilities of what he would do with it, but she wasn't prepared for his question.

"Tell me where you burn the hottest?" When she didn't answer, he touched the ice to her navel. She jumped and tried to free herself but he held her fast.

"Tell me."

His sensuous voice distracted her to the point that she could barely speak. "I...I...everywhere."

"Here?" He dragged the ice down her belly. The shock of the cold made her twist and struggle once again.

"Tell me."

"No...lower," she gasped.

"Here?" He touched the ice to her pubic bone, tracing the very top of her plump lips.

"L-lower." She couldn't breathe, couldn't think.

"Ahh...here." He slid the ice inside her. She shrieked. He fucked her with it, sliding it in and out, making her squirm both from pleasure and the need to escape. The cold sensations were sharp, piercing, but rather than cooling her, they made her hotter.

"Or would this be better?" He rubbed the nearly melted ice over her clit. Then he bent and gave her a firm lick with his scorching tongue. Instantly, she went over the edge, tumbling into a world where flames burned around a frozen lake.

When she opened her eyes, Avran was holding a knife. Frightened, she tried to scoot away. "What are you doing?"

He smiled and laid his hand on her leg, holding her still. "Don't' be afraid. I want to give you my heart blood. For my kind, letting someone drink from the heart is the ultimate sign of union."

She shook her head as he brought the knife to his chest. "Avran, you don't have to do this."

*****

As Avran watched her, love showed plainly on her face. It made him want her all the more. Quickly, he made an inch long cut over his heart. He hardly felt the sharp pain. It couldn't overpower his hunger or his need to be inside her.

He dropped the knife to the floor and slid his body over Liz. Lifting her head, he brought her to his chest. "Drink."

She did. The sweet pull of her lips nearly made him come before he entered her.

He positioned himself against her tight, wet entrance and thrust deep as he pressed her back down against the mattress. He felt her hunger in her mind. She was already nearing her peak again.

Taking her arms, he stretched them over her head and lowered himself so he could sink his fangs into her wrist. Her body jerked upward when he did. Her hips bucked against his, forcing him to increase his pace. He took her in wild, hard strokes as her hot blood filled his mouth.

She was hanging, almost ready to fall into the abyss. He could feel the effect his lips had on her. Fire raged from her wrist all the way down to where he stroked her with abandon. He forced himself to slow down and make teasingly shallow strokes. Then he pulled out all the way and slammed into her to the hilt. He could feel himself inside her, stretching her almost to the point of pain. Her muscles spasmed around him. Any second she would take her release.

She thrust her hips against him, crying out again and again. The last layer of her mental defenses dropped, and a rush of images beat against him. As he poured himself into her, he felt all her inner longings—her pain, her pleasure, her fear, her hunger and, rising above it all, her love for him. Her love became his, and he reflected it back into her. The intensity brought tears to his eyes.

Only the briefest flicker of sanity in the midst of this union stopped him from drinking too much and forcing the Change on her. With the deepest despair he'd ever felt, he let go of her wrist and pulled his chest away from her lips, giving up his last chance to make her his for eternity.

She fell back against the bed, eyes closed, chest heaving. When he'd closed both their wounds, he lay down beside her and pulled her into his arms, stroking her back and feeling her tears run over his chest. Their salt stung the remnant of his cut.

A few moments later, Liz sat up, a look of panic on her face. "Avran, I feel really strange."

Fear seized him. If he'd let her take too much then the Change was already beginning. He'd have to finish it.

She was looking around the room, her eyes wide and frightened. He gripped her shoulders and turned her to face him. "Tell me exactly what you're feeling."

She took a deep breath and managed to meet his eyes. "Somewhat like last time, but more so. It looks almost bright outside, like it's day. I can see everything. And I feel restless, hungry."

"What are you hungry for?"

"I...I don't know. I...it's like when I need you inside me, but it's not sex I need."

She was in the early stages of blood hunger. He was sure of it, but what did it mean? Was she Changing? Was she craving his blood? Or was she simply taking on more of his qualities since she'd drunk more blood?

He lifted his arm to his mouth and bit it gently, making only a small incision. Taking a drop of his blood on his finger, he held it out to her. "Is this what you need?"

She took his finger and licked the blood off, but he saw none of the crazed hunger of the addict on her face. "Mmmm, it's fabulous, but no, I need..." She looked stricken and a little sick.

"Liz, what is it? What do you need?"

"I...I don't know how I know this, but I need human blood." He thought she was going to cry, but she held herself still and took a deep breath.

"It's all right. Take some deep breaths and tell me what else you're feeling." He rubbed his hands up and down on her arms, but she pulled away.

"I don't know. It's just so strange." She looked all around the room, obviously overwhelmed by her heightened senses.

"Liz, I need you to concentrate. Tell me everything that's going on in your body. This is very important."

He felt her fear. "What's wrong?"

"Please, concentrate. Do you feel any pain or nausea?"

Liz closed her eyes for a few seconds and then opened them and focused on him. "No, I feel great, like I have enough energy to run for miles."

He exhaled slowly. If she were Changing, she'd be in pain. She was probably only taking on more vampire qualities than a normal human would. "As much as you drank, you could probably run all night without stopping."

"Avran, what were you so worried about?"

He debated whether or not to tell her, but finally decided he'd better. "I was afraid you'd drunk too much and that you'd begun to Change."

"But I haven't?"

"I don't think so." He studied her face. She almost looked disappointed. "Liz—"

"No! Don't ask me now. I can't bear to talk about it now."

Avran felt residual heat from their lovemaking drain from his face. "It's dark. We should get ready to leave." He knew his voice was cold, but he couldn't help it. Even looking at Liz was painful.

Pulling on his jeans and allowing himself one last glance at her tear-stained face, he turned toward the door. "I'll go ask Gregory to help me round up the tools we will need. Can you handle the hunger? If not, I can get you some blood, but—"

"No!" Panic crossed her face again, but she got it under control. "I'm fine."

"Okay. Meet me downstairs." Then he left as fast as he could so he wouldn't turn back and pull her into his arms again

*****

A sense of deja vu washed over Liz as she stood outside the maintenance entrance to the Mercer Building. Fear and doubt collided in her mind, making it hard to concentrate on the simple magic that would help her unlock the door.

Would they actually find the silver? Would she be able to neutralize its power? Would Avran be able to fight the silver's effects? Where were Liftkin and Rosalia? Why hadn't they made any moves after the disaster the night before?

"Liz, are you all right?" Avran laid a hand on her shoulder.

She realized she'd been staring at the lock for a very long time. Before she answered, she completed the movement of energies that allowed her to shift the lock. "I'm fine. I was just having trouble focusing." She opened the door and walked slowly toward the stairs that led to the basement. It was pitch dark, but she was able to see clearly without a light.

Using her exaggerated hearing, she stood still and concentrated, trying to listen for any sounds that might alert her to another human presence. None of her senses indicated anyone else was around, so they began their descent.

When they reached the grate, Liz reversed her spell far more easily than she'd expected to. With the new infusion of blood, even the most complex spells seemed simple. She jumped down, not feeling the impact. What would it be like to have such enhanced physical abilities all the time? She immediately shut down that line of thinking.

Avran lowered the tools into the opening then dropped to the ground. He nearly tripped trying to get up, and he was still unsteady when he got to his feet. She felt pain gripping him. "You don't have to stay down here where the silver can hurt you. I can dig on my own and neutralize it before I bring it up."

He shook his head. "I'll be fine."

"You can wait in the room above. You'll know if anyone is approaching. Please. I can't stand to see you in pain."

"I'm not leaving you."

She had to turn away so he wouldn't see the tears in her eyes. If only he could stay with her forever. She took a slow breath before she spoke. "If you become incapacitated like you did last night, I'm forcing you back up even if I have to throw you."

A day ago, he would have laughed at her, but his voice remained eerily neutral. "With my shields up, I'll be able to handle it."

Liz would rather he were angry than distant. She'd seen images from his most powerful memories, happy ones and agonizing ones, and she felt what he'd felt. Never could she have imagined being so close to another person. But now he'd shut her out completely in an effort to make their parting easier.

Her heart was going to break when he left, no matter how he treated her for the next few hours. She wished he would at least open up to her, but now was no time to argue. She had to keep digging and get to the treasure.

Avran stood near the entrance. She heard him breathing in slow, long breaths. She felt the tension that poured off him as he fought against the pain. He needed to leave, to stop pushing himself, but she didn't have the energy to argue with him.

Finally, her shovel hit something hard. "I found something." She reached into the hole to search. Her added strength allowed her to loosen the packed earth around it with her hands.

"I t-think you...found it," Avran gasped, and she looked up. He was whiter than she'd ever seen him. He'd lowered himself to the ground. The cords in his neck stood out, and he fought to draw in air.

"Avran?"

He didn't respond.

"Avran? Can you hear me?"

"Y-yes."

She took the ladder and leaned it up against the entrance. "Can you pull yourself up with this?"

"Actually, we'd prefer him to stay right there." Liftkin's face appeared at the entrance to the chamber.

Avran's pain had distracted her. She hadn't heard him coming. And she wasn't prepared for the burst of energy he sent out.

She'd expected the bolt to hurt, maybe even kill her. Instead, he'd paralyzed her, surrounding her with a field of energy. She could neither move through it, nor draw on her own reserves.

When had he gained such a power? Then she saw Rosalia behind him and realized they were combining their efforts.

"We appreciate you finding the silver for us, dear," Rosalia cooed. "Now, we'd like you to go right ahead and finish digging it up."

Liz knew she couldn't panic. When she began to relax her defenses and stop fighting against the energy hold, she felt a shift in the forces. Suddenly, she realized how to use the force field to her advantage. By drawing the energy in instead of pushing against it, she could build up her reserves and possibly strike back as well as revive Avran. It was a gamble, but she didn't have many choices.

"N-no. I can't." Liz tried to project fear and panic, wanting them arrogant and unguarded.

She didn't dare try to look down at Avran. She'd stepped in front of him before Liftkin had zapped her, and she was able to reach a hand behind her slowly and touch his shoulder.

Rosalia sent a bolt of energy into him, he jerked, but he stayed on his hands and knees. Liz used a tiny bit of power to help him steady himself. She hoped he was getting the signal that she wasn't as powerless as she seemed.

"Do as we ask or I'll show your little vampire pain he's never dreamed of." Rosalia's lips turned up in a wicked smile.

Liftkin dropped through the hole and grabbed Liz by the arm, probably planning to drag her to the silver. Instead, she sent a hot burst of energy toward him, reflecting the power that had trapped her. At the same time, she shot a line of healing energy into Avran.

Liftkin dropped to the ground. Avran grabbed Rosalia as she lowered herself into the chamber, pinning her arms behind her back. He ripped her head to the side and sank his teeth into her neck. She screamed.

Liz dove for her bag and the gun she'd hidden there, but Liftkin recovered too quickly. He grabbed her by the hair, slamming her body against his. She felt the cold metal of a knife pressed to her throat.

"Let her go," Liftkin ordered Avran.

Rosalia looked frighteningly pale. Liz wondered if Avran had already killed her. How long would it take him to drain someone?

Avran released Rosalia. She fell to the floor at his feet. She didn't move, but with her heightened vision, Liz saw her chest rise and fall.

"Get over here and start digging." Liftkin motioned toward the uncovered box.

Not knowing if her power burst would hold if Avran got any closer to the silver, Liz's mind raced for a way out. Trying to buy time, she said, "You don't have to do this. If enough of us turn against Rosalia, she won't win."

"Why would I be so foolish when I'm finally close to my ultimate goal?"

"The power in these coins caused their maker and numerous others to lose their sanity. Why risk that?"

"Red Bird didn't have Rosalia's strength. The coins are for her. She's promised me far more than a momentary power burst."

"What has she offered you that's worth breaking all the rules that keep our people safe?"

Liftkin smiled. "The one thing I've always longed for and thought never to have, a seat on the Synod."

"But there aren't any vacant seats and even if there were—"

"Duncan is old. He refuses to see the sense of Rosalia's vision. His influence is keeping others from joining us as well. None of his heirs have inherited his power. Rosalia promises his seat will be vacant soon."

"He's old, but I've not heard that he's sick or..." She stopped, realizing what Liftkin meant. Rosalia thought that with the power of the coins she would be strong enough to kill the most powerful member of the Synod. And Liftkin was right, without Duncan's influence, others might be swayed.

Rosalia stirred and began to drag herself away from Avran. "Kill her, Avran," Liz shouted.

"Move and she dies." Liftkin jerked Liz's head back by her hair, giving himself better access to her throat.

Liz thought she could break free of his hold, but she didn't want him to have a chance to attack Avran. Rosalia had to be taken out. Her own life mattered less than that.

"Forget about me. Just do it."

Avran knelt and grabbed Rosalia's leg to restrain her.

Liftkin pressed the knife against Liz's throat. She felt stinging pain and a trickle of blood ran down her neck.

"I love you!" she shouted to Avran.

Chapter 23

Bang!

Liftkin's knife clattered to the floor, and he crumpled.

"I love you, too." Avran held a gun in his hand that Liz could only guess had come from Rosalia's pocket.

Liz whirled around to see Rosalia disappearing through the hole in the ceiling.

"Quick, grab her!"

Avran shook his head. "We can't risk it. The police are coming. We've got to get this area sealed off.

Liz listened carefully and heard the distant sirens. "She's planning to kill Duncan."

"We'll find her later. She's in no condition to fight with anyone tonight. And she doesn't have the silver."

"I know, but she'll find another way."

"Not before we've gotten her. We've got to hurry. They're getting closer."

Liz took a step toward Liftkin's inert form.

"Don't!" Avran laid a hand on her arm. "It's messy. Get the silver and do what you need to with it. I'll deal with Liftkin's body."

"So he's dead?" Liz asked, careful to keep her eyes focused on Avran.

He glanced behind her and then nodded slowly. "Yes, he's definitely dead."

Unable to stop herself, Liz turned around. Avran had hit him in the forehead, and a gaping hole stared back at her. She took a step back and leaned against the wall, thinking she was going to throw up. But after a few gasping breaths, she steeled herself against it. She had to accept what they'd done, even the most gruesome details.

"I tried to warn you," Avran said, but he projected comfort and tenderness in his voice.

"I know. I'll be all right. I had to see for myself that he wouldn't be back."

Avran gave her a sympathetic smile. "Move the silver. I'll bury him."

"You're going to leave him in here?"

"Yes, the police won't find the body here. Besides, it seems rather fitting, doesn't it?"

"I suppose I just—"

"Trust me."

"Okay." She finished digging up the box of silver, but her hands were still shaking from her narrow escape and it took her longer than it should have.

"Take it up to the basement and deal with it there. I'll finish here and join you."

She did what Avran asked. Neutralizing the silver's magic was easier than she'd thought it would be. Her own natural powers, combined with the enhancements from Avran, enabled her to do things she'd never thought possible. She hadn't thought it could happen, but at that moment she was confident her power outweighed Rosalia's and maybe Duncan's.

The things she could do if she focused this explosive combination of magic for good. A nagging voice told her all she had to do was let Avran Change her, and she would be like this for eternity. Eventually, she would even be stronger. She ignored the voice and closed the lid of the shoebox-sized metal container filled to the brim with bars of silver.

Avran emerged from the hidden chamber, and Liz drew in her breath. Would the silver affect him now, and if so, how would she ever get them out? Sirens wailed just outside the building, and she heard the scratch of tires on the asphalt.

"Can you seal this so they won't be able to open it or preferably even notice it?" Avran pointed to the grate.

"I think so. Are you feeling all right?"

He tilted his head to the side for a second and then answered, "I can't feel a thing. The silver's power to affect me must have drained away with the magic. Letting my shields down would be risky, but with them up I'll be fine."

Liz bent over the grate, using a sealing and cloaking spell which came as easily as breathing with her new understanding of her power. Then Avran directed her into a supply closet as they heard the maintenance entrance open above them.

Liz put the box of silver on the floor and let Avran pull her into his arms. The feel of his warm breath against her sent a sudden bolt of lust down her body. The adrenaline pumping through her fueled her desire for him. She wanted to rip his clothes off and take him right there with cops searching right above them.

"They're coming down here," he whispered, and Liz heard the footsteps on the stairs. "I might need to direct them away from us. I have to let my shields down, so I'll need you to do whatever you did in the chamber that helped me overcome the effects of the silver."

Liz nodded. She fought against her hunger for him and gathered her power as she had before, praying she could reconstruct what she'd done.

They heard two policemen come down the stairs and begin to approach their hiding place.

She felt the warm healing energy gather and holding his hand in hers, let it race down to her palm and jump the tiny gap to enter his body.

His head fell back against the wall.

"Are you all right?" she whispered close to his ear.

"More than all right." His voice held its seductive edge once more. Apparently, when he wasn't in the grip of pain, her energy not only strengthened him, it aroused him.

An officer spoke from just down the hall. "I don't think there's anything down here. That woman must have been mistaken about what she heard."

A second man answered, "She was sure she heard gunfire. We'd better be damn sure she was wrong before we leave. We don't want to have to come back out here."

As they moved closer to the closet, Avran squeezed Liz's hand. Her heart pounded in her chest. What would they say if the police found them?

The cops stood right outside the door. "Look, there's nobody here, let's go. This old basement gives me the creeps."

"What about the car outside?" Liz's heartbeat accelerated. She forgotten they'd left Avran's SUV parked right outside the door they'd entered.

"Probably one of the lawyers that works next door. He must've walked home or headed down to one of the bars."

"I guess you're right. It sure looked like a lawyer's car. I wonder what that woman really heard."

"There's no telling, but whatever it was, there's no sign of any guns being fired here."

Their steps receded back up the stairs and out the door. When the engine of their car started, Liz let out the breath she'd been holding.

Avran squeezed her to him. "Let's go. I'm taking you back to my house. I want to see you clean and well-fed, and I need to make sure there aren't any lasting effects from the blood before—"

"I have no intention of going anywhere until I find Rosalia."

"Liz, she's in no shape to harm anyone tonight. You've got some time. She'll need to find another source of added strength now that the silver is gone."

"I can't just let her go."

"Liz, think about how quickly your power faded last night. You aren't in any condition to do this. Be thankful we found the silver and got rid of Liftkin."

Liz took a steadying breath. She could already feel her energy draining, and her night vision wasn't as keen. Avran was right, but the thought of letting Rosalia have even another moment of freedom sickened her. And without Avran, without his blood, Liz wasn't sure she'd be able to catch her later.

Resigned, Liz said, "All right. I'll wait until I've rested, but I want to go to my own house."

"Liz, I—"

"Please."

✶✶✶✶✶

Reluctantly, Avran nodded his assent. He wanted her with him, where he could watch her fall asleep. He wanted to pretend he didn't have to leave.

He parked on the street in front of his house and reached for his door handle.

"You can let me out here." Her voice was very soft and small.

"I'm going to pretend I didn't hear that." He jumped out and closed his door more forcefully than necessary.

Ares and Saffron demanded attention when they got inside. Once they were well rubbed and fed, Avran searched for something to say, anything to forestall their inevitable parting. "What are you going to do with the silver?"

"I'd like to get it converted into a more usable currency and give it to a charity, maybe set up a scholarship fund."

"That much silver could raise a lot of questions, but I can put you in touch with my financial advisor. He'll help you arrange for it to be exchanged."

They fell into an awkward silence. Several times, Avran tried to force himself to tell her good-bye and walk away, but he couldn't do it.

Then they both started to speak at once.

Avran nodded. "You go first."

"I feel fine. I'm tired, but I will be all right after I sleep. I promise I won't go after Rosalia tonight. You don't have to stay."

He saw the shimmer of tears in her eyes before she was able to turn away, and he turned her back toward him and took hold of her hands. "Tell me you'll reconsider—"

"Avran—"

"No, listen to me. The idea of saying goodbye is hurting you as much as it is me. You saw what you were able to do tonight. Think how easily you could find Rosalia if you Changed."

"I can't Change simply to gain power."

"Would you do it for me?"

Her tears spilled over and began to run down her cheeks. She let go of his hands and stepped back. "I should say no."

"Don't."

"What if I said I would think about it? I know that's prolonging our pain and—"

He held up a hand. "I'm willing to wait. I'd rather leave here tonight with hope, no matter how small."

"You have to promise you won't contact me. I don't know how much time I might need, but I want to be sure of my decision. And to do that, I need time alone."

"I will stay away until you've made your decision, however long that is. But you must promise to call if you need me."

She nodded. "I promise."

As he turned to leave, his heart beat far faster than normal. He wanted one last kiss, one last taste of her. If she ultimately said no to the Change, and he didn't dare hope she wouldn't, he might never hold her again.

He turned back to face her. But she held up her hands before he could speak.

"Please, I can't touch you right now. I have to know I'm making the right choice for the right reason."

Avran ran for his car, moving so fast no human could have seen him. When he reached it, he braced himself against the roof and tried to slow his ragged breathing. He'd been so close, so close to taking her against her will. The pain he'd felt when he lay dying on the field at Agincourt had been nothing compared to this.

What would happen to him if she turned him down again?

Chapter 24

Before she could allow herself to do any serious thinking about Avran, Liz needed to figure out how to stop Rosalia. Should she call Duncan and warn him? Would he believe her?

She went in search of her address book. She'd never called Duncan before, and she'd only met him once, but Elspeth had made sure she had his phone number in case of an emergency. He was the only council member Elspeth had trusted implicitly.

Duncan lived in Edinburgh, and it took her a few moments to negotiate the complexities of dialing a foreign number. Finally, the line began to ring, and she took a deep breath. He answered, and she began to explain who she was, but he stopped her, assuring her he'd heard plenty about her from Elspeth.

"Oh, okay." She tried her best to halt the shaking of her voice. "I'm sorry to disturb you, but I need to tell you something very serious. It may sound unbelievable, but please hear me out."

"Rosalia's been to see you."

Liz gasped. "Do you know what she's planning?"

"It is often convenient to appear more idealistic and serene that one actually is."

Once her initial shock passed, Liz felt the tension drain from her. If Duncan knew what was going on then the whole burden of stopping Rosalia no longer rested on her shoulders. "She was here. She'd recruited Max Liftkin to help her gain control of a cache of magical silver."

"Did she succeed?"

"No, we...I mean, I managed to get to the treasure first and neutralize its energy."

Liz had almost mentioned Avran. How could she be so careless? Fortunately, Duncan didn't mention her slip, nor did he comment when she told him Liftkin was dead. He assured her Rosalia was being watched and while he might require Liz's help soon, she needed to take a week or two to recover from the stress she'd been under.

After she hung up the phone, she still had a few hours before she needed to go to her store. The morning air was sweet and cool. She decided to sit in the wooden swing that hung from a huge oak in her back yard.

Hardly anyone else in the neighborhood was stirring yet so it was quiet and peaceful there. The fence around her yard gave her privacy. Eventually she abandoned the swing and lay down on the ground to meditate. But every time she got her mind stilled, images of Avran rushed in to fill the void. She deliberately brought the vision of her and Avran with the Lord and Lady to her mind, the one they had told her to study.

The revelation hit her within seconds. While it could be a picture of them being sent on a quest, it could also be a wedding. She knew without a doubt this vision showed the possible future the Lady had spoken of, a future where she not only worked with Avran but where she was bound to him for eternity.

The Lord and Lady approved of her Changing.

How could she have been so blind to it before? Looking more closely at the scene, she saw herself smiling. She had fangs. Had that been there before, or was it a confirmation of her thoughts?

She heard the Lady's voice in her mind. *It will not be easy, but there will be many rewards if you choose to walk this path.*

I choose it. She responded with absolute certainty. Joy and peace like she had never felt settled in her heart. She knew the Lord and Lady had been preparing her for this moment all along. Somehow, she would convince Duncan that what she'd done was right and that she still intended to help him preserve the old ways of Deep Magicians.

She wanted to see Avran immediately, to throw herself into his arms and tell him, but he would be asleep. She could try calling him, but he needed to rest after last night and she needed to settle her own affairs before she took this step.

The first thing she did was call Stephanie since she was the only person to whom Liz could confide the true story.

"Hello?" Stephanie sounded groggy, and Liz realized how early it still was.

"I'm sorry I woke you, but I really need to talk now."

"I'll be right over."

"You don't have to come. I can tell you now."

"No, if you're about to say what I think you are, it needs to be done in person." Stephanie hung up before Liz could wonder how she knew.

When her friend arrived, Liz explained what had happened the night before and what Avran wanted of her. She even confessed she was a Deep Magician and explained what that meant. What had once seemed like an earth-shattering revelation was anti-climatic after all Liz had been through.

Stephanie admitted to encouraging Avran to Change her and gave her whole-hearted approval of Liz's decision.

"What should I do with the store?"

"You don't have to give it up."

"No, but I don't think I'll be able to work there during the day."

"You might be."

"True but even if I can walk in the sun, I'm going to have to go after Liftkin's accomplice and I may have other similar missions."

"What if you keep ownership but let Cindy manage it? She still hasn't found a job, and she probably won't any time soon. This way she can work on her art at the store or at night, especially if she hired someone else to help her."

"That's a great plan. Would you help her initially?"

"Of course I will. I'll go in with you today, and we can explain that something's come up and you might have to go out of town for several weeks."

"Thank you, Stephanie." Liz gave her a hug. "Whatever happens and wherever I go, I'm going to stay in touch with you. Where else could I find someone whose so blasé about the existence of vampires?"

Stephanie laughed and gave her a tight squeeze. "I'm going to love having two vampires for friends. Where else could I find such excitement?"

Cindy was elated about the opportunity. Once Liz got the particulars settled and showed Cindy all the things she needed to know about the system for doing inventory and filling orders, she had lunch with Stephanie at her favorite restaurant followed by a cupcake at the bakery. She savored every bite in case it was her last. Then she returned home alone.She tried to call her mom but her mother had already left the hotel listed on her itinerary. Oh well, Liz hadn't really expected to track her down. It wasn't like her mother would worry if Liz disappeared for a while. She'd probably think how great it was that Liz was getting out for a change.

Next she called her grandparents. She explained that a friend needed her assistance, and she would have to be out of town for a while. She promised to check in with them regularly and visit as soon as she could.

She hung up the phone and curled up on the couch with Saffron. Ares lay on the floor below her. She'd considered asking Stephanie to take care of them while she helped find Rosalia, but then she'd remembered how much Gregory had enjoyed having them around and decided she would leave them with him.

Everything was in order now. There was nothing left to do but wait for the late afternoon when Avran would wake.

*****

When the library door creaked, Avran looked up from his seat at the desk to see Liz standing in the doorway, her long blond hair unbound, a purple velvet skirt flowing about her legs. She looked primitive, untamed. He was reminded how much he loved the wildness in her, how it called to him. He didn't dare hope she'd come with the answer he longed for, and he couldn't bring himself to speak.

"I've decided."

He could hear her heart beating and smell the hot blood rushing through her. He gripped the edge of the desk to keep from running to her and taking her before she had time to tell him her answer. "I didn't expect you back so soon. If you need more time to think about this..." He wanted to stall her, postpone the inevitable.

"I don't need more time to I know I can't live without you. I'm willing to take any risk necessary, give up whatever I must for that. Change me."

The wood of Avran's desk threatened to splinter as he tightened his grip. She couldn't really mean it, could she? But with all of his heart, he hoped she did.

Knowing once he touched her there'd be no going back, Avran forced himself to give her one more chance to change her mind. "Liz, are you certain? Once I start this, I won't be able to stop myself. I believe you will be one of the strongest among us. You should be able to go out in the sun, to awaken at any time of day, to take a little food, but I can't be certain. I can't promise you what will happen."

"I know. You've warned me before, but it's worth it. I love you and that matters more than food or sunlight or anything else I may have to give up."

He couldn't hold back any longer. He was suddenly before her, pulling her into his arms, letting himself revel in her scent and the soft feel of her body. "After six hundred years, I'd given up on finding a woman who could claim my heart. And then I found you, and I knew I would lose you. I never thought you'd choose this."

She pulled back and looked into his eyes. "We were meant for each other. I see that clearly now. Ever since I met you, the Lord and Lady have been sending me visions of us together. At first I denied what I felt. Then I thought they were telling me to ask you for help against Liftkin, but last night, I realized they wanted me to Change. They've been preparing me for this. I must warn you though I think there is something in store for us once I've joined you, some mission they will send us on. Are you willing to accept that?"

Avran ran his knuckles across her smooth cheek. "Liz, I'm willing to accept anything to be with you. And if you are as powerful as the legends say, we will not be able to avoid dangerous missions. Every vampire or werewolf or other magical creature who doesn't want to kill us will look to you for protection." He studied her reaction, praying his words wouldn't change her mind.

"Then I will have to try to live up to their expectations. As long as you are with me, I feel like I can conquer anything."

"I love you, Liz."

"I love you, too." She tilted her head to the side, exposing her neck to him. "Take me, Avran. I don't want to wait any longer to be yours in every way."

Pure desire overwhelmed him, and the soft pulse at her neck became the focus of his world. He lifted his wrist to his mouth, sank his fangs deep and then offered his blood to Liz. As she began to suck, he reached for her mind and bit into the soft flesh of her neck.

His thoughts melded with her and he sensed the last of her doubts dissolving. She surrendered to him completely, lost in the exquisite pleasure of their exchange.

Two weeks later

Liz licked and nibbled the blood-warmed skin of Avran's abdomen, coming teasingly close to the head of his cock. He lifted his hips and groaned. When she didn't respond to his silent pleas, he fisted his hands in her hair and attempted to guide her mouth to wear he wanted. With no more than a thought, she slipped rings of pulsing energy around his wrists and ankles and pinned them to the bed.

He growled and thrashed, fighting the restraints. "What have you done?"

She smiled down at him. "Just a little magical experiment I wanted to try."

The bed shook with his efforts to get loose. "Let me go."

"Not until I'm done with you." She let her tongue glide slowly along his cock.

He arched his hips. She knew from their mind link he was desperate for her to suck him deep, but she refused to give him what he wanted. Instead, she nipped gently at the base of his shaft then shifted her attention to the soft skin of his inner thighs. After laving him with her tongue and teasing him with several nips that just failed to break the skin, she sank her fangs deep in one delicious bite.

He cried out, but the hot pain turned to pleasure as she deepened their mind link and began to suck at the wound.

"Ms. Carlson."

Liz jumped as Gregory's voice drew her out of her fantasy.

He frowned. "I didn't mean to frighten you, "

"Don't apologize. I was just day-dreaming."

"I have those treats you requested. Shall I leave them on the table."

Liz smiled, recovering herself. "Yes, please. I must have been dozing.

Gregory placed the box from Eccles Bakery on the small round table beside the Adirondack chair where she lounged. "Do you need anything else?"

"No, thank you for bringing these."

"Anything for you." He smiled before slipping back through the sliding door that separated the balcony from her bedroom.

Liz closed her eyes for a few seconds and let herself soak up the warmth of the afternoon sun, appreciating it as she never had before. Then she reached for one of the cupcakes Gregory had brought. She couldn't resist a smile as she licked away some of the chocolate icing. Thank the Lord and Lady she hadn't had to give these up.

Ares looked up longingly from his place at her feet. "Sorry, boy. This one is all for me." Saffron gave him a look of disdain. As if to say, she would never stoop to eating human food. Liz smiled. She was glad both animals had adjusted easily to living at Avran's house. Even Saffron hadn't made a fuss about spending several days in Gregory's care.

She had spent her first week after her Change in a haze of bloodlust. Most fledglings suffered from uncontrollable hunger for months, but her magical abilities had made it easier for her learn how to control her desire for blood. Avran taught her to think of the hunger as any other energy she needed to transform.

She'd yet to drink from anyone besides Avran. Since her body could still digest food, she had less physical need for blood than normal vampires, though she felt the same gnawing hunger when she woke. She knew eventually she would have to fully embrace her new nature and learn how to feed on her own. She would deal with that when the time came. She'd known what she was getting into when she asked Avran to Change her, and she had no regrets about her decision.

Liz had enjoyed the dream-like existence of her last few days. She'd yet to leave Avran's home and they'd spent all his waking moments together. Now that they knew she could withstand the sun as well as renew herself with very little sleep, nothing prevented her from returning to her shop.

Sooner or later, Duncan would call on her, and she would have to face the council's wrath when they discovered what she had become. She hoped Rosalia laid low and licked her wounds for a bit longer. Liz wanted to gain more knowledge of her new powers and finish recovering from the toll the Change had taken on her body.

Whenever and however the call did come, she had every confidence she and Avran were up to the challenge. Nothing had ever felt as right as Avran's blood flowing through her body. The Lord and Lady had been correct, as usual, in recommending she surrender to her soul-deep need for Avran. And if the Divine forces blessed their union then no Deep Magician, no matter how strong, would separate them.

She felt Avran's mind questing for hers and stood to go inside. She called to him, asking him to join her in the bed they shared when he didn't need protection from the noonday sun. Later that evening, he would teach her more about how to control her new abilities, but first, she intended to enact every one of the fantasies that had wandered through her mind while she waited for him to awake.

She laughed as she thought of how he would react to the last one. Nothing gave a woman confidence like knowing you could surprise a lover who had six hundred years of experience.

Silvia Violet

Silvia Violet can often be found haunting coffee shops looking for the darkest, strongest cup of coffee she can find. Once equipped with the needed fuel, she can happily sit for hours pounding away at her laptop. Silvia typically leaves home disguised as a suburban stay-at-home-mom, and other coffee shop patrons tend to ask her hilarious questions like "Do you write children's books?" She loves watching the looks on their faces when they learn what she's actually up to. When not writing, Silvia enjoys baking sinful chocolate treats, exploring new styles of cooking, and reading children's book to her wickedly smart offspring.

Silvia writes erotic romance and erotica in a variety of genres. She recently won Angela Knight's Golden Stiletto contest with a hot excerpt from one of her books.

You can find Silvia on the web at http://violet.chaosnet.org or reach her by email at silviaviolet@gmail.com

If you enjoyed Magic in the Blood, look for...

Six Feet Under
© 2006 Mackenzie McKade
An erotic vampire romance from Samhain Publishing.

He found her six feet under...and unearthed a passion beyond their wildest dreams

Buried six feet deep is not what Private Investigator Charlene Madison, had expected when she agreed to meet an informant at New Orleans' most famous cemetery. Neither was encountering the devil himself when Devin Leduc rescues her, only to imprison her in his arms. She can't explain her attraction to him, especially once he reveals his secret.

After centuries of darkness, Devin has found his light. Charlene makes his body burn with desire, along with his temper when her penchant for justice and her stubborn nature lead her straight into danger. Together they will unmask a killer and discover a love so fulfilling, nothing, not even death, will quench the flames of passion.

Warning: This title contains hot, steamy explicit sex, ménage a troi, and violence told in contemporary, graphic language

Samhain Publishing, Ltd.

It's all about the story...

Action/Adventure
Fantasy
Historical
Horror
Mainstream
Mystery/Suspense
Non-Fiction
Paranormal
Red Hots!
Romance
Science Fiction
Western
Young Adult

http://www.samhainpublishing.com

Printed in the United States
56750LVS00008B/25-75